ADVANCE PRAISE FOR *LAST STO.* ~.. ...

"Bravo to Patricia Dunn for creating this uniquely powerful journey from which it is nearly impossible to turn away."

MARY CALVI, author of *Dear George, Dear Mary: A Novel of George Washington's First Love*, Emmy® award–winning journalist, anchor for CBS 2 News and *Inside Edition*

"If you like quick-witted, fast-talking, and street-smart characters who have big dilemmas and even bigger hearts, look no further than Patricia Dunn's *Last Stop on the 6*. This is a story of wars we fight, ones in faraway lands as well as in the places we call home. For suspense, humor, and that singular variety of Bronx-born tough love with a little hope mixed in, give this a read."

KATHY CURTO, author of *Not for Nothing: Glimpses into a Jersey Girlhood*

"*Last Stop on the 6* is a rip-roaring love song to the Bronx, a coming-of-age story about the places that make us, that we try so hard to leave, and that so often pull us home. Set at the dawn of the Gulf War, it tells the story of a young woman grappling with warring identities: that of her upbringing in working-class, Catholic, Italian American Pelham Bay and her new life as a Birkenstock-wearing, vegetarian anti-war activist in Los Angeles. At turns deeply poignant and uproariously funny, it asks whether we can reconcile the selves pressed upon us and those we build on our own—if we can ever really go home, and if we ever really leave. Part raucous caper, part *My Brilliant Friend*, and simmering like a meaty Sunday gravy with the depths of hope and grief that live in the promise of the American Dream, *Last Stop on the 6* explores the limits of loyalty and faith—to family, to country, to God—and how far we'll go to protect the people we love. You don't have to be a working-class Italian American with roots in Naples to love this book, but if, like me, you are, you'll find yourself startlingly seen in these pages. Beyond those borders of identity, though, Patricia Dunn has written a powerfully universal story of family, love, and belonging that, no matter where you come from, feels a lot like coming home."

MELISSA FALIVENO, author of *Tomboyland*

"*Last Stop on the 6* is the return of the prodigal daughter to a world of long-buried hurts, political complexities, and female resilience. Dunn has introduced me to characters all possessing questions for which there are no easy answers—only the slow and steady re-awakenings of familial bonds and moral responsibility. A heartfelt work of art."

CAROLYN FERRELL, author of *Dear Miss Metropolitan* and *Don't Erase Me*

"In this fiercely tender portrait of a Bronx family, *Last Stop on the 6* follows Angela, a community activist who goes home for her brother's wedding after ten years away. Painful emotions resurface as she realizes the people she left behind aren't that different, and while on a humorous hunt for her missing brother, she reckons with how one terrible night changed the siblings' lives forever. A moving story with lots of lighthearted moments, *Last Stop on the 6* shows us how making amends with our troubled past may be the only way to grow closer to the ones we love."

BROOKE LEA FOSTER, author of *Summer Darlings*

"*Last Stop on the 6* has a heroine, Angela, who knows what's good for everyone else. And like Emma, she learns the about the limitations of her power and her vision, as this dazzling, perfectly paced novel turns like a kaleidoscope, with each chapter revealing something subtly different about the neighborhood, her family, their relationships, and her past. We read with delight because *Last Stop on the 6* is artful and elegant and we experience what we read as just like real life, because our view of these people and the world around them keeps changing. *Last Stop* is both painful and comedic, a perfectly paced dance through politics, aspiration, family, and Italian American life in the Bronx. You'll be happy when you're reading it, and sad when you are done."

MYRA GOLDBERG, author of *Whistling*

"A dazzling and heartening plunge into a complex Bronx family, generous with secrets and ambitions to save each other and the world. Dunn writes with verve and eloquence in this deftly told, gorgeously crafted story that crackles with wry humor and remarkable observations about love, departure, and its aftermath."

JIMIN HAN, author of *A Small Revolution*

"*Last Stop on the 6* is one of the funniest books I've read—laugh out loud funny—and one of the wisest. The narrator, Angela Campanosi, brings into teeming and uproarious life the neighborhood where she grew up when she returns after a decade away and learns some of the ingredients of a long-postponed reconciliation with her family: restored memory, humility, and a willingness to be loved. And fluttering around the novel is the holy moth whose story of capture and escape illuminates all the others. A miracle."

KATHLEEN HILL, author of *Still Waters in Niger, Who Occupies This House,* and
She Read to Us in the Late Afternoons

"At times hilarious, at times heartbreaking, Pat Dunn's new novel *Last Stop on the 6* is a highly original and penetrating story of the everlasting reach of family and home. Set against the backdrop of the Gulf War, the novel follows activist Angela Campanosi as she returns home for her brother's wedding some ten years after a tragedy that sent her fleeing. Fast-paced and peopled with a colorful and entertaining cast of characters, the book is a unique and thoroughly enjoyable read that will leave you thinking about your own family story—and how much of it, to this day, still makes you who you are."

BARBARA JOSSELSOHN, author of *The Lily Garden*, *The Bluebell Girls*, and *The Lilac House*

"All families—but Italian American families in particular, it seems—have their dramas and their conflicts. Patricia Dunn has created a fictional family into which we want to be invited as guests, despite their problems, confusions, and intrigues. The Bronx, New York family Dunn has rendered is one in which love ultimately prevails, whether it's tough love, romantic love, or familial love. These are characters you will want to know and live with through her novel. Get on that 6 train now and take it until the last stop."

DAVID MASELLO, executive editor of *Milieu*, author of *Architecture Without Rules*, *Art in Public Places*, and a forthcoming book from Rizzoli

"Why do families consist of people telling each other what to do? This implacable human mystery is the heart of a surprising, outrageous, and terrific novel about a prodigal daughter's return to the Bronx, armed with regret, muddled memories, and integrity. A superb book that I couldn't stop reading."

JOAN SILBER, author of *Secrets of Happiness*, *Ideas of Heaven*, and *Improvement*, winner of the National Book Critics Circle Award in Fiction and the PEN/Faulkner Award

VIA Folios 152

Last Stop on the 6

Last Stop on the 6

Patricia Dunn

BORDIGHERA PRESS

Cover painting by William Papaleo.
Cover design by Mike Tepper.
Author photo by Gary Gershoff.

Library of Congress Cataloging-in-Publication Data

Names: Dunn, Patricia (Creative writing teacher), author.
Title: Last stop on the 6 / Patricia Dunn.
Other titles: Last stop on the six
Description: New York, NY : Bordighera Press, 2021. | Series: VIA folios ; 152
   | Summary: "'Last Stop on the 6' is the return of the prodigal daughter to a
   world of long-buried hurts, political complexities, and female resilience. Dunn
   introduces characters of all possessing questions for which there are no easy
   answers - only the slow and steady re-awakenings of familial bonds and moral
   responsibility"-- Provided by publisher.
Identifiers: LCCN 2021018983 | ISBN 9781599541730 (paperback)
Subjects: LCSH: Homecoming--Fiction. | Italian American families--Fiction.
Classification: LCC PS3604.U5627 L37 2021 | DDC 813/.6--dc23
LC record available at https://lccn.loc.gov/2021018983

Printed in the United States.

Published by
BORDIGHERA PRESS
John D. Calandra Italian American Institute
25 W. 43rd Street, 17th Floor
New York, NY 10036

VIA Folios 152
ISBN 978-1-59954-173-0

To the memory of my father, John Joseph Dunn, and of my godfather, Eugene Michael Petilli, who both inspired me to dream big

CHAPTER 1

It was the night of January 12, 1991, after the largest protest in Los Angeles since Vietnam. We had three days left to stop a war. I'd been center stage, had shouted until my face flamed, until thousands chanted, "NO BLOOD FOR OIL." Now I found myself in a holding cell, sharing a cold concrete bench with another woman, who hadn't meant to stab her pimp in the neck. She'd been aiming for his eyeball. The guard called my name and unlocked the cage, but instead of walking me in the direction of the processing desk, where in the past I had been given my release papers along with my confiscated belongings – a wallet with five dollars, a week-from-expired driver's license, a business card for a National Lawyers Guild attorney, and my worn Birkenstocks – I was taken to the showers. This was the first time I was hosed down naked, checked for lice, and had to endure a cavity search.

When the guard handed me a gray jumpsuit, I kept calm and demanded to see my attorney, to which I was told, "Keep your mouth shut or you can visit the nurse."

I was about to have my first prison sleepover.

In the line to the dormitories, I recalled what my recent bench-mate with the bad aim had warned me: "Sleep with your eyes open. They'll stab you for kicks." But I wasn't worried. I was the Bronx Girl, the cliché – stubborn, loud, and tough. I could stand up to a wall of LAPD in riot gear without blinking an eye. Not much unnerved me.

The guard called out, "Theresa Angela Campanosi," my legal name. Everyone called me Angela. Theresa was a name my mother hated but was guilted into by her mother-in-law, who'd lost Baby Theresa to sudden infant death syndrome.

"Here!" I raised my hand, ready to face my perilous fate.

"Your release papers came through," the guard said.

An hour after my release, I returned to my studio apartment in Venice Beach, California – a community known more for its bodybuilders, artists, and punks, than its canals. On the ground in front of my door was a cardboard FedEx envelope. I picked it up. Written in Mommy's perfect Catholic schoolgirl script, my middle name, Angela. Last name: Campanosi. Address: 25 Park Avenue, Venice Beach, CA, with smiley faces in place of the *a*'s in *Park* and the *e*'s in *Avenue*. The smog index, Mommy always said, was the reason she would never visit, so I let her imagine some upscale equivalent of New York City's Park Avenue instead of the sketchier Lower East Side doppelgänger that was my neighborhood. If Hollywood Hills was where working actors moved to on their ascent to stardom, I lived where falling stars landed after they were extinguished.

The threat of a stranger stabbing me for kicks didn't make me sweat. And yet, it took three shots of tequila at the corner bar to muster the courage to tear the perforated edge off that FedEx envelope. Good things come in small packages, but my gut knew that only trouble could come by express mail from my mother.

The envelope was now open, but I still couldn't bring myself to look inside.

"Another shot." I shoved the envelope at the bartender with the surfer's tan. "What's inside?" He reached in and pulled out a plane ticket to New York. I grabbed the ticket out of his hand. "Tomorrow? One-way?" I shoved it back into the envelope and mumbled, "Is she crazy?"

"Hey, that's you!" yelled the man sitting on the stool to my right.

On a nineteen-inch distorted color television screen was the woman with the fashion model features: five-eight, 119 pounds, high cheekbones, and a nose so perfect that strangers stopped her on the street because they had to get the name of her *guy*, and they never believed there was no *guy*, and her nose was the nose she was born into.

It was her eyes, the color of dark chocolate, semisweet, that Hollywood agents and talent scouts called her best feature. With eyes round and wide, a lovesick cartoon character or a can't-find-my-mom-in-the-supermarket five-year-old, she exuded a vulnerability that could sell anything.

I was that girl, but I didn't feel pretty or vulnerable, and on that small blurry screen with both fists raised to the sky, I wasn't selling lingerie or perfume or lipstick that promised sex, love, and a Malibu beach house. I was selling justice.

The bartender raised the volume but before the words "No Blood for Oil" or "We Don't Want Your Fucking War" or "President Bush, Shame on You" were chanted, the image on the screen shifted to the five warmongers standing across the street from the anti-war rally. "Today, as Congress voted to support Bush should he declare war on Iraq, the public also showed their support of the president."

"Lies! There were thousands of us, thousands." I slammed my fist down hard, spilling every drink on the bar.

Following my rant about lies and the press and the deep pockets of the corporations that owned them, and how cheap oil was good for business, and war made money, and if Bush wanted public opinion to support bombing Iraq, well, that's the story the media was going to spin, the bartender escorted me out of the bar.

"Pretty girls like you are good for business when they keep their traps shut."

I glanced down at my NO BLOOD FOR OIL T-shirt, worn and washed so often over the past six months that the blood red had faded to cotton candy pink, and said, "Who you calling pretty?"

He slipped the envelope under my arm. "Go to New York. You need a vacation."

I staggered over to the sand next to the sign about the toxic water and swimming at your own risk, and plopped down. A vacation. Prison would be more of a vacation than going to the neighborhood I hadn't seen in ten years. Go back, tomorrow? Why after ten years would I?

I reached into the envelope, and sure enough, on my mother's real estate company's stationery, under the logo – two loopy *L*'s for *Lane and Lane* – in Mommy's perfect script was my answer: *Your brother's getting married. . . .* His wedding would be on Wednesday, January 16, the day after the deadline the U.N. Security Council with Bush leading the charge gave to Saddam Hussein to pull out of Kuwait, "or else." I couldn't understand how my brother planned to get married on the day after we might go to war. Then again,

Jimmy, and my relationship with him, stopped making sense a long time ago.

The only other thing my mother wrote was *Get on the plane. You owe him.*

I did owe him. Jimmy would never walk again because of me. There are some debts that can never be repaid.

In LA, I was the Bronx Girl – stubborn and tough – an activist with only three days to stop a war from happening. In the Bronx, in Pelham Bay, I was the sister who ruined her brother's life.

The idea of returning home made me wish I were still in prison.

"No Blood for Oil," I said under my breath.

CHAPTER 2

There were too many blanks to fill in during a thirty-minute ride from LaGuardia, the airport with the runways too short and too close to the water, so I insisted I would take the train and two buses home. My mother insisted back: "That's not the way we treat family in New York." Did she really think families in LA didn't pick their relatives up at the airport? Nevertheless, with my right hand holding the same brown suitcase I used when I ran away to LA ten years earlier, and my backpack slung over my left shoulder, I walked past baggage claim and through the sliding glass doors to passenger pickup area A.

"Shit, it's freezing." My words hit the cold air forming tiny clouds. New York winters were a distant memory, and the coat I'd worn on the plane to LA had long ago been donated to a homeless shelter. I wasn't dressed for East Coast weather. I wasn't ready to be back.

I had no trouble spotting Dad's white van before frostbite set in – it was emblazoned with a huge green glow-in-the-dark rat, black lettering painted on the side: DON C AND SON EXTERMINATING.

Dad's name was James, but "Don C" was a nod to Don Michael Corleone from *The Godfather* movies. Dad loved that his customers and all the local wiseguys called him Don. He also thought "Don C and Son" rolled off the tongue easier than "Don C and Daughter," so I was the "and Son." Jimmy was the star.

Underneath the company name, painted in blood red, was our motto: WE FORCE PESTS TO THEIR KNEES, AND THEN WE KILL THEM.

My brother, Jimmy, and I had come up with it one night after we'd had too many, but when Dad got all teary-eyed over what he thought was a gesture of love, we didn't have the heart to tell him it was a joke. Of course, Mommy had no problem telling him what she thought: "It's ridiculous. Cockroaches don't have knees." Dad was the dreamer and Mommy was the sledgehammer who smashed those dreams into smithereens.

What I loved most about the van was what Jimmy despised: the faux rat's tail jutting out the back. Whenever Dad drove us to school, Jimmy insisted Dad drop him two blocks away. I, on the other hand, would have let Dad drive me into first period. Jimmy was the insecure actor who cared way too much about what others thought; I had no shame. With my middle finger held high, I walked by all the idiots chanting "Rat Girl, you want a piece of cheese?"

The girl who cared what people thought but did what she wanted to anyway wasn't the woman freezing in passenger pickup A. I wanted to be anywhere but here.

Dad, who prided himself on never getting a ticket, not even for an expired meter, waited in the airport's loading and unloading zone, apparently ignoring the security guard who waved and shouted at him to move on. Maybe some things do change. I hurried toward the van. I was sure he would be taking off any second. I slid the side door open, threw the suitcase and backpack in, closed the door, and climbed into the front passenger seat in time to hear, "She's here, now fuck off, please." The driver – clearly not Dad – leaned over and kissed my cheek, and I was smacked in the nostrils with Aramis, the cologne worn by the guys of Pelham Bay. "My God, Billy, I didn't recognize you."

"The beard?" He swiped his hand over his chin.

"You look great," I said. What I didn't say was how hot he looked. My brother's best friend, my best friend, since elementary school had gained enough weight to fill in his once-hollow cheeks, and his blue-black hair had a sexy streak of gray draping over his right eye. His eyes were hazel-green and almond shaped, nice but nothing extraordinary until he looked at you, and then they could make your heart stop.

"Funny how breaking a heroin addiction does wonders for your complexion." He flashed the smile that had always made me trust him, and something started beeping.

"What is that?" I asked.

"Seat belt," he said.

Billy was wearing a seat belt, and when I reached beside me, I was surprised to see the seat belt was there. My dad had this recurring nightmare where he was stuck in a car at the bottom of the ocean and he couldn't get out because the seat belt was jammed. After seat belts were no longer optional and came standard in every car, Dad systematically removed them. When Jimmy and I were little, we sat on the floor in the back, which Dad believed was the safer option.

"I had them reinstalled," Billy said.

"And Dad was okay with that? I have been gone a long time."

"Too long," Billy said.

Before I had a chance to respond or change the subject, airport security banged on the window; Billy flipped him the finger and peeled off.

"So the rumor's true," he said, middle finger raised to his side mirror, where I assumed the security guard was still in view.

"What rumor?" I asked.

"Hollywood folks only eat sprouts."

I glanced down at my flat stomach and chest – before LA, cup size D, now cup size barely a B. Over the past decade I had lost ten pounds, a pound for every year away, or two pounds for every member of my family, Mommy, Jimmy, Dad, Mike (Mommy's second husband, and from what Mommy's told me, now Dad's best friend), and Billy.

"Seriously, you look good. Hot, even."

The only time Billy had ever commented on my appearance was to tell me my eyes were bloodshot or my gait was wobbly, to warn me I was too stoned to go home.

"You can turn on the radio." I didn't know what else to say. I was embarrassed.

"Was stolen." He stuck his hand into the empty hole in the console where the radio would have been. "Twice in the last few months. Not worth replacing."

He hummed and tapped. "Name that tune." He resumed humming and tapping.

"Sorry." I shrugged.

"You don't know 'Blues from a Gun'?"

I shook my head.

"Jesus and Mary Chain?" he said.

"Christian Rock?"

"What? No. I can't believe that never-to-be-called Theresa Angela Campanosi doesn't know The Jesus and Mary Chain. You knew every alternative band there was. Hollywood keeps you too busy to be cool?"

"Social injustice," I said.

"Never heard of them."

"Heard of what?"

"Social Injustice. Great name. I'll have to get their CD."

I stared out my window, trying to calm my nerves. Seeing Billy felt comfortable. I missed him more than I had realized. Still, I couldn't help but feel this was the calm before the storm, a level-five shitstorm. All I wanted to do was crawl inside my suitcase and roll three thousand miles away. Of course, my suitcase was pre-wheels.

"You know I really did mean to get out there." Billy shifted his eyes from the road to me. He had never been able to drive and talk without turning to look at you, even if you were sitting in the back seat, which was why Jimmy or I always drove.

"I can drive," I said.

"You must be exhausted."

I was. The Benadryl was supposed to help me sleep, but instead it made me jittery, so I spent most of the flight pacing the aisles. My internal organs were knotted, twisted, and mangled – in less than thirty minutes I'd have to face my family, especially my brother – I didn't want it all to end on the Van Wyck Expressway. "I'm fine to drive."

"I even bought a ticket." This time when he spoke, he kept his eyes on the road.

"And you didn't come?"

"Shit happens."

Shit was always happening to Billy, especially since I left. All those calls in the middle of the night, stoned, promising he was getting his life together, for real this time, and he was coming out to see me and the Pacific Ocean. At first I believed him, of course I had. It was Billy, the one who had my back, no matter what. After the accident, he was the only one who saw my pain and understood why I had to leave. Eventually it became clear that Billy was never coming to visit. He needed to tell those stories to get through another day.

The last time we'd talked was over a year and a half ago. Billy was in some rehab place, which surprised me. In our neighborhood, rehab was for pussies. Addicts had two choices to get clean, cold turkey or death. I was his one and only phone call. He begged me to fly to New York and get him out. It was the closest I'd ever come to returning, but when I called Mommy to ask if she would lend me the money for a ticket, she said Billy didn't need me to enable him. Actually, what she said was "He needs tough love, not a pity party." I hated her for that, even though I knew she was right.

I looked at Billy, and I could still see the wide-eyed optimist who always tried to make everyone happy,

"You're working for my dad now," I said.

"We have an arrangement."

"You could never fill my shoes." I smiled.

"I've missed that," he said.

"My gorgeous smile?"

"How you laugh at your own dumb jokes." He reached out and lightly brushed my cheek with his knuckles. "Your face is so thin. I didn't realize you had such high cheekbones."

What the hell? Was Billy flirting? He'd always been touchy-feely with me, so I couldn't be sure, but there was definitely a flash of heat in my groin. Billy had been my first kiss, my first fuck, and in all the years of knowing him, my body had never responded to him the way it did right then.

"What do you think?" he said.

"Excuse me?"

"About my idea."

Clearly I had been too distracted to hear a word he said, so I gave him the most noncommittal response I could think of. "Interesting."

"Glad to hear you say that. I think it could really work. I've already done quite a bit to increase business with the direct mail campaigns I initiated—"

"That's great, Billy."

"You know us addicts, we got the head for numbers. We even got the metric system down."

"Excuse me?"

"How many grams can you snort and for how much?" He was smiling, but I could feel he was still raw. I leaned in, but before I could hug him and tell him all was forgiven, he said, "Your dad tells me you got a part on some television show."

I recoiled.

"A pilot, right?"

"Oh, yeah, probably won't go anywhere." Acting and show business, or the "biz," as Dad called it, wasn't for me, and it had been years since I last auditioned, but I couldn't bear to tell my parents, especially my father. He had sounded so sad recently that I told him I had gotten a small part in a pilot, *Paranoid in Pasadena,* about a talking hamster in Pasadena who creates chaos in the life of a typical American family. It sounded too ridiculous to ever make it to air.

"Fingers, toes, and heart crossed for you," Billy said, and I felt guilty lying to him. Billy, a loyal a friend, couldn't keep a secret. Acting opposite a talking hamster my family would respect; acting to prevent a war was for rich liberals and hippies who needed to get jobs. Billy checked his rearview mirror and then, in a forced casual tone, asked, "Boyfriend?"

"Not right now," I said. The truth was there had never been one, only a lot of one-, sometimes two-night stands, but the only serious relationship I'd had in the past ten years was with the Coalition to Stop the War. What had started as something casual was now a full-blown commitment. "Girlfriend?"

"No, no girlfriend."

I was happy to hear this. Way too happy. What was going on? Billy was family, a brother to me, except those few times we fooled around, but that was practice so we would be prepared for when we had real sexual relationships. The funny thing was, after Billy, I had been sexual with many, maybe too many, men and a few women, but it never felt more real than it had with him.

"You awake?" He pushed against my shoulder.

"You need me to drive?"

"I thought you dozed off."

"What's she like?" I asked.

He turned to look at me. "There's no girlfriend."

I nudged the tips of my fingers against his chin until his eyes were back on the road. "Jimmy's girlfriend."

"You mean fiancée," Billy said.

"This wedding came out of nowhere," I said.

"You'll like Julie."

"Who?"

"The bride. She's sweet. She really seems to love Jimmy."

"She's okay with everything?"

"Your mom's a lot to take, and when she and your dad and Mike get going, it's *The Three Stooges,* if one was a platinum blonde." Billy pushed his fist against my knee.

"I mean with his . . ." I paused before I said, "Challenges."

"You mean is she okay with Jimmy being a cripple?" Billy kept his eyes straight ahead now.

"That's offensive," I said.

"You think *challenges* isn't? Jimmy would be the first one to tell you, or anyone, where to put the ultrasensitive lingo. Shit is shit, no matter how much lemon Glade you spray on it."

"Well, she can handle him?" I asked.

"Angela, I don't know anyone who can handle Jimmy, but she sure seems to love him enough to try."

"It takes more than love to make things work," I murmured.

"There's the cynical Angela that I know and love."

I didn't have to ask him to explain. But I wanted to tell him I had changed. I was an activist. I was organizing and giving speeches and getting arrested because I believed we could stop this war from happening. But I didn't feel as sure as I had yesterday in LA, under sunny skies, and it was as though the moment I stepped back into New York, any growth I'd achieved over the past ten years had blown away.

"Listen, I know it's none of my business, but this wedding is happening very fast," I said. "Unless it isn't happening so fast."

Billy kept his eyes on the road. I couldn't believe it had taken until now, eighteen full hours, to realize my brother didn't want me here. Why else did I only first hear about the wedding yesterday, and from my mother? Why else didn't I get a Save the Date a year before the wedding? Where was my formal invitation printed on heavy paper stock, addressed by hand in calligraphy with a stamped return envelope for me to RSVP no less than three weeks prior to the wedding date and include my dinner menu choice – prime rib, baked salmon, or chicken stuffed with spinach, which as a vegan would be *none of the above.*

My brother may have changed in the past ten years, but there were two things I knew would never change. Jimmy believed in Pelham Bay, PB for short, tradition, and superstition. It was part of his DNA. To plan a wedding less than a year in advance was not PB etiquette and was bad luck.

"I know Jimmy didn't plan for me to come to his wedding."

Billy turned to me and stared a second too long.

"Watch out," I shouted, and he swerved, narrowly avoiding a head-on collision with a Good Humor truck.

I paused to find my breath. "Who buys ice cream in the winter?"

"Addicts," he said.

"Pushup pops and fudge bars help with withdrawal?"

"Actually, yes. But I was referring to how these trucks are used as fronts to sell."

I nodded, thinking about the guy with the ice-cream truck near my apartment. He was always out of everything. I could never understand how he stayed in business. I didn't understand until right then his business was not ice cream.

We drove without talking until we got to the Whitestone Bridge and an accident or construction or both forced traffic to a standstill.

He turned to me again.

"Billy, please, eyes on the road."

"Okay, but we're hardly even moving."

"You don't have to go fast for an accident to happen," I said, and immediately regretted it. We both knew I was referring to Jimmy's accident. There was no car involved, but that whole night the three of us had moved in slow motion.

"I don't blame him for not inviting me to his wedding," I said. "Please tell me he knows I'm here."

Billy pulled over to the shoulder, turned off the engine, and clicked on the hazards. He stroked his beard several times and said, "Angela,

I can't tell you what Jimmy's feeling."

"You can't or you won't?"

"You've been gone for ten years."

"I know. I'm a fucking coward. I ran away. Not a day goes by when I don't think about that night and what I did."

"What do you want me to say?"

Say that Jimmy forgives me for that night in the park, for destroying his chance to be a star, for ruining his life and then running off to Los Angeles, the city that was supposed to be his dream. Yes, I wanted Billy to lie to me. To hug me.

The knock on my window startled me. "It's a cop," I said.

"Roll down your window," Billy said.

I did. The officer looked past me and directly at Billy. "Car trouble?"

"The engine was making a strange sound."

"Start the car," the cop said.

Billy turned the key in the ignition.

After several seconds, the cop said, "Sounds okay to me, but I can follow you to a gas station."

"Thanks, officer," Billy said. "I can have my guy check it out. We're close to home."

"Careful getting back on the highway." He slapped the side of the van. We waited until he got back into his squad car before we took off.

As Billy merged into traffic, I thought about how, yesterday, I was in sunny LA, had stood in front of ten thousand people chanting, "No Blood for Oil," and they chanted back, because they were listening, listening to me. Together we would stop this war from happening. Now, less than five miles to the place where I grew up, all the good I thought I was doing, and all the change I thought I had been making, was evaporating into the cold air. I was back to being Jimmy's older-by-thirteen-months sister, and there wasn't anything I could chant, or say, to get him to listen and to make things right.

What I needed was a miracle. The problem was I had long stopped believing in miracles.

CHAPTER 3

Billy double parked in front of the house. "Welcome home," he said with enough sarcasm to sink to the bottom of the Long Island Sound what little hope I had that it might all be okay. From the car window I stared at the stoop, with its black iron railing that my mother tethered me to when I was a toddler so I wouldn't run out into the street. I clutched his forearm. "I don't think I can do this."

He put the van in park, took my hand and squeezed, not tight enough to hurt, but tight enough for me to know this was not a romantic gesture. "Sorry, sweetie, but seeing them for the first time in all these years, well, it's going to suck hard."

"Thanks for the ride." I reached for the door handle, he pulled me to him, and before I had a chance to protest, he pressed his lips against mine. When our tongues touched, there was nothing familiar about it; this was new and exciting, and even though his beard felt scratchy, I was ready to let him take me into the back of the van and . . .

He pulled away. "Welcome home," he repeated. This time, the sarcasm was clear.

I slammed the door on Billy's self-satisfied grin and gave him the finger as he drove away; the fucker was testing me.

Billy knew there was something about this place that evoked the Angela who made bad choices, said stupid stuff, and hurt the people she loved the most. Screwing Billy in the back of Dad's van would have proved I was the same self-centered Angela who had fucked Billy whenever she needed a distraction from the crisis of the day. The same self-absorbed Angela who found it easier to pretend Billy was happy with our "friends with benefits" relationship than to deal with the messy truth. Billy was in love with me, at least he had been. Now, I wasn't sure about anything.

I wanted to believe I had changed. I was a better person with more empathy for others, but if Billy hadn't pulled away, I wasn't so sure I would have passed his test.

It was time for another moment of reckoning.

I walked over to my front stoop, climbed the three steps, grabbed the handle of the rust-colored, never-locked security door, and froze. I couldn't quite bring myself to take the inside staircase to the top floor apartment to face the discordant soundtrack that was my family, but what choice did I have? I turned back to the street – maybe I could leave – but my ride was gone. Besides, my mother didn't send a return ticket and the change at the bottom of my backpack wasn't enough to buy a subway token. My backpack! I left it and my suitcase in the back of the van.

I plopped down onto the stoop.

The sun was setting, and in the second-story windows of the nearby buildings, with their red-brick exteriors, mirror images to mine, with their two legal apartments and one illegal basement apartment, I could see silhouettes of the infamous Beach Chair Ladies, BCs for short. From Memorial Day until the first snow, the BCs, a dozen or so women from the block, gathered to gossip on the sidewalks and sat in low-to-the-ground plastic-and-nylon discount store beach chairs. They pocketed every one of our pink balls that bounced within their reach. Sometimes one of them would run into the street and steal our stick right out from the batter's hands. If we dared to ask for it back, they cursed and chased us. It was the price we paid for acting like kids.

The BCs didn't only police the children. They also determined who was and wasn't allowed to rent on this block. Only if you were a hundred percent Italian did they give the landlords their approval. Only Italians who had emigrated from Southern Italy were approved. My family was the one and only exception. Mommy and Dad each had Italian parents, but they'd been born in Parkchester, only a few miles away. In the minds and mouths of the people on this block, my parents and their offspring were as American as McDonald's. Mommy had charmed her way into this neighborhood, the way she charmed her way into, or out of, everything. For the most part, Jimmy and I were tolerated, spared the evil eye. But we did have to endure frequent slaps to the back, administered to encourage us to speak in Italian. "Speak Italian. No English!" the BCs commanded. Whenever something went missing, we were the first accused, and called thieves, in English and Italian. Then Jimmy did his first commercial, and he was taken into the fold. TV stars transcended nationalism. I became the number one suspect, though still never guilty of robbing anyone's purse or home. I was the only kid on the block who had never climbed a backyard fence and stolen a fig or a tomato. In my teen years, I earned my reputation and stole other people's boyfriends, a few girlfriends, and the occasional married man.

I hugged myself for warmth. The temperature was dropping, but I couldn't bring myself to stand up and go inside. And so, grasping the bottom of the banister, I shut my eyes and willed forth the toddler in me who had run for her freedom into the street, as well as the woman in me who had yesterday stopped traffic and marched for justice. I needed to get off my freezing butt cheeks, climb those stairs, and stand up to my disappointed mother, whose three-months-shy-of-thirty-years-old daughter still hadn't found *a man* to take care of her and didn't need one. I needed to tell my fragile father that I may have lived the past decade in the city where he believed miracles and lucky breaks happened every day, but I didn't believe in miracles, and the only breaks I ever witnessed were when the LAPD cracked their batons over the skulls of peaceful protestors. Mostly, I had to find the courage to come face to face with the brother I had crippled and abandoned. This felt more impossible than anything I had ever imagined myself doing. I had spent the past decade letting guilt fester in my heart because I was too afraid to risk an unaccepted apology.

"Angie, is that you?"

I opened my eyes. It was Dad's voice behind me. He was waiting in the doorway. I stood and turned to face him. He was wearing the same Yankees cap he'd worn the day he drove me to the airport, and when he opened the screen door he kissed me on the cheek like it had been only a week since we'd seen each other, and not ten years. There they were, the gray-blue eyes, the only thing Mommy ever complimented him about – "It's a shame none of them have that color," she had often said. Only my mother could compliment Dad and express regret about her children at the same time.

"How's my big Hollywood star?" he asked.

"Far from it," I said.

"You know what they say, there are no small parts—"

"Only a lot of big-mouth actors." I finished his sentence like no time had gone by at all.

"Exactly."

"Dad." I paused to muster the courage to tell him the truth about my life in LA. I wasn't an actor, but growing up the sister of a child actor meant a childhood spent on sets and watching the production assistants, the directors, and the camera, lighting, and sound people. All this prepared me for my work as an activist, where I was the "producer," running a show we hoped would save the world. Ratings mattered. And I wanted my father to be proud.

I inhaled so deeply I felt the oxygen pull up from my toes and into my throat, and on the exhale I managed to squeeze out, "In three days—"

"Your brother is getting married," he interrupted.

Before I could explain I was referring to the UN's deadline to Hussein, and how I had been working to stop this war from happening, he asked, "You talk to your brother?" Dad sounded nervous. I couldn't blame him. Having his two kids estranged from each other had to be ripping him apart even after all these years.

"No, Dad, I haven't." In the past I would have been disappointed, Dad asking me about my brother, always about my brother, and not about me, not even a "How was your flight?" The possum in me was grateful for the reprieve.

He took a deep breath, the way he always did when he and Mommy were fighting and he was afraid of saying something he couldn't take back.

"Everything's okay," I said.

He let out his breath, and in the white air there was the familiar smell of beer. "Where's Billy?" he asked.

"He took off."

"I hope he's not doing stops on Sunday," Dad said. "You start giving up your Sundays—"

"And your life is no longer your own," I finished. We both smiled.

"I'm happy Don C and Son are doing well," I added.

"Billy's really got a head for the numbers," Dad said.

"I'm glad you have him," I said, feeling a tinge of jealousy. Exterminating had been our thing. The one thing Dad and I did that wasn't about Jimmy.

"You remember the Deli on the Square?" Dad asked.

"The stop we lost because you refused to sign off?" Business owners who thought the smell of pesticides was bad for business would try to bribe Dad to sign the health inspector sheet without spraying. Dad knew it only took one customer spotting a roach scurrying up a wall or across a floor for a business to go under. He was a man with some principles, and "No spray, no sign" was one of them. This man, I thought, might understand why I was more interested in getting coverage on the six o'clock news than I was in getting a part in a commercial or sitcom.

"The board of health should have shut him down," Dad said.

"Too much payola for that to have happened," I said.

"The owner's youngest son had a bit of a gambling problem, ran up their debts."

Dad always had this around-the-block way of making a point, but I had been away too long to grasp what he was trying to tell me. "What's your point, Dad?" I asked.

"One way or another the roaches of this world will take you down, if you don't take them out first."

"But, Dad, it wasn't the roaches. It was the son who put the deli out of business."

Dad opened his mouth to speak, but the only thing that came out was a stronger smell, beer with a hint of Scotch underneath.

"Dad, is something wrong?"

He looked me straight in the eyes. I suddenly felt cold, as if an apparition had rushed through me. Did Dad know the truth? I wondered. Jimmy and I had never spoken about what happened that night. The one time I tried, he told me to shut up and then we swore on Saint Jude, the saint of desperate situations, to never speak of it again. "It's our secret," he said. "The kind you take to the grave."

Maybe Jimmy had broken our promise? If so, I wouldn't have blamed him.

"Dad, what's wrong?" I asked. "Please tell me."

"The wedding will be fine," he said. "Your mom has it under control." These words were code for "the shit has hit the fan," and my mother was getting someone, or *someones* – usually my father and my stepfather, Billy, and me, when I still lived here – to clean up and sanitize the mess.

"Caterer plans on using frozen and not fresh shrimp? The florist can't get the flowers to match the color scheme?" I was grasping at possible wedding blunders I knew would put my mother over the edge. She handled the big stuff calm and collected. The time I fell off my bike and my femur was jutting out through my skin, Dad threw up and almost passed out, while Mommy took one look and said, "It's nothing to worry about." I stayed calm and treated it as if it were only a paper cut. The little stuff, the curtains she ordered for the living room arriving two days late and looking more eggshell than white or my borrowing her earrings without asking, were nuclear attacks. She panicked and overreacted.

"You gonna tell me what the crisis is?"

"I'm late for my meeting."

"A church meeting?" Dad had dragged us to Mass every Sunday, but after he and Mommy divorced, church was limited to Christmas, Easter, and before every game the Yankees played during the playoffs.

"You've been away for so long, I forgot." He stepped off the stoop. He lifted three fingers on his right hand. Was he giving me the official Boy Scout salute?

"AA, three years sober."

"That's great, Dad," I said, but I wanted to ask: *If you're sober for three years, why do I smell alcohol on your breath?* Confronting my father head-on would have only forced him to retreat and drink more.

"Catch you later." He made it as far as the next step down before he turned back to me. "Your headshots up-to-date?"

"I'm good, Dad," I said.

"A professional photographer owes me a favor—"

"You handle a roach infestation for him?"

"Vermin, Angie, he had rats. You know those nasty city rats, if cornered they'll jump six feet in the air—"

"And bite right into your jugular," I said.

Dad smiled. "I'll give him a call and set up a time for a photo shoot."

"I'm leaving the day after the wedding."

He nodded, but I knew he didn't understand.

"You don't want to be late for your meeting." I desperately wanted to redirect the subject away from an eight-and-a-half-by-eleven glossy of my face, with the only real acting credit listed on the back being "Girl with Pocketbook Who Walks Alongside Three Other Girls with Pocketbooks Singing the Show's Theme Song Before the Opening Credits of a Pilot that Never Made It to Air."

I stepped off the stoop, in no rush to go upstairs, and was about to insist that I go with him, but on second thought I wasn't sure they let nonalcoholics into AA meetings, and if they did, I didn't think I was ready to watch my father stand in front of a room full of strangers and announce, "My name is James and I'm an alcoholic."

Dad walked off into the gray late Sunday afternoon, DON C AND SON EXTERMINATING embossed in red on the back of his jacket. I didn't have Dad's passion for bugs, but Don C and Son got me through the worst year of my life. While I was out on a job, I wasn't obsessing about my brother in the hospital, then the rehab center, and then at home. Or about the father who refused to get out of bed after he tried, and failed, to inspire Jimmy to roll his wheelchair back in front of the camera.

"Dad," I called out to him.

He stopped and turned in my direction.

"Are there possums in the Bronx?"

"Can't say I've ever seen one or had a customer need me to trap one. If you think you saw one, it could have been a big rat."

"Thanks, Dad," I said. He tipped his Yankees cap and went on his way.

Possums wouldn't survive in the Bronx, definitely not in this neighborhood. Those who played dead were kicked to the curb, or buried alive, though in that moment going upstairs and facing Jimmy terrified me more than either of those possibilities.

CHAPTER 4

I watched Dad turn the corner, and as I started to gather my courage to head inside, a Mercedes came rolling down the street in the wrong direction. After three hundred and thirty-two collisions, the city had installed a one-way sign on the corner of the block. Three hundred and thirty-two became the number many block residents played, and lost, every week in the lottery, until the crescent-moon night the sign disappeared. No one complained. Convenience had always been welcomed over safety in this neighborhood.

Now the one-way sign was back, and the Mercedes double-parked in the wrong direction – which meant the driver had to be someone who had lived here in the "good old days." The only person I knew who was rich enough and stupid enough to buy a car with as high a theft rate as a new Mercedes was the landlord. The last time I had seen him was the night before Jimmy was supposed to fly to LA for the role of a lifetime – his first feature film. I was here on the stoop, holding a fifth of rum and a liter of Coke, insisting Jimmy allow Billy and me to give him a proper send-off at Pelham Bay Park.

The landlord had whacked Jimmy on the back and said, "You too big a shot to celebrate with your family? Take my car." He tossed his keys to Billy.

I knew if I saw the landlord now, the rest of what happened that night would play out in my mind, a horror movie where the teen girl ignores the audience shouting, "Don't go down to the basement," and she does and she's stabbed, diced, sliced, or chain-sawed in half. I had been the one not to listen when Jimmy insisted he didn't want to go to our park hangout to party the night before he was supposed to fly to Hollywood for his screen test, his big break. He wanted to stay home and turn in early. I was the one who hadn't listened, but it was Jimmy who was severed. I walked away in one piece, one physical piece anyway.

I stood up quickly and opened the security door. At the bottom of the staircase was a chairlift. I was hit by a tsunami of images I thought I had long ago erased from my memory. No warning and nowhere to go but under. There was Jimmy, spitting at the wheelchair I had rolled to the side of his bed, shouting, "I'd rather crawl." Only, with a severed spine crawling wasn't an option, so Billy and I would carry Jimmy down the two flights of stairs, to the front stoop, and into the car every time he had a doctor or specialist appointment, dozens every month. Jimmy swung at us, once breaking Billy's nose and twice cracking one of my ribs. Finally, Billy had to straddle and hold Jimmy down until I could strap his arms to his sides. Cracked ribs and swollen eyes were a lot easier to manage than the Jimmy who stopped fighting and would lie in his bed, refusing to move or speak. I'd since trained activists in nonviolent resistance techniques. I'd demonstrated how to go limp when the police, a cop, was taking hold under each armpit and dragging you into a cop car or paddy wagon. You weren't cooperating, but you also weren't giving them any excuse to bash your head. Passive resistance was empowering. Jimmy had given up. He wanted to be left alone to die.

I took the stairs two and three steps at a time, as if getting to higher ground as fast as possible would stop me from drowning.

I turned the knob to our front door, and it opened; no matter how many reported burglaries there had been in the neighborhood we never locked doors. Our familial connection – we all lost keys. "Hello," I called out. "Anybody home?"

Jimmy's bedroom door was closed. Still, after all these years, it had JIMMY AND ANGELA on it – a little cherub in place of the last *A* – which Jimmy painted for my thirteenth birthday. I wondered if Jimmy left it because he had been too lazy to remove it or too tired to fight Mommy, who would have insisted he not touch one of the few remaining visible signs that her children had once been close. I lifted my fist, bracing myself for the inevitable. The moment my brother would look up from his bed, or chair, and say, "Get the fuck out of here." I had no delusion Jimmy wanted me here. I knew this was all about what our mother wanted. Still, I owed him, even if it was an apology that he would never accept. I knocked.

"Is that who I think it is?" I turned around as the kitchen door swung open, the smell of garlic and virgin olive oil slapped my face, and there was my stepdad, Mike, Mommy's second husband, wiping his hands on the front of a black apron with the words REAL MEN COOK QUICHE embossed in purple.

"Nice apron," I said.

He pulled at the Q in *Quiche*. "A joke from your brother." He smiled. It was hard for me to picture Jimmy playful enough to give a gag gift. When I left I thought he'd never smile again.

"The joke is on him. My quiche is delicious." Mike was a great cook, but he had always been a meat-and-pasta-with-red-gravy man. It was hard for me to imagine Mike making anything with a flaky crust. Mike, standing six foot three, bent down, reached out, and gave me one of his big bear hugs, warm and comforting. "Your eyes still shine smart." Mike always knew how to make me smile.

"You need a haircut," I said. I loved to make him smile back. At fifty-eight, Mike had thick, black hair with only a bit of gray. A gray that looked dusted from having his head under someone's dirty sink, rather than distinguished. He loved his hair. He also feared it. Feared it was someday going to abandon him the way his first wife had.

Mike tilted his head in the direction of Jimmy's bedroom. "You can take your old bed."

Sharing a room with Jimmy again didn't feel right, definitely not the best of ideas.

"You know, I was thinking I'd crash at my dad's place."

"This is your dad's place." Mike forced a smile.

"He's living here? Since when?"

"It makes the most sense." I didn't have to ask how having your wife's ex-husband living under your roof made any sense. Once you were in this family, there was no escape; divorce and distance only got you paroled temporarily.

I did want to know, though. "What happened to his place?"

"You know your dad."

"He said he's three years sober?"

Mike opened his mouth but didn't say anything. I suspected what he was almost going to say was something my father didn't want me to know. He wasn't sober. He was drinking, the same drunk he'd always been. Mike was not a rat. He was the only one in this family who could ever keep a secret, except from Mommy. She was a human truth serum. All she had to do is inject her *you better not be keeping a secret from me* tone into a conversation, and we told her whatever she wanted to hear. I had needed three thousand miles between us to keep my real life from her.

"I guess these days," Mike finally spoke, "shit is happening to all of us." He put his hand on his lower back and winced.

"You okay?" I asked.

"Good days and bad days. I hope to get back to work soon."

"You got hurt?"

"Your mother didn't tell you?"

I didn't answer him. We both knew Mommy never shared bad news.

"I was installing pipes, copper, the best, on this big job and the roof collapsed. My back's a mess. Two minutes under a sink, and agony. The worst part is how little disability pays. I promise you this: I'd rather never make another meatball than to fill it with bread crumbs or white Wonder Bread. The name is meatballs, not bread balls." Mike was a good plumber, but his passion was his food.

"Mike, I'm sorry."

"Shit happens." Mike looked down at my feet.

"Your mother's going to love those," he grinned.

"Birkenstocks. They're comfortable." The words came out of my mouth, and I wished I could have pulled them back. With Mommy, fashion took precedence over comfort.

"No luggage?" he asked.

"Back of the van," I said.

"If it wasn't attached, you'd lose your . . ." He patted the top of my head. If anyone else had done this, I would have given explicit instructions as to where to shove their condescending gesture. But this was Mike, one of the most endearing people I'd ever known. The same man who talked about his time stationed in Japan, not long after World War II, as if the Japanese people were grateful for us dropping not one, but two atomic bombs on their country. He now had to be in favor of us going to war. When it came to fighting the good fight, he never could, nor would, see *The United States of America* as anything less than one hundred and twenty percent in the right. At the same time, he distrusted all politicians, Democrats and Republicans, so he refused to vote. He was a man of contradictions, but he loved this family, mothered us all, and I couldn't help but love him.

"Billy will be back," he said. "He never misses a Sunday dinner. Or Monday, Tuesday, Wednesday . . ." He smiled. It was nice to hear that something hadn't changed. After Billy's father died, his mom checked out and Billy spent most of his days and nights here. It was comforting to hear he still did.

"It's settled," he said.

"What's settled?"

"You take your old bed, and your dad the couch."

"Mike, really, I'd be more comfortable on the couch."

He glanced over at Jimmy's door and then looked into my eyes and said, "You must be starving."

I couldn't remember the last time I'd eaten, except for a few rice crackers and hummus I brought with me on the plane. My stomach had been too flip-floppy for me to eat. There was no refusing Mike when he wanted to feed you. In that way, he was more the stereotypical Italian nonna. Mike wrapped his bear arms around my shoulders and walked me into our kitchenette, with the swinging door that hit you on the way in and on the way out. The space was so tight that by the time I was four, I could no longer lie across the black-and-white-checkered linoleum floor without bending my head to the side. By the time I was eleven I had to squish my body into a fetal position to fit. By the time I was twelve I had started dating boys behind my parents' back and stopped lying on the kitchen floor.

The only thing this kitchenette ever managed to hold comfortably was Mommy and Dad, usually arguing over how much oregano to add to the sauce or salt to the pot roast. There was comfort in familiarity, and this love scene played over again and again until one day the fighting stopped. The silence hurt for longer than forever, at least it felt that way, and then one Sunday, Easter Sunday morning, I heard my parents fighting in the kitchen, but it wasn't over how to season the Easter ham. It wasn't over Jimmy, and how Mommy wanted Dad to let Jimmy be a kid, and Dad wanted Mommy to get out of the way of Jimmy becoming a star. They were fighting about Mike. Mommy was having an affair with a man she had shown an apartment to, and over the crown molding they'd fallen in love, or at least that's the story Mommy told.

Even in those early years, I didn't hate Mike. I knew it was a betrayal to my father not to, but I was selfish; when Mike was around, my mother was happy, and when my mother was happy, she wasn't acting unhappy with me.

It took Jimmy longer to accept Mike into our lives, especially because Jimmy cared so much about what people in this neighborhood thought of us. I did too, but I was better at acting as if I didn't. In this neighborhood, where murder was believed to be less sinful than divorce, our mother's affair with Mike was the hot gossip. Whenever Jimmy and I were within earshot, our mother's name, Rose, was punctuated with the word *puttana*. Slut. Jimmy was ashamed, and I was angry. Until one day, when they still thought I didn't understand they were calling my mother a whore in Italian, I walked over to their chairs, pulled down my tube top, and flashed my boobs. "No, I'm the putan'."

It only took one bite for all of us, including Dad, to accept Mike's cooking every time.

On the stove was a ten-quart pot too big for the burner. "Is that what I think it is?" I asked.

"You know it." Mike tore off the end of a loaf of bread resting on the counter and handed it to me. Arthur Avenue bread, from the other side of the Bronx and known statewide as the ultimate in Italian bread, was light years from what they called bread in LA. They said it had something to do with the minerals in the water. The ultimate bread came from the bakery around the corner. Dominick's bread was hard, but not crack-a-tooth hard – firm on the outside and fluffy on the inside. One bite, and all your troubles were forgotten. When eaten with Mike's gravy, which had the power to pacify a dysfunctional family, you had a religious experience.

"Go ahead, dip," he said. "You know you want to."

Of course I wanted to. I missed Mike's gravy almost as much as I had missed Mike.

"Use a" – before he could get the word *potholder* out, I had lifted the lid barehanded – "hot" – and flung it into the sink. "Very hot."

Mike turned on the tap and stuck my scorched fingers under the running cold water.

"It's okay." I shut the faucet with my dry hand.

Mike dipped the pointed end of the bread into the vat of red bubbles, topped inches deep with virgin olive oil, and extended his hand to me. "For you."

"I better not spoil my appetite," I said. The truth was, as much as I had wanted to believe I was no longer a superstitious Pelham Bay Catholic, in my heart I knew my tender fingers were a message, a sign. I had to talk to my brother and make things right, or at least own up to all I had done to fuck things up, before I could chew on Dominick's bread topped with Mike's gravy without regurgitating.

"One bite," he said.

"I need to see Jimmy."

Mike shoved the gravy-soaked bread into his mouth and spat it right out into the sink. "Hot." He turned the cold water back on and stuck his tongue under. Mike, the man who was thoughtful, and careful, and used potholders, had burned his mouth on his gravy. This was another sign, a bigger sign, that something was not right in the two-bedroom apartment of Marchesi-Campanosi-Petrolli.

"Mike, tell me what's going on?"

His long silence almost brought me to tears. Of course Jimmy was hiding out in his bedroom, didn't want to see me, didn't want me here. I knew what I had to do. Face him. Apologize. Shut up while he told me to shove my *sorry*s up my ass. Then I would leave. I'd have to get Mommy to lend me the money for the return ticket, but then I would go back to LA, where I could still make a difference. It was too late to repair my relationship with my brother, I was sure of that. It wasn't too late to stop this war from happening.

I pushed past Mike and rushed to Jimmy's bedroom, the room he and I had shared our whole lives, until my last few months at home when I'd slept on the couch. Jimmy said he needed privacy, but I think he knew I was the one who couldn't bear to lie in the bed next to his when he couldn't, or wouldn't, do anything for himself. Jimmy, the strong one, the smart one, the one everyone thought would make it out of the neighborhood, grew too depressed to wipe his own ass and had to be force-fed by Mike.

This time I didn't knock.

Inside, there remained the evidence of my first conscious act of defiance. Mommy had wanted her little girl to sleep under a yellow polka-dot canopy and play with Barbies. Instead she got me, who, at the age of seven, clogged the toilet with doll heads, and yelled, "Timber!" after taking a hacksaw to all four of my bedposts.

So little had changed, which was almost as upsetting as what had changed – the need for the stack of adult diapers in the corner.

There was a hospital bed that had replaced the race car with the mattress inside. The yang to my yin. Where was Jimmy?

"He's not here." Mike came up behind me.

"Where is he?"

Mike didn't answer, so I waited, my eyes focused on the portrait of Mommy and her brother, which Jimmy and I had thought was a *paint by numbers*, until in high school when Billy talked us out of going bowling and into taking a trip to the Met. We took one look at a painting translated from French to English, *Circus Sideshow* by Georges Seurat, and we knew the artist who painted the portrait of our mother and her brother used his technique of pointillism. For a brief moment we thought Seurat himself was the artist, but Billy pointed to the plaque on the wall. Seurat had died a hundred years earlier. Still, Jimmy and I went home that night hoping that it was another famous artist, but Mommy debunked us. The artist, she said, was unknown and the only value the painting had was sentimental.

The two pairs of eyes didn't follow me around the room, but the painting still creeped me out. The faces were sad and angry, and as hard as I tried, I could never imagine these two children playing with toys, or each other. I would have stuck the painting in the back of our closet long ago, but Jimmy wouldn't allow it. He hated the portrait even more than I did, especially because it replaced his Gene Simmons–with-the-tongue-spitting-fire poster. He understood this portrait, which had been painted by some street artist in the middle of Times Square, was the only tangible proof that our mother had a brother, the uncle we had never known.

"Out," Mike finally spoke. I knew there would be only two reasons for Mike's coyness. He didn't want to hurt me, or he had been ordered to keep his mouth shut.

I turned to face him. "Out where?"

Mike's expression went flat. He opened his mouth, but instead of words he blew air between his teeth, and then we stood there, daring each other to make the next move. I couldn't take it any longer. "What is it?"

"I forgot the seltzer in the car." He slapped his palm against his forehead. "You know your mom has to have her seltzer." He kissed the top of my head. "Don't worry, your mom will explain," he said, and dashed off. When I heard the downstairs door slam shut, it was time to get answers from the one person in this apartment who wasn't afraid to talk. My mother.

CHAPTER 5

I marched the twenty-five feet from my childhood bedroom to my mother's sanctuary, or as Jimmy and I had called it, the leave-me-the-fuck-alone room. It was also where she slept, conducted business, watched her shows, and I assumed, though preferred not to think about, had sexual relations with my father and then stepfather. She only locked her door when she needed to get away from me.

I turned the knob. The door wasn't locked. I stepped inside. A chill went up my spine. It was freezing in there. Mommy, because of her allergies, kept the air conditioner in her bedroom running year-round. Even on cold winter days like today she refused to open her bedroom windows. Mommy didn't trust the air the outside world breathed.

All I could see of my mother was ten tiny blood-red-polished toenails.

Blocking my view was a four-drawer metal file cabinet and several FOR SALE signs. Mommy now used her bedroom to run her real estate business. The only indications that Mike shared this room were the red-and-blue-striped necktie and the man's white T-shirt sticking out of the middle drawer.

"That's double the estimate. . . . The value of the property isn't worth it. . . . I know the clock is ticking. . . . You'll get your money."

"Ma, I need to talk to you."

"I gotta call you back, my baby's here. . . . Yes, the movie star." She slammed the receiver down. "Idiot contractors. They're all extortionists. Angela," she called out. "Why are you hiding? Come here."

And there it was: Mommy's call to arms, to her arms.

I stepped around the file cabinet and there, in full view, was Rose Maria Marchesi-Campanosi-Petrolli, half sitting, half lying on her bed – three pillows propping her up, her empty plastic cup with a straw in her right hand (she never let anything but disposable plastic touch her lips), and in her left hand, the television remote control.

The only thing unfamiliar about this picture was that the woman with forever-dyed platinum hair and a feather cut that hadn't been in style since Farrah Fawcett was a Charlie's Angel, was fat. My two-inches-short-of-fame-and-fortune model-weight mother, who all summer wore yellow and pink tube tops, was wearing a box-shaped lavender housecoat, slightly torn at the shoulder. This woman resembled the mother Jimmy had always wanted, a mother who wanted to feed you, not fuck you.

I had waited all my life for this moment. The moment when I could throw in my mother's face the words she'd said to me more times than my churning stomach would let me remember, words that told me what a great disappointment I was to her: *You're lucky you have a pretty face.*

I moved closer to my mother, but before I could say anything, she said, "Yes, your mother is fat. Go ahead, say it."

As usual, she beat me to the kick in the gut, and instead of wanting to take her down, I wanted to give her a kiss. But I knew better. If Mommy wasn't the one to initiate the kiss, she recoiled like a rattlesnake.

She grabbed my hand and placed it on her belly. I was expecting something inside to kick. "This is because those doctors put me on this medicine for my breathing."

"Can you breathe better?"

"Yes."

"That's great," I said, but I wasn't convinced. Mommy was whistling, which was what she did when her breathing wasn't, as she put it, "cooperating."

She reached up and tugged my bangs.

"Ouch." I swiped her hands away.

"They need more wisp." She pinched my cheek.

"What are you doing?" I swiped her hand away again.

"Trying to give you some color. You're as pale as a ghost. I thought it was always sunny in LA."

"Nice color on you," I said, the first sincere thing that popped into my head.

"This?" Mommy pulled on the front of her housecoat. "It belonged to Rita Malenetti."

"Your friend from the salon?"

"I helped her husband sell the house last year."

"Ma, she's dead."

"Exactly why he had boxes of her stuff to give away."

"You always said buying secondhand clothes was disgraceful. When I brought the wool coat home from the Salvation Army, you called me disgusting and threw it in the garbage."

"You didn't know who that coat belonged to."

"Wearing your dead friend's clothes is okay?"

"They're two completely different things."

I opened my mouth, but on second thought decided to let it go. If I had any chance of staying sane over the next few days, I would have to pick my battles wisely.

"Where's Jimmy?" I asked.

She muted the television. "How was your flight?"

"Fine," I said.

"No turbulence?"

"None."

"Did you drop at all?"

"Not at all."

"Oh." Mommy sounded disappointed. She'd never flown, but she'd always had this need to know about every bit of discomfort someone else felt. It was as if she believed the more discomfort they felt, the less there would be for her when she finally did fly.

"Mike said you would explain?"

"Since he's been home, the man is driving me crazy."

"Why didn't you tell me about Mike?"

"What about him?"

"His back? Ma. He can't work. Why didn't you tell me?" I looked at my mother, who called me every week to broadcast the weather in New York, LA, and some random places, the Dakotas or Syracuse.

"You were in California. What could you do?"

"I can't do anything about a tornado in Kansas City, but you never hesitate to call me when one touches down."

She stretched out her arms, now the thinnest part of her. I stiffened and held my breath, hoping to disappear. "Come." She took hold of my wrist and pulled me to her chest; there was a balloon between us that could pop at any moment. Where was this newly found display of affection coming from? I remembered from past experience: she wanted something from me. But it was something my mother couldn't demand, and that made me afraid.

She released me and scooted over. "Sit."

I was too jet-lagged to put up a fight. I also needed her to tell me what was going on with Jimmy.

She punched the pillow next to her. I sat. "Relax." She pulled the back of my shirt until it was resting against the headboard. I kept my feet on the floor.

"What are you doing? Put your feet up," she said.

"I'm okay," I said.

She bent over and lifted my legs onto the bed. "What are those?" She was pointing to my Birkenstocks. I kicked them off.

"They're comfortable," I said.

"Angela, there's more to life than comfort." She said this as she handed me her plastic cup to put on the fax machine, stretched her arms overhead, and unmuted the television. We remained silent during the commercial with cats meowing for the food on a silver tray. Mommy grabbed my hand and pulled me closer.

"You don't thank family," she said. "The ticket, my gift to you."

"You want me to thank you for the *one-way* ticket?"

"What did I say," she said. "No thanking me."

"I'm not thanking you," I said.

"I didn't get you a return ticket yet because I wasn't sure when you were going home."

"After the wedding," I said.

"I thought you might want to spend a little more time with your family." More time? I wasn't sure how I would make it through the next few days to this wedding. Already the walls in Mommy's bedroom were closing in on me.

"Where is the groom?" I asked.

"My show's on," she said, and I instinctively leaned forward to change the channel on the television; most of my childhood had been spent as my mother's pigtailed remote control. Before I could do my job, she clicked and changed the channel herself.

"The Italian Renaissance, you idiot," she yelled. Mommy had a head filled with facts and information that only *Jeopardy!* contestants needed to know. "What was the name of the game show you were on?"

She knew the name. *Say It, Don't Spray It* had been her favorite show, that is, until I was a contestant and let her down. The object of the game was to name the celebrity scandal, based on some obscure tabloid headline, or you could choose to hose down your opponent with slime. If your opponent knew the answer, you were slimed and lost a turn. Thanks to Mommy, who used *Cosmopolitan, People, Star,* and *National Enquirer* to find her bedtime stories when Jimmy and I were little, I got every question right. I lost the bonus round because I inadvertently called Demi Moore, Deby Moore. I went home with green slime in every nook, cranny, and crevice in my body, but I did walk away with thirteen thousand dollars.

Mommy didn't care about the money. She cared about the fame.

Serial killers are famous, I had told her when she called me from New York to insist that if I wanted to be discovered, I had better get my hair styled and wear at least a three-inch heel for the taping. She didn't find this as amusing as I had. She didn't find this amusing at all. In fact, she berated me for my insensitivity to the plight of our community. Ten years earlier, the .44 Caliber Killer, later called Son of Sam, had shot two of his victims around the corner from our house. I apologized, which I instantly regretted. My admission of guilt didn't earn my mother's forgiveness; it simply supplied her with more ammunition to use against me in the battle of why her daughter hadn't found a man yet. "Men don't want women who say stupid shit." And I'd thought that's all men wanted.

"*It is* a damn shame," Mommy reminded me now.

"Too bad nothing came of it." I beat her to the punch line.

"It is too bad. Talent scouts spot people on game shows and make them stars all the time."

"That's not how it works," I said. Actually, it did. After the show a Hollywood producer, the real deal, approached me. He offered me a leading role in his next movie. He said he could relate to my persona. I had no clue what he meant, but I figured it had something to do with the tough-Bronx-girl vibe, who at the time still said *youse,* the Bronx plural of *you,* and wasn't apologetic about it. I turned him down.

I had spent my entire childhood wishing on every birthday candle to be Jimmy, the star. Wishing I had been the baby that a commercial photographer discovered on the subway. Wishing that as a favor to Jimmy, his agent had sent me on a handful of auditions, and I had been "right" for the part, at least one. Instead, I was too tall, or too short, and always too chubby. Not fat. There was a market for fat kids. Not thin enough or fat enough, I was ordinary. I knew if my wish had come true, I would be the star and my father would pay attention to me.

In the moment the Hollywood producer was ready to grant my wish to make me a star, I remembered my brother with his head over the toilet right before every audition. It wasn't nerves, anxiety, or bad eggs; Jimmy was a natural, and acting came easy to him. He was sick to his stomach because our father would start drinking, or drink more, for every part Jimmy didn't get.

I hadn't been careful about what I wished for, because when I finally got it, it was clear I didn't want it.

I'd only been in LA a little over a year at that point, and far from ready to face home, but there was nothing for me in the City of Angels. The morning I was to going to buy a ticket back to New York with the money left from the game show winnings, which wasn't much after paying a whole lot of overdue bills, I saw an ad in one of the free weeklies: VOLUNTEERS WANTED TO BUILD HOUSES IN REVOLUTIONARY NICARAGUA.

I took this as a sign, or an excuse, for me not to go back home and face my brother.

I didn't know a lot about Nicaragua, or most of the world, unless a celebrity scandal was involved. Building houses, helping people, made sense to me. It would give me purpose and a break from the guilt I had lived with every day since the accident. I bought an airline ticket to Nicaragua, which was cheap since there wasn't a lot of tourism for a country that I would soon understand had been under attack by a US-fabricated-and-financed counter-revolutionary group, known as the Contras. In the company of five carpenters, two electricians, and a structural engineer, I, the unskilled labor, went to help the people of war-torn Nicaragua. The experience opened my eyes to a new world. Not to mention, it was the start of my activist career and my learning geography-fact: Nicaragua is not on the same continent as South Africa.

I could hear Alex Trebek's voice in my head. *"Please pick a category."*

Angela's Life for $200, the price of a one-way ticket back to Los Angeles.

"At the apex of her activist career, three days before Bush, with congressional and UN support, may get us into another unjust, money-grubbing, innocent-people-used-as-collateral-damage war, Angela is sitting on her mother's bed watching a game show where declarative statements — 'We Don't Want This Fucking War' and 'No Blood for Oil' are wrong answers. . . ."

What is another bad life decision?

"That's a trick question," Mommy yelled.

"Excuse me?" I said.

"The Library of Alexandria is in Egypt, not Greece. Can you believe she's a Harvard graduate?" Mommy waved the remote at the contestant in the middle. "Maybe you'll get the part in that television show."

Of course Dad would have told her about the pilot and my imaginary audition. Dad told her everything.

"Most pilots never make it to air," I said.

"A hamster that talks. I'd watch that. It's funny," Mommy smiled. "Why wouldn't it do well?"

It was time to slow down the fantasy train before it derailed, and get us back on track. "What's up with Jimmy?"

"He's getting married."

"I know that. Where is he now?"

"Out," she said.

"So I heard. Out where?"

She pointed the remote at me. "I'm not your brother's keeper." Mommy may not have been my brother's keeper, but she was his Lojack. She knew where he was at all times. She and Dad were homing devices when it came to Jimmy, and this was even before he got hurt, his childhood. It was different with me, probably because I didn't have to be anyplace that was going to cost me some commercial or sitcom or movie, another opportunity of a lifetime. Besides, I was usually with Jimmy. On the set, or at home helping him learn his lines, or trying to get him to ditch rehearsal and do something fun. I either played the supporting role in Jimmy's life, or the fun-loving sidekick who goaded him into taking risks and making bad choices.

"Ma, I know Jimmy doesn't want me here. I get that."

"Why would you say that?"

"You sent me a one-way ticket, yesterday. No formal wedding invitation, which I would have received at least three months ago. This is too off-script even for him."

A whistle could be heard beneath her deep sigh.

Mommy pointed the remote back at the TV and hit mute. "Do any of us know what we want?" When Mommy got philosophical on us, only one of two things happened – she would go off on a rant about something unrelated or she would go off on two rants about two things unrelated. It was time to leave the room. I started to get up but Mommy pulled me back. "Why are you still single?"

Bingo. Not only an unrelated topic, but also one for which there was no right response, even if I put it in the form of a question.

"There are Jews all over Hollywood." Mommy waved the remote around the room. "Why can't you find a nice Jewish man?"

I couldn't believe she was still harping on my marrying a Jewish man – the answer to all of the questions she had for my life. Jewish men, like Catholic men – with the rare exceptions of Dad and Mike, she always emphasized – cheated on their wives. But Jewish men gave their women everything they wanted in order to make up for it. Of course, the children would be raised Catholic.

We'd been here before, and I knew no matter what I said, she'd insist that something she considered a compliment couldn't be racist.

"Don't do this," I begged.

"What am I doing?"

"Changing the subject—"

"What subject?"

"Dad and Mike both said—"

She popped up into an erect seated position, turned to me, and through her teeth said, "What did those morons tell you?"

"They didn't tell me anything."

She let out a wheeze.

"It's what they weren't saying. What do you have under control?"

"Theresa, enough!"

This shut me up.

"You'll like her."

"Who?"

"Julie, the woman your brother's marrying."

This time I got up. I knew if I didn't leave immediately, I would revert back to the hysterical teenager I was when I left ten years ago.

"Get me the shoebox." She pointed to the always-off-the-track closet door on the other side of the file cabinet. I should have run, but shoes were Mommy's Valium. I thought if she felt calm and happy, she might give me a clue to what was going on around here. I struggled to slide the closet open. A black shoebox hit me in the head.

"Careful, those shoes are expensive."

The closet was jammed with shoes still in their original boxes. Mommy insisted shoes lived longer that way. "The blue one to your right," she said.

I pulled it off the shelf, miraculously not disturbing any of the trillion other shoes. It was all I could do to hold back from asking her if she had any idea how many people in this world, in this country, in New York State, couldn't afford even one pair of shoes.

SIZE 9 was printed on the front of the shoebox. Since my mother was barely a size 6, I knew whatever was in that box was for me. The only thing that made her happier than buying shoes for herself was buying shoes for someone else.

"Open it." She smiled widely, somewhat resembling The Joker from *Batman*.

Inside the box was exactly what I didn't want – six-inch slingback stiletto heels. Mommy thought my five-foot, eight-inch model height was my best feature, and accentuating it was, she claimed, the main reason she focused on my achieving model weight. The only feature these shoes were meant to accentuate was a latent desire to join the ranks of prostitution. But the height of the heels wasn't the most disturbing part of the shoes. They were dyed to match a color – mauve. Dyed-to-match mauve shoes meant there was a mauve dress I was expected to wear – a bridesmaid's dress? Was this the big secret Mommy didn't want me to know yet? She expected me to be a bridesmaid? I don't know if I was more relieved or repulsed, but I was certain my brother and the bride-to-be had no intention of my being part of their wedding party.

I dropped the shoes back into their box and reached up over the closet to touch the hanging crucifix, which had instilled fear in me since my First Holy Communion. With the exception of a tiny black mole on his cheek, which Jimmy had put there with an indelible Magic Marker, this Jesus's features were erased. His head leaned to one side, and he was missing the fake-blood color in all those places where he had been nailed to the cross.

After I made my First Communion, everything was Jesus to me. Every day, I'd climb up on a chair so I could kiss Jesus on each wound – the palm of his right hand, the palm of his left hand, and the place where his ankles crossed. Then, one day, Jesus slid down and fell off the cross. Convinced I'd broken Jesus, I started to cry, until Jimmy came into the room, stepped up onto the chair, and standing at my side, demonstrated how Jesus slid up and down.

"See, his body is a panel, hiding a secret compartment."

The inside of Jesus was empty.

Mommy later told me the secret compartment once held a vial of holy water and two candles, which a priest would need to perform last rites. "Priests don't need to break glass in case of an emergency, they need to break Jesus open." It was rare for her to make a joke, and I wanted to encourage her, so I laughed extra loud before I asked, "Who died?"

"No one died." She stopped smiling. "The candles and holy water vanished."

When I asked her if Jesus was a magician and could make things disappear, she bent down and whispered in my ear, "Only children who misbehave."

"Theresa!" Mommy was sucking on her inhaler.

I rushed back to her. "You okay?"

She looked down. The remote had fallen to floor. I picked it up and handed it to her. She grabbed my hand and said, "I am so sorry I beat you and your brother when you were little."

"Ma, you never beat us."

"You know what I mean." Unfortunately, I did. People in this neighborhood, in my family, didn't say sorry for what they did wrong. Instead, they apologized for what they didn't do. Mommy didn't beat us, not with her hands or with a spoon or belt. Her choice of weapon had been her tongue, the master of psychological warfare. In that sense, I supposed she had beaten us, and I wondered if a belt would have left less of a scar.

"It's freezing in here." I walked out.

"Where's the winter coat I bought you?" Mommy called after me.

CHAPTER 6

The dining room was painted red, a color Mommy insisted represented royalty, and she refused to acknowledge it was also a color popular in restaurants because it dulled the palate so patrons wouldn't taste the imperfections in the food.

Both ends of the six-foot-long glass-top dining table, bought for Mommy's fantasy dining room, a room three times the size of this one, fit flush against the walls, so no one sat at the head. There was also no way for me to walk around the table to get to my seat. I had to crawl under the same way I had when I was three. Crawling at almost thirty was harder on my knees and my self-esteem.

All the usual suspects sat in all the same places – Mommy directly across from me, with Dad on her right and Mike on her left. The only ones missing were Jimmy and Billy. After that afternoon's kiss, I was relieved this wasn't most nights, and a part of me was still relieved Jimmy wasn't here either. At the same time, the feeling I had waiting to see Jimmy made me even more anxious than I had been about the looming war – faceless, voiceless, a creature in the shadows clawing at my soul. I couldn't tell myself what I already knew, with our troops on the Iraqi border and Congress giving Bush the thumbs-up, we were already at war. I wouldn't admit what I was sure Jimmy would do when he first saw me. My biggest fear was he would go into his room and lock his door, and I would knock until my knuckles bled and he still wouldn't let me inside.

"Your favorites." Mike lifted the plate of antipast' in front of me.

Mommy stuck her fork into the sharp provolone and took a bite. "You went to Angelo's?" she asked.

"The best," Mike said.

"His prices are outrageous."

"Since when?" Mike said.

"Since we have a wedding and other expenses."

My mother had never worried about money. Whenever she bought something she clearly couldn't afford, she always said, "God gives us what we need." It was the same belief she took to Atlantic City. Sometimes God took a while to pay back the losses.

"Well, we can't return it," Mommy said. "Angela, eat."

Before I could explain that I was a vegan now, and what that meant in the context of Mommy's world, where you ate meat or died, Dad and Mom gave each other "the look." They were players in some spaghetti western, both reached for their guns, or in this case, the remote. Mommy, with the fastest reflexes this side of her bedroom, got it and clicked on the nineteen-inch color television mounted to the wall at the head of the table. *Wheel of Fortune,* her second-favorite game show, appeared. Dad wasn't staying down, though. He climbed up onto his chair and changed the channel old-school.

"It's the playoffs."

"It's always something." Mommy clicked back to *Wheel.* Dad changed the channel back to the team in green on the fourth yard line. The back-and-forth went on until Dad lost his balance and, to save himself from falling off the chair, kicked Mike's wine onto the antipast' and splashed marinated-mushroom juice onto the front of Mommy's housecoat.

"That's it." Mike stood. "James, get down from that chair and sit." And without having to be asked, Mommy relinquished the remote to Mike.

"We could watch the news," I said.

"The news," they said in unison, looking at me and my three heads.

"The news will give you agita before you eat." Mike clicked off the TV. "In honor of your homecoming, no television."

Dad mumbled something about the game and Mommy glared at Dad. It was always his fault.

"Angela, I'm sorry, it's ruined," Mike said, picking up the wine-drenched salami, prosciutt', provolone, and moozarell.

"The wine gives it flavor," Dad said as he reached for a piece of cheese.

Mommy slapped his hand. "What are you doing?"

"I was joking." Dad pulled what I thought was a poker chip from his pocket. "Three years sober."

"So you told me," I said. But the father who'd gulped, not sipped, the sacramental wine when taking communion being a recovering alcoholic was still surprising to me.

"You missed a lot living out there in La-La Land," Mommy said in her unsubtle accusatory tone.

Mike took the plate of antipast' back to the kitchen.

"Dad?"

"Things got a little out of control . . . ," Dad said.

"You wrapped the van around a telephone pole," Mommy said. "It's a miracle you're alive."

Another *what-could-you-do* my mother had never mentioned in our weekly phone conversations.

"What matters," Dad said, "is one day at a time. I'm okay."

"Thank God for Billy dragging your ass to a meeting," Mommy said.

"Did someone say my name?" a voice called from the doorway.

"Billy!" I practically squeaked. Mommy glared at me, but whatever comments lingered on the tip of her tongue she kept to herself.

Billy stood inside the front door wearing the skewed smile that made his face imperfect enough to be sexy and not ugly. The front of his jeans was covered in dried yellow paint.

"You're moving in now?" Dad lifted his glass of Coke in Billy's direction, and when I leaned forward, I saw that my backpack and suitcase were at his feet.

"It's nice seeing you around again," Mommy said.

"Kid is working hard, Rose. Give him a break," Mike said.

"Dropping off Angela's stuff." Billy glanced over at me. "I don't want to interrupt your dinner."

"Since when?" Dad said, smiling.

"Leave the bags there and come, sit and eat." Mommy pointed to the empty seat to my right, which was where Jimmy had sat until the wheelchair.

Billy crawled under the table and took the seat.

"I love the beard." I was flirting with Billy. He looked hotter than he ever had, but Billy was my brother from another mother, except we had sex once, or five times. We were experimenting, helping each other prepare for the outside world. I wasn't sure what I was doing now.

"Don't encourage him." Mommy reached out and tugged on Billy's beard. "He needs to shave and stop hiding his handsome face."

"Don't shave." I gently ran my smooth knuckles, not my fingers, calloused from using a staple gun to post NO WAR, NO MORE flyers on every SWIM AT YOUR OWN RISK sign along LA County beaches, over his beard.

Billy pressed his palms together and with restraint I admired softly said, "Why don't we let me worry about my facial grooming?" He dropped his hands and reached out to Mike, who was back and balancing a huge family-size bowl of rigatoni in one hand and a gravy boat in the other.

"Any luck?" Mike handed the pasta to Billy.

"Now is not the time," Mommy said.

"Let him speak, Rose." Mike dropped the gravy boat, splashing red onto the gold tablecloth. Mommy was too focused on Billy to notice.

Billy shook his head.

"You asked the guys at the—"

"Mike, enough. Time to eat." Mommy ladled pasta from the bowl, still in Billy's hand, onto my plate.

"What am I missing here?" I had to ask.

"Not your concern," Mommy said as she now ladled more pasta onto my plate. I extended my hand to stop another scoop from coming my way. If Mommy was force-feeding me, then there was no doubt that I should be concerned. Billy set the bowl with the remaining pasta on the table. Mommy served him two scoops and herself one.

"Hope it's not overcooked." She bit into a tube, oblivious to the shock that ricocheted around the table from her words. Mike picked up the bowl of remaining pasta, and from the way the corners of his mouth lifted straight up as he scooped rigatoni onto Dad's plate, it was clear he was upset. Mike's pasta, always al dente to perfection, was one of the only things Mommy didn't openly doubt and judge.

"It's fine," she pronounced, and I could hear Billy sigh with relief.

Now I knew something wasn't wrong, but *very* wrong in the house of Marchesi-Campanosi-Petrolli. It was time to talk about the elephant in the wheelchair.

"Is Jimmy coming home for dinner?" I tried to sound as casual as possible.

There was a moment of silence, a long moment, maybe the longest silence this family had shared since our parents sat down Jimmy and me, and Billy too, to tell us they were getting a divorce. Then Mommy scrunched her face and said, "Eat."

"You must be starving." Mike poured gravy over the mound of pasta on my plate, and that's when I saw the pieces of shredded flesh.

"There's meat in this gravy?"

"I bet you went to Angelo's for that, too," Mommy said. "Perfectly good supermarket right around the corner."

The supermarket? Mommy had always said supermarkets were for cleaning products and toilet paper. If it was something you put inside your body, you bought it from a store owner whose home address you knew.

"What else would there be in a meat gravy?" Mike laughed.

As Mommy's eyes rose toward me, I said, "All great," deciding I would eat around the flesh. I had been vegan for several years, and as much as the thought of eating red meat stabbed directly into my social conscience, I couldn't bring myself to criticize Mike's gravy. I'd save the discussion of the evils of meat for later in the meal, after I found out why no one was answering my very simple question.

"Is someone going to tell me where Jimmy is?"

More silence, which I would have attributed to their mouths being full if Mommy had been eating instead of staring at the television's blank screen.

The sense of doom in the air was so pervasive that I swallowed a piece of rigatoni whole, and the tube got stuck in my esophagus.

I forced myself to cough but couldn't get it to come up.

"Drink this." Billy handed me a glass. I gulped, a combination of wine and Coke sprayed out of my nose, which forced me to cough harder.

"Do something," Mommy shouted.

"Hit her on the back," Dad yelled.

"Stand," Billy ordered. I listened, and he pushed my chair to the side and squeezed behind me. He wrapped his arms around me, and with both his fists, hit me smack center in the gut. The tube shot out of my mouth and onto Mommy's plate. Dad and Mike both crossed themselves.

"Thank you." I sat back down, thinking this wasn't the first time Billy had been there for me.

Mommy flipped her hair, and turned her head so fast in my direction I expected gravy to spew from her mouth. "Say what you need to say."

Dad and Mike sat frozen, the proverbial deer in the headlights: *If they don't move, she won't see them.* Billy gently put his hand on my thigh, his way of telling me to let it go – but if he remembered anything about me, he knew I couldn't let most things go, and this was no different.

"Where's the fucking groom?" I managed not to keep my voice steady and calm.

"Watch your mouth!" Mommy stabbed her fork into a piece of rigatoni. She had to be fucking kidding me. She and everyone in this neighborhood said *fuck* so often, it was used as an adjective, a verb, and a noun.

"Rose, we have to tell her," Mike said.

"He's right." Dad reached for more pasta and Mommy slapped his hand.

"There's nothing to tell. And I don't want to hear another word about it."

"Jimmy doesn't want me at his wedding, I get it. It doesn't make any sense to make things worse and force him and his fiancée to make me a bridesmaid."

"A bridesmaid!" Mommy looked happier than I had ever remembered seeing her. "Did Julie call and ask you?"

"The mauve shoes, Ma."

Disappointment washed over her face, the shadow of death in *The Ten Commandments,* Jimmy's second-favorite movie. "I thought in case—"

"You have to stop this, Ma."

"Stop what?"

"You invite me to his wedding, knowing he doesn't want me here."

"I know no such thing." Her voice cracked. If I didn't know her, I would think she was going to cry.

"I only got the ticket yesterday?"

"They only got engaged two weeks ago." Mommy hit her fist against the table, and Billy reached out and grabbed her plastic cup of Diet Pepsi, saving my pasta from the same ill fate as the antipast'.

I put my hand over Billy's and pressed it into my thigh. "Two weeks? Jimmy?"

"Don't you ever give up?" Mommy stood. "Let it go, for Christ's sake." She stalked to her bedroom and closed the door. The lock clicked and there I was again, an eight-year-old girl at her mother's door, begging, "Let me in, please, Mommy. Say you love me. Please, say you love me!"

Billy pulled his hand out from under mine. "Ange."

"Billy, what's going on?"

Mike plopped down into Mommy's seat and Dad dropped his head, both shot in the heart with the same bullet.

"You see . . . ," Mike started.

"Three days ago . . ." Dad looked up.

"Jimmy disappeared." Billy brought it on home. Of course, I had no idea what he was talking about, but before I could ask, he continued, "Thursday morning—"

"Wednesday," Dad said.

"I think it was Thursday," Mike said.

"I could have sworn it was Wednesday. . . ."

"Please, it doesn't matter." I could feel the adolescent bubbling up inside of me. "Billy, tell me what happened."

"Jimmy called me to ask if I could give him a ride, and it couldn't have been more than thirty minutes before I got here. He had already left."

"His bed was made," Mike said. "Since your brother has never made a bed in his life, he probably was up all night, sitting in the chair."

"I drove down to the El," Billy continued. "Figured I'd catch him before he got on the train, but he wasn't around, and when I asked Frank—"

"Frank?" I asked.

"He replaced Vinny in the token booth," Mike said.

"Vinny's dead," Dad said.

"Dead? How?"

Mike shook his head. "He moved to Florida."

Dad shrugged. "Like I said, dead."

"Anyway . . ." I could hear the frustration in Billy's voice, which surprised me; he'd always had so much more patience for this family than I did. "Frank said he hadn't seen Jimmy in months, so I drove around a bit to see if I could find him, when I remembered that Jimmy hadn't asked me to play his number that morning, so then I went to the candy store to see if he had gone there himself, and Nick said his number hit. Paid out $5000."

"What did the police say?" I asked.

Now everyone was staring at the blank television screen.

"You're telling me that Jimmy's been gone since Wednesday and no one called the police?"

"Thursday," Mike said. "I'm sure it was Thursday."

"Pretty sure it was Wednesday," Dad said. In the past I'd found Dad and Mike's "Who's on First" routine amusing, especially because, as devoted fans as they were of Abbott and Costello, they had no idea they were doing it. But in that moment, I wanted to "Who's on First" them across their faces.

"You call the police when a person has been missing for more than twenty-four hours."

"I think for adults it's forty-eight hours," Dad said.

"It's twenty-four," Mike said.

"Are you sure?" Dad asked.

"Are you all out of your minds? We need to call the police now!" I slid off the chair and crawled under the table to the other side, but Mommy's swollen ankles blocked me from getting out. I wasn't sure when she'd reappeared from her room.

Mommy banged her fist against the glass above me. I cringed, afraid it would come crashing down on me.

"Stop making this about you," she said.

"You have got to be joking." I crawled over to Dad's feet but Mommy shouted, "Block her!" And he did.

"Sorry," he mumbled. I looked up through the glass. Billy, staring down at me, mouthed something I couldn't make out. There I was, back in my old life, a sitcom one episode away from cancellation. I started punching, then kicking, up at the glass.

"Stop!" Mommy shouted. "If it cracks—"

"What? You're going to let me disappear too?"

"Stop being so dramatic! He left a note." Mommy pulled a folded piece of paper from her pocket and shoved it under the table at me.

"You'd think you would have started with this." I unfolded the paper, and in Jimmy's controlled Catholic-school always-stay-within-the-lines handwriting were the words *I'll be back.*

"This is it?" I looked up at Billy.

"That's it," he said.

"Who does he think he is, Arnold Schwarzenegger?" I said, doing a very bad impersonation of the Terminator.

"I didn't think of that." Dad smiled, and I knew he saw this as another sign that Jimmy wanted to act again.

"God help us," I said, and she did. The phone rang.

Mike reached over and picked up the receiver from the phone mounted to the wall. "Hello," he said, unraveling the cord, which was long enough to reach the bathroom.

Mike looked terrified. "Let me get Rose." He covered the receiver and mouthed, "It's Julie."

"What does she want now?" Mommy asked.

"Her missing fiancé?" I said.

Mommy kicked her two-inch beige pumps at me but missed, and I came close to shouting, "Your shoes don't match your outfit." There were some things you couldn't take back.

"What do you want me to say?" Mike's knuckles whitened as he gripped the receiver.

Mommy tapped the glass, and when I glared up at her, she said, "If you say anything to upset this girl . . ." Her mouth, like a bottle of Windex, sprayed saliva across the table. That was the last spit. It was time for me to grow up, but first I needed the nerve to crawl out.

"Julie doesn't know," Dad said.

"Are you kidding me?" But I knew he wasn't.

"Jimmy's not missing," Mommy said.

"Rose, what do I tell her?" Mike interrupted.

"I'll talk to her," Dad said.

"Don't you dare! The last thing we need is you screwing this up."

"Hey, I'm no Al Pacino, but I certainly have enough talent to pull this off," Dad said, doing a poor impression of Al Pacino in *Godfather II*. But he couldn't even pull off Al Pacino in *Godfather III* – the embarrassment of the trilogy. Dad may have sat in on every acting lesson that Jimmy took, and memorized every one of Jimmy's lines, but his delivery was always off. Dad couldn't even lie. Whenever he tried, he deepened his voice, Darth Vader on steroids.

Mike stretched the phone cord to Mommy.

I could hear the whistle as she took a deep breath. "Julie, how are you?" Mommy's right foot tapped faster and faster and then she switched to her left and then back to her right. I thought she might at any minute break and do a full Broadway dance routine. "You know the rules. No talking to the groom before the wedding." Her face beamed with deceit. "I know four days is forever when you're in love. . . ."

"I knew it was Wednesday," Dad mumbled.

"He's not even here right now, but you know who is?" Silence. "That's right. Angela." Silence. "A few hours ago. She'd love to say hello." Mommy shoved the phone under the table, but I scooted out of her reach. I had no interest in talking to Jimmy's fiancée, especially when she had zero idea that the man she was planning to marry in a few days was missing.

Mommy stomped her right heel. I shook my head real fast, and my adolescent self was now my toddler self.

She waved a half-opened hand at me. She couldn't be bothered to commit to the whole fist. "I'm sorry; she's in the restroom." Silence. Mommy hung up. "She's coming over."

"Are you crazy?" Mike said. "You told her to come over?"

"She *told* me," Mommy said, and if I hadn't witnessed it, I wouldn't have believed it. No one told Mommy anything.

"I better get going," Billy said, and instinctively I reached out and grabbed onto his calf.

"You can't," I said.

"Sorry, but I have" – he hesitated for only a second, but I knew whatever he said next would be a lie – "a stop to do."

"On a Sunday?" Dad may have stopped going to church, but he never stopped treating Sundays as sacred.

"Five Star Deli in Riverdale," Billy answered a little too fast. "Mice," he said.

"You know the good news about having mice," Dad said.

"You don't have rats," all of us said in unison, the way we had a million times before.

"Yup, they don't cohabitate." Dad always had to get in the last line when it came to vermin.

Please, don't go, I mouthed to Billy. I wasn't ready to be left here with my family and a fiancée on the way.

Billy got up from his chair, crawled under the table, and stood by Mommy.

I tried to grab his leg again but he moved out of my reach. I needed him to stay.

Mommy stuck her fist under the table and shook it in my face. "Your brother won some money and he's somewhere blowing off pre-wedding steam. He's probably in Atlantic City. Nothing for Julie to worry about, so keep your mouth shut."

It wasn't hard for me to believe that Jimmy was in Atlantic City. For Jimmy and Mommy, gambling was therapy. They claimed it calmed and cleared their minds. It was impossible for me to understand why Jimmy would be getting married two weeks after he got engaged. Unless Julie was . . . "She's pregnant!"

"Your brother told me it was none of my business."

Mike walked over to Mommy. "Sweetie, he didn't say that."

"What did he say? Tell me?"

"He asked for your support." Mike tried to put his arm around her, but she pulled away.

"When have I ever *not* given him my support?"

Dad sighed. Mommy spun her head in his direction faster than Linda Blair in *The Exorcist;* I expected pea soup to spew out of her. "My wanting his obsessed father to back off on the acting nonsense was supporting him."

"Nonsense." Dad stood.

"Not the time," Billy said. Dad sat back down.

"It makes sense," I said.

"It makes sense that my son won't confide in me?" Mommy said.

"If he got her pregnant, of course he'd do the right thing and propose. He probably freaked out and ran away."

Billy knelt, touched my cheek, and looked at me pleadingly. "You don't understand."

"You've seen him? Talked to him? Do you know where he is?"

"Don't make this about you."

I stared at Billy. Having my mother imply that I was self-centered was comical, but hearing this from Billy stung.

Billy rose to his feet. "He will be there to roll down the aisle."

"How do you know?"

"You have to trust—"

"Billy, enough." Mommy pointed at the door. "Go and take care of business."

CHAPTER 7

Without as much as a "See ya," Billy left. Mommy slammed the door behind him; I saw my escape and climbed out from under the table. Mommy got right in my face, so close our noses almost touched.

"What is he thinking, doing a stop on a Sunday?" Dad said, more to himself than to any of us. "Once you agree to work on a Sunday, they want all your Sundays. I told him that a thousand times. . . ."

"He's not spraying today," Mommy scoffed, but she kept her eyes on me now. "You saw the yellow paint on his jeans."

"What is he doing, cheating on the exterminating business?" I said. "And painting apartments on the side?"

"He's doing some art thing," Mike muttered.

Mommy had the twinkle in her eyes she always got when she knew something that I didn't know. "He started when he was in rehab," Mommy said.

"Idle hands are the devil's workshop," Dad said.

"Better to have a paintbrush in your hand than a hypodermic needle," Mike added.

I was going to ask them to tell me more, when Mommy said, "Julie will be here any minute." I unclenched my fist, exposing the now balled-up note. *I'll be back!* "That is something you write when you go out to get milk or bread or cigarettes, knowing you're never returning."

"Or you're planning a comeback." Dad stood and, bending deep from the waist, bowed the way the leading actors always do at the end of the play. "You have to admit this was a very dramatic and bold choice. This could be his way of getting his feet wet."

"Please." With one word Mommy said what we were all thinking: *Let it go. Jimmy is never returning to the screen or stage.*

"It's still possible." Dad returned to his seat but this time with his back to us.

"I never even met this woman, but she has the right to know Jimmy doesn't want to get married."

"Angela, I'm asking you to please don't say anything. Please." Was my mother pleading? Begging? This was a first. Mommy only ever demanded.

The desperation in her eyes gave me no choice. "Okay." I put the balled-up note in her housecoat pocket.

Mommy opened her mouth and a sharp wheeze blew out. "Thank you."

Another first, I thought.

Mike tried to put his arm around her, but she pulled away. "Let me get your inhaler," he said.

"Stay out of this," she told him.

I excused myself and went to my childhood sanctuary, the only room in the house where we were allowed to lock the door. The bathroom.

I sat down on the crocheted toilet seat cover and waited for the knock. As often as Mommy locked us out, she couldn't bear for us to do the same to her. She was sure to demand I come out so we could "sit down and discuss the situation," which meant she'd tell me exactly what she wanted me to say when Jimmy's fiancée arrived, and how if I didn't go along with the plan, I would be betraying the family and my brother, who, in case I had forgotten since the last time she reminded me, I owed.

A lifetime of covering for Jimmy wouldn't even begin to repay my debt to him. Besides, I wasn't so sure that Jimmy wanted me to cover for him – I may have not seen or talked to my brother in ten years, but I knew Jimmy better than any of them, and I was convinced this was his cry for help.

I had to admit that the note he'd left was so Jimmy. He wasn't one for monologues. He used as few words as possible. He was the listener. I was the talker, the rambler. I had the compulsion to explain everything. The day I left home I told everyone, "Need a change of scenery. See you in two weeks." I had no idea when or if I would be back, and no one asked. In fact, it took Billy several years to convince the family that Mommy's silence on why I left wasn't because she didn't care. She saw my life in the Bronx as a broken garbage disposal. It made a lot of noise but the scraps swirled around and around and went nowhere until they rotted. I was sure she borrowed the metaphor from Mike, but it was true; I needed to get away, far away. Distance didn't make the guilt vanish, but it had made life bearable enough for me to take action, make changes, and be a better person.

I got up and turned on the right faucet of the double sink. No water. The left faucet worked. For as long as I could remember, one of the two was broken. You'd think with a plumber living here, it wouldn't be a problem, but Mike had enough on his hands keeping this family fed and from falling apart to worry about our plumbing.

See? I reassured myself. *Nothing's changed.*

I splashed water on my face, avoiding my reflection in the mirror. I knew I looked worse than shit. An Amnesty International documentary I'd seen demonstrated how sleep deprivation was an effective means of torture; between pulling an all-nighter planning for Saturday's rally, and failing to get any shut-eye on the plane, I was almost forty-eight hours without sleep.

I dried my face on the same green-and-red hand towel Mommy put out every Christmas season as far back as I could remember. The towels were for show and the occasional guest only, but Jimmy and I used them whenever Mommy was out of the house. Right now, it didn't matter that Mommy was home, because I was a guest.

But when I looked up and saw the lift device attached to the tub, reality slapped me in the face – hard. I had a choice about being here. Jimmy didn't. He would come back and go through with the wedding. He would marry a woman he probably didn't even love, because he had nowhere to run, nowhere to hide. If Mommy, and Dad, and Mike, and even Billy, his best friend, weren't there for him, what choice did he have but to get married?

Then came the knock, and I made myself look at my reflection, and I told myself out loud, "You fight for social justice, and sacrifice for others, you get things done by any means necessary. You are an activist." And for the first time in ten years, I wanted to see Jimmy.

Because right then and there, I had the solution to Jimmy's problems: I was the solution. I had figured out a way to make up for – not everything, but for some things, maybe most things. I'd bring Jimmy to California, where I knew several organizers with physical disabilities, and they would help us get whatever services he needed and connect Jimmy to a community of people where he could be himself. Maybe by seeing what was possible, he would believe he could again do what he loved most in the world: acting. Dad had been right not to give up on the dream. Jimmy could still be a star.

Of course, I told myself, he couldn't, nor would he want to, abandon his soon-to-be-born child, but people raised children bi-coastally all the time. Didn't they? We could visit him or her in New York every other month and the baby could stay with us for part of the time, which would be good for the mother. Everyone needed a break. After Mom and Dad's divorce, it was rare for Dad to have had it together enough to take Jimmy and me for a whole weekend, but when he did, Mommy was always happier and more relaxed when we returned home.

I nodded at my reflection. I was an activist, and the two things any activist worth their shit needed I had: a clear mission and a plan to carry it out. My mission – stop this wedding. The plan – find Jimmy and take him to California.

There was another knock. This time I was ready to open the door, but when I did, instead of my short, newly rounded mother sneering in my face, a model-height-and-weight bleached blonde wrapped her arms around me and squealed, "Sister!"

CHAPTER 8

The meat was almost served.

Mommy stood and offered Julie her seat, a gesture I had only seen her make once before, when Father Roberto, our neighborhood priest, dropped by to solicit money for the third church restoration in two years. Mommy had offered her seat, and as soon as Father Roberto sat, she stood, lecturing him about the Crusades and how it wasn't their love of God, but their greed that led to their raping and pillaging. Of course, Mommy didn't give Father Roberto a dime that day, but she did give him a cannoli to go.

"I'm good," Julie said, and I wondered if she knew about Father Roberto. "I was in the neighborhood."

"That's how you got here so fast." Mommy's smile was as tight as a botched plastic surgery.

"I was ordering the cake from Dominick's and I weakened. I wanted to hear Jimmy's voice, so I called from a pay phone." She paused, and when she glanced over at Mommy, her face lit up with the glow of an angel's, or of someone gullible enough to marry into this family. Telling her about Jimmy would be doing her a favor. Of course, I knew it would be difficult and confusing at first, but if she really loved him, she would want him to be happy. And if she didn't love him, and was only marrying him because she was pregnant, well, screw her. It was her choice to have this baby, wasn't it?

"Angela!" Mommy snapped me out of my head. "Wasn't it nice of Julie to come by to see you?"

I opened my mouth to say something, when the innocent one interjected, "When I heard that my future sister-in-law was here . . ." Julie paused and hugged me again. "Jimmy's told me so much about you."

"I hope it wasn't all bad," I said, assuming, of course, it was.

She stepped back and held me at arm's length. "You're so your brother. Same sense of humor."

I didn't know how to respond to that. Jimmy was a lot of things, but humor had never been his strong point, irony was nearly impossible for him, and his sarcasm contained no wit and all bite. Unless she knew a side of Jimmy I wasn't aware of, she had insulted me.

"Speaking of my brother, I haven't seen him yet. How is he?"

"You haven't seen him yet?" Her voice rose at least one octave, and I almost felt ashamed for "pulling a Republican" on her. That's what I called pulling the rug out from under someone.

"Of course not," Mommy said through gritted teeth. "He couldn't risk running into you." She put her arm around Julie's shoulder and guided her toward the table. I could see from Julie's face that she was trying to make sense of Mommy's explanation, which had more holes in it than Ollie North's testimony at the Iran-Contra hearings.

"Julie, we're so glad you're here." Mommy went for the diversion tactic.

"Mrs. Petrolli . . ."

"Rose, please."

"Rose." Julie took in a deep breath, and held on until she said, "I didn't even know I was coming over until a half hour ago."

I couldn't wait to see how Mommy was going to talk her way out of this one. If I had been sitting, I would have leaned back in my chair and crossed my arms, but I was standing, and crossing my arms felt awkward, so I instead tried to casually lean up against the back of Dad's chair. This time it was Mommy who pulled a Republican. She stepped closer to me, wrapped her arm tightly around my waist, leaned her head against my bicep and said, "It's so good to have my baby girl home." Julie flashed a polite smile while Mommy continued, "I told Jimmy that I was going to call you and insist you come over to meet Angela." Her fingers pressed into my ribs. "I tried calling you, but obviously you weren't home because you were already in the neighborhood." She's good, I thought. "I was about to leave you a message when I was interrupted by one of these two." She tilted her smile toward Mike and Dad. "Some days I can't tell them apart," she said with a laugh.

I revised my earlier opinion. She wasn't good – she was great. The master manipulator.

Julie bought it, hook, line, and sinker. Her earlier suspicions instantly dissipated and relief poured over her face.

"I told you on the phone," Mommy continued, "bad luck to see the bride."

"It's sweet that he's so traditional," Julie said.

I didn't know whether to slap her or help her escape; though, at that moment, I was the one caught in my mother's death grip. Then again, I thought, people believed what they wanted to believe. They wanted simple stories. Saddam Hussein was an evil dictator and President Bush was doing the right thing by standing up to him. Simple, white bread goes down easy, and the aftermath of consuming empty calories is a problem to worry about down the road. The morality of innocent people dying to keep the price of oil cheap was too complicated to process during the twenty minutes a day most people listened to the news, which included the weather and traffic updates.

Jimmy was gone because he didn't want to get married. I had to make Julie see that.

"Jimmy's always been big on tradition – kind of superstitious, really," I said, piling it on. "Especially when it comes to weddings. So I was surprised to hear that he was getting married so quickly. You know, without the traditional year of planning."

"If circumstances were different," Julie began, and this was it, I thought; finally she would admit to the pregnancy, and then I could help her see that a loveless marriage wasn't good for any child.

But of course, Mommy wasn't giving up that easily. "James," she screamed, "it's bleeding!"

Our heads turned in unison, all trains of thought interrupted, exactly as she'd wanted. Dad cut into the roast.

"Looks delicious," Mike said.

"Give me that." Mommy grabbed the knife from Dad's hand and lifted the crown roast to the sky, then shoved the platter into Mike's hands. "Do you know how many germs there are in the blood?" Of course none of us, including Mommy, knew, but there was no arguing with a mother who believed the only proper way to eat red meat was brown and overcooked.

Dad gave Mike his *please save us both* look, and Mike hesitated. Then Mommy blinked, and Mike hurried off to the kitchen, leaving a trail of rare roast drippings behind him. Dad looked as if he might cry.

"Julie, please, you must sit and join us for some pasta." Mommy gave a Vanna White hand gesture to the remaining rigatoni in the bowl. Maybe I needed to buy a vowel, I thought.

"It's so hard for me to turn down your gravy." Julie smiled, still standing.

"Mike's gravy," I said.

"What about my gravy?" Mike burst in from the kitchen.

"I think when two people are married they get to take credit for each other's accomplishments," Julie said.

Mommy stuck the tip of her tongue out at me.

"My gravy is your gravy." Mike wrapped his arm around Mommy's shoulders and kissed her on the cheek. This time she didn't push him away.

"Get her a plate," Mommy said to Dad.

Dad stood.

"I'm fine." Julie flashed the palm of her hand at him. Dad sat. "As much as I would love to, I have to fit into that dress," she said, patting her stomach. I looked down, but her coat was too bulky to tell how far along she was.

"You shouldn't be worrying about weight," Mommy said, probably for the first time in her life.

"Thank you, Rose."

"Can I take your coat?" I asked.

"Where are our manners?" Mommy said. "Please, Julie."

Julie took off her coat and handed it to Mommy, who handed it to Dad, who stood up and asked, "Where do you want me to put it?"

"The bedroom."

Dad walked toward Jimmy's room.

"And take Angela's bag in there too." Without skipping a beat, Mommy turned to Julie and said, "Let's get you something to eat."

I looked down at Julie's abdomen. Flat as a board. She wasn't showing. Maybe not having this baby was still an option, I thought. "Are you Catholic?" I asked.

"Excuse me?" Julie sat in Mommy's chair.

"I was wondering if you were having a church wedding," I said.

"Justice of the peace," Mommy said.

"You're not Catholic?" I asked.

"A church wedding would be great, if there was enough time."

"Enough time?" I jumped almost a foot closer to her.

Mommy stepped between Julie and me and put both hands in full "Stop! In the Name of Love" position, only she didn't sing the way Jimmy, Billy, and I had when we jumped in front of cars as kids. She spoke slowly, pronouncing every syllable, so there would be no doubt as to what she had said. "There will be time to talk about the wedding after this girl gets some food into her."

"Rose, I'm really okay. I ate a late breakfast."

"Of course you'll have a little something." Mommy wasn't going to give up.

"Julie, tell her you're not hungry," I prompted.

"Don't tell her what to say," Mommy said.

"I'm not telling her what to say."

"You just did."

"Well, you told her what to do!"

"Rose," Julie said, and I detected a slight bit of frustration. For a split second, I felt hope for her yet, and then she said, "I could eat a little something."

I huffed and puffed until Mommy turned to me. "That LA air, I told you, it's causing damage to your lungs."

It was all I could do to stop myself from yelling and stamping my feet, but a temper tantrum wasn't going to help Jimmy. And oh, did he need my help. Julie was all wrong for my brother. Jimmy needed a wife who could stand up to his mother, not some sweeter-than-saccharine wimp, a woman who tasted delicious but was carcinogenic.

"You'll have to have some roast, then," Mommy said, and I could hear how pleased she was with herself.

"I thought you knew I was vegetarian," Julie said, and I nearly shouted, "Me too." But before I could, Mommy got right up in Julie's face.

"You're anti-meat?" She had the same self-righteous tone the right-to-life protestors used on me when I had done clinic defense work. Abortion was against God, but pushing a scared pregnant teen to the ground and kicking her in the face to avoid damaging the fetus apparently was okay in the eyes of their Lord. I wanted to speak up and defend Julie, but if Mommy was against Julie, it would be so much easier to stop this marriage. So I went against my core principles as an activist, and kept my mouth shut.

"It's not so much that I'm anti-meat," Julie said. "There are so many healthy alternatives that it doesn't justify the damage it does."

"What damage?" Mommy said.

"It's burning." Dad had stood up, and now he rushed past us. "The roast. I'll save it." He pushed open the kitchen door and smoke billowed in our direction. Everyone but Mommy coughed. The interesting thing about her allergies was that they only seemed to be irritated by nature and stress. A room filled with man-made, or rather, Mommy-made smoke didn't bother her at all.

There was a loud crash of unidentified objects and two "oh shits," followed by another crash and two "Jesus Christs."

"Mike, please go see what he's doing." Mommy pointed at the kitchen.

Mike nodded and went after Dad.

The three of us kept our eyes on the kitchen door until Dad reappeared, carrying a platter of burnt meat to the table. "Saved the middle."

"Let's adjourn to the living room for dessert." Mommy stabbed the knife, still in her hand, into the heart of the roast.

"The meat is edible." Dad popped a piece of burnt roast into his mouth as Mike returned from the kitchen. We all watched as Daddy chewed, and then spat into a napkin. "Dessert would be great."

Mike walked back to the kitchen, mumbling inaudibly under his breath.

"I wish I could stay," Julie said. "I have a dozen errands still left to do, but I have a favor to ask of Angela." She stood and smiled at Mommy, and when Mommy smiled and nodded back, I felt a spasm in my gut.

Julie stepped in between Mommy and me, cupped both her hands over my right hand, and said, "Angela." She paused to clear her throat. "Angela," she repeated.

"Yes, Julie?" I said.

"It would be a great honor—"

She's going to ask me to be a bridesmaid, I thought, or worse, a maid of honor. An ugly mauve gown flashed before my eyes.

"Julie, listen, you hardly know me—"

"Theresa Angela," Mommy snapped. "Don't interrupt." There was that twinkle. She knew exactly what Julie was going to ask. She probably already had the mauve dress in her closet.

"Julie, please continue," Mommy said, taking her seat at the table.

Julie looked at her and then at me, and it was clear she had no idea what was going on, but I had to give her credit for not skipping another beat. "Angela, will you be Jimmy's best man?"

Mommy coughed. Turned out she was the one who'd been Republicaned.

"I don't have to wear mauve, do I?" I thought the more I rubbed in Mommy's face this complete disregard for all that was sacred in Pelham Bay wedding tradition – girls were bridesmaids, not best men – the more she'd turn against Julie.

"You can wear anything you want," Julie said.

"A tux?" I asked.

"One of my customers has a tux rental shop. We can get matching tuxedos," Dad said.

"What do you think, Ma?" I smirked at Mommy, who was being uncharacteristically quiet. She opened her mouth, but all that came out was a deep wheeze followed by more coughing.

"You okay?" I asked.

"She's going to cough up a kidney," Dad said.

"Get her inhaler," Julie said. Before I could react, Dad ran into Mommy's bedroom.

"Raise your arms above your head. Now," Julie ordered.

Mommy did as she was told and the coughing subsided.

"Got it." Dad ran out of Mommy's bedroom holding her inhaler in the air. "Thank God we have a nurse in the family."

Julie took the inhaler and put it into Mommy's mouth. "Breathe in." She depressed it once and Mommy sucked in. "Now hold."

To Julie's count of five, Mommy held her breath. "One more time," Julie said, and they repeated the ritual.

Dad looked how I felt. Lost.

"You okay?" Julie asked, and sat down next to Mommy.

Mommy nodded and then gasped. "Best man!"

Mommy was shocked and I was dumfounded. Where did she get off asking me to be my brother's best man as if it were Jimmy's idea? I hadn't been my brother's best anything in over ten years.

"Who wants a honey ball?" Mike was carrying a large tray of one-inch dough balls drenched in honey. Mommy reached out, grabbed a handful, and shoved them into her mouth.

I couldn't have found a better time to pop the question. "Julie, when is the baby due?"

Julie looked at me. "Baby?"

Mommy spat what she hadn't already swallowed of the honey balls into a napkin. "She's not pregnant."

"Please, Ma." I put my hand on Julie's shoulder, hoping to give this poor woman some comfort in her time of need-to-get-the-hell-away-from-this-loony-bin family. "It's okay to say she's pregnant. We're adults."

"It would be okay," Julie said. "If I was, but I'm not."

"I grew up here. We all knew someone in high school that went to Italy and came back right at the time their mother gave birth to their baby brother or sister."

"I knew two of those someones in middle school," Julie interjected.

"We're adults," I said, even though I was afraid if I looked in the mirror right then, I would see the child banging at her mother's locked door, begging to be let inside.

"You don't understand," Julie said.

"You're a grown woman. It's 1991. You don't have to hide your pregnancy. You don't even have to have it."

Mommy stood, and Julie grabbed her hand before her palm made contact with my face. I was shocked. My mother had never tried to hit me before.

Mommy scooted back into her chair, scraping the black and white linoleum tile with the bottom of the chair. The remorse for what she'd almost done was so clear I almost told her I was sorry.

Julie had at least three inches on me. I had to tilt my head back to look her in the eyes.

"Angela, I'm not pregnant."

"Then what's the rush on the wedding?"

"Julie's going to war." Dad was back, and I was confused.

"What does he mean?" I held eye contact with Julie.

"If you knew anything about what was happening outside of La-La Land," Mommy interjected, "you'd know we are going to war with the Middle East."

"Iraq," Julie and I said in unison.

"Isn't that the Middle East?" Mommy was peeling honey balls stuck to her fingers.

"It's in the Middle East, not the whole region," I said.

"Since when have you become a world affairs expert?"

"Rose, there are many countries in the area that are our allies. The Middle East is a misnomer. Depends on your perspective. It's the Middle of East of what and to whom?" Julie smiled at me. I wasn't sure if she had come to my defense or insulted me. The irony of my mother educating me about politics, or the world outside of Pelham Bay not reported on *Entertainment Tonight,* wasn't lost on me. The irony of Julie, a woman I had known for all of a half hour, if that, correcting my knowledge of the region I had spent the last six months trying to prevent this country from bombing felt insulting.

"You're going to war?" I glared into the chocolate in her eyes. "What does that mean?"

"Julie's in the reserves." Dad reached between us and grabbed a honey ball from Mommy's middle finger and popped it into his mouth. "If we go to war, Julie's flying out the day after the wedding."

"Are you out of your fucking mind?" The words left my mouth before I could stop or censor them.

"The verdict is still out," she laughed.

Dad and Mommy joined her, though they weren't using their ha-ha laugh, which rarely happened at the same time. This was their we-are-uncomfortable-and-want-this-situation-to-go-away laugh. Mike sat quiet, too quiet. It was as if he was bracing himself for the storm only he knew was coming.

"I don't understand how you could support this war. It's wrong."

"Wrong?" Mommy and Dad both said in unison. I don't remember them ever standing on the same side of anything until now.

"He's a brutal dictator that must be stopped."

Mommy grabbed the edge of the table as if she was going to use it to stand but then plopped back into her seat.

"He has been warned," Dad said. "If he doesn't back off, then he deals with the consequences. The world can't see that we're weak." Dad had almost as much conviction in his voice as he had when he talked about Jimmy's career and how some director was an idiot for not casting him.

"He kills babies," Mommy continued.

I sat in the chair next to her and took hold of her sticky hand. "Do you know how many babies, innocent children, will die if we start bombing?"

Mommy pulled her hand out from under mine.

"Do you really think this is about us doing the 'right' thing?" I glanced over at Dad, who was eyeing his half-empty glass of Coke and wine.

"What's wrong with that?" Mommy and Dad again spoke the same words at the same time. What was happening? This war was bringing my parents together? Something two children and almost fifteen years of marriage couldn't do.

"Didn't we learn anything from Vietnam?" I asked.

Now Mommy got up quickly. On her tippy toes, she stretched her neck and kissed Julie on both cheeks. "I'm going to rest. You may want to rethink this best man choice." With Mike following behind, Mommy went to her bedroom. The door slammed behind them. I didn't have to turn the knob to know the door was locked.

Julie took Mommy's seat. "Angela, I don't expect you to understand my decision."

"Do you even love my brother?"

"More than anything."

"Then why would you marry him and leave knowing there's a good chance you won't come back? Don't you think he's been dealt enough shit in his life?"

One tear rolled down her cheek. Instead of feeling sorry for her, all I could think was that if she's able to cry on command, she could have a future as an actress.

Julie wiped her eyes with the back of her hand, took a deep breath, and on the exhale got to her feet and said, "It would mean a lot to your brother if you would be his best man."

I let her walk out of the apartment without my saying another word.

"She forgot her coat." Dad startled me. I had forgotten he was there. "Sometimes we can't see what's right in front of us." Dad lifted the glass of wine and Coke to his lips and chugged.

CHAPTER 9

I popped a honey ball into my mouth, for fortitude, and headed straight for Mommy's room. Her unwillingness to even consider that her runaway son didn't want to get married made sense to me now. My mother wasn't losing a son; she was gaining a private nurse. Jimmy marrying a nurse was even better than him marrying a doctor. Nurses aren't afraid to get their hands dirty. But this wasn't any nurse. This was a woman who soon might go into combat. If she did come back physically intact, it was unlikely she would come home emotionally and psychologically unscarred.

In any event, Jimmy didn't need a nurse. He had me now.

Dad stepped in front of me. I pushed past him and reached for Mommy's doorknob.

"NO!" If my father wasn't standing right in front of me, I wouldn't have believed that roar came out of him. Dad had never once raised his voice to me. Not even the time I lost our best customer because I was too hungover to show up and clean out the mousetraps on health inspection day.

"Angela, leave it be for tonight." His voice returned to a subdued tone.

"We have to stop this wedding."

Dad looked as if he wanted to reach inside of me and pull out the two-headed snake he was convinced was in there. "Let me help you get settled." I hesitantly followed him to Jimmy's room.

"I changed the sheets for you this morning," Dad smiled.

"You're living here now?" I wanted to hear it from him.

"Drinking got hold of me." Dad fingered that AA chip again. "If it weren't for Mike letting me stay here, I don't know what I would've done."

"You must be a huge help to Jimmy."

"If your brother hadn't turned me on my side all the nights I blacked out, I would have choked on my own vomit."

A rash of surprise spread across my face. My father always drank, a lot sometimes, but I don't remember him ever passing out.

"The legs don't work, but the rest is powerful. I wish he'd give the acting a chance again."

"Maybe he will."

"Miracles do happen." Dad threw his chip up in the air, and I caught it.

"I didn't know," I said, making eye contact.

Dad looked farther away than ever. "It's a lot better now. Billy's done wonders with the business."

"That's great," I said, but there wasn't anything that felt great about all this.

"One day at a time," Dad took his chip from my hand, and before I could think about whether or not I should ask about the alcohol I smelled on his breath earlier, and the glass with Coke and wine he drank, he said, "Sobriety isn't always perfect."

I didn't know what to say. I thought sobriety had to be perfect; one slip and you were a mess again.

"It would be nice for you to come to a meeting sometime," he said.

"Dad, I only have an occasional beer now."

He laughed. "Family is welcome for special meetings. It would be nice to have you there, you know, to hear my story." I didn't know, but I was sure I didn't want to hear his story.

"If we go to war, she's going to leave the day after the wedding. Jimmy's been through enough—"

"People get married all the time during war," Dad said. "People who wouldn't have gotten married otherwise. It's betting on the future. Trying to influence fate."

"Don't you think him taking off means he doesn't want to get married?"

"We'll get you measured for the tux in the morning." Dad was doing what he had always done, acting as if all was perfect in Jimmyland. Dad was a better actor than I gave him credit for.

"Tomorrow I have some stuff to do in the morning, but you meet me at Carmela's."

"She's still in business?"

"Only the good die young." He kissed my forehead. I sighed with relief that the scent on his breath was coffee and cannoli cream, though I didn't remember Mike serving cannoli. The damn honey balls distracted me.

Dad closed the door behind him. I kicked off my shoes, picked up the remote, and clicked the TV on to find the president standing at a podium with two fingers raised in the air. For one hope-filled moment I thought he was giving me the sign of peace, then I raised the volume. "Out or else," he said. Two fingers for two days left before we go to war. I clicked the TV off.

I was exhausted, too exhausted to open my suitcase and change out of my street clothes, and faced with the choice between the thirty-year-old mattress on the desecrated canopy bed and the therapeutic mattress, I plopped, headfirst, onto the latter and was swallowed. A pig in a blanket.

There was a knock at the door.

"Help," I shouted.

Mike came to my rescue, pushing an empty wheelchair into the room. Jimmy came back, I thought, my arms flailing.

"It's an air mattress," he said.

"Where's the air?" I said.

"The pump is off." Mike flipped a switch at the front of the bed. The surface under me began to harden. Mike took my hand and as he pulled; I pushed myself up and onto my feet. "Jimmy, where is he?"

Mike looked down at the empty chair. "This is the spare from my trunk. I was afraid of it getting stolen." He patted the seat. "This model would get you a few hundred at least on the street." I tried to imagine the hustlers I grew up with peddling wheelchairs and wondered if there was a whole nursing-supply racket that I wasn't aware of.

"Do you need anything?" Mike asked. I needed to find Jimmy, but I knew there was nothing Mike or anyone could do about that tonight.

"I'm good."

"You sure? I can make you a sandwich."

"Really, I'm good, Mike. Thank you." I wanted to ask Mike if his silence earlier was his way of telling me he agreed going to war would be wrong. He didn't talk about his time in the army often, and when he did, it was about food he loved or couldn't stomach, but he always ended with a shake of the head and a mumble, "Waste of life."

"Sweetie, can I ask you for a favor?" he asked.

Mike didn't ask for favors often, so when he proceeded to ask me to try to not upset my mother while I was here, I gave him the most sincere smile I could. I loved Mike, and Mike loved this family, but there was no one on this earth he loved more than Mommy. And when I didn't hate her, I loved her too.

Mike didn't push my promising to do something we both knew I couldn't. Not upsetting my mother meant agreeing with her about everything, and that would be impossible for me. Mike had to ask and I had to pretend to try.

"You have been gone a long time." Mike leaned over the wheelchair, and as he kissed the top of my head, he knocked the plastic saints from Jimmy's nightstand onto the floor.

Before Mike could bend down, I said, "I'll get them."

"You really do have the smartest eyes of anyone I've ever known." He walked to the door and with his back to me said, "Make sure they're lined up exactly, you know your brother." He closed the door behind him, and I jumped over to the closet, and when I slid the door open I was reassured. I did know my brother. While Billy and I had collected baseball cards, Jimmy collected six-to-eight-inch plastic statues of Catholic saints. There they were, right in front of me, hundreds of statuettes waiting in bubble wrap for Jimmy to need them. When called upon, the designated batters would be un-bubbled and placed on his bedside table.

"Oh, when the saints go marching in," I sang as I went back to the side of Jimmy's bed. I pushed the wheelchair out of my way and got down on my knees. From under the bed, where it had fallen, I pulled out Saint Anthony, the saint we prayed to when we lost anything – money, the gold cross I got for my First Holy Communion, the speaking part in the Toys R Us commercial Jimmy had wanted because of all the toys he thought we would get. We thought maybe if we prayed hard enough, Jimmy's agent would call back and say they'd decided not to go with the redhead-and-freckles look after all.

When Jimmy lost the use of his legs, though, I didn't pray to Saint Anthony because I knew it wouldn't help. I stopped believing in the power of saints after Cathy, my best friend in fifth grade, died of leukemia. I had prayed day and night to Saint Catherine, her namesake, to save her, but she died anyway. Jimmy said I had prayed wrong. "You don't pray to a saint because of their name, you pray to a saint because of their job." He told me I should have prayed to Saint Bernadette, the patron saint of illness. Still, I thought if saints were as powerful as Jimmy believed, Saint Catherine would have saved my friend. Years later, the news broke that the hill near Orchard Beach, which was part of Pelham Bay Park and which we often climbed and pushed each other down, had been an illegal dumping ground for toxic waste. Instead of cleaning it out, the city's solution was to grow grass over it and spray mega gallons of air freshener. It turned out the area where I grew up had one of the highest leukemia rates in the country.

After the accident, Jimmy refused to have any saints on his bedside table, so I assumed that he too had stopped believing. Rubbing Saint Anthony's bald spot now, I wondered what Jimmy had wanted Saint Anthony to help him find. I reached under the bed again, and this time found Saint Genesius, the patron saint of actors. Whenever there was a part Jimmy wanted, or he was nervous about the opening of a show, Saint Genesius would be de-bubbled and set on the dresser; for the last few years before Jimmy was hurt, Saint Genesius remained out all the time. Despite Dad's wishful thinking, I didn't believe Jimmy's *I'll be back* note was a sign he wanted back in the business, but Saint Genesius? For sure.

"Angela." I looked up at the closed door. "Now!" It was Mommy. I dropped Saint Anthony and Saint Genesius on the nightstand, and when I opened the door, there was Mommy with her dress halfway over her head, covering her face.

I didn't even try not to laugh.

"It's stuck," she grumbled.

"That's clear."

"Do something." She was using her this-is-serious-and-no-laughing-matter tone, and, of course, it made me laugh harder.

"Theresa Angela!"

I tried to lift the dress over her head. "It's caught on something."

"Tell me something I don't know."

I tried to pull the dress up again.

"Ouch. My hair."

"Ma, it will be easier if you're sitting." I guided her to my bed, she sat, and I took a step back to survey the situation. "It's stuck on something."

"My bra." She was going to cry. Mommy never cried.

"We can do this," I said, trying to reassure myself as much as her. "Let's unhook your bra, and then I can probably get it over your head."

Mommy reached behind her but couldn't get to the clasp. "I'll do it," I said. I reached around her and unhooked her bra. The gel pack she used to fill her right cup so the world wouldn't know what was missing fell to the floor.

October of my junior year in high school, Mommy was diagnosed with breast cancer, but it wasn't until late winter, when she started losing her hair from the chemo, that I realized she was ill. Mommy embraced her cancer as she did all of her physical limitations. If I hadn't already been convinced she was invincible, I was after she beat breast cancer.

Mommy put her hand over mine. There was a slight tremble. What was she afraid of?

After I managed to get her slip over her head, she thanked me, which felt strange – Mommy never thanked family and never let family thank her. But at that moment, with me standing in front of this woman wearing only white cotton briefs and gold hoops, we weren't mother and daughter, we were two women, letting it all hang out, our vulnerabilities. If ever there was a right time to talk to her about Jimmy and how this marriage would be the second biggest mistake of his life, it was now – the first was him relenting and going out drinking that night, when he had made it clear that what he wanted to do was go to bed early. It should have been me who fell off the stadium stairs and cracked her spine. Not Jimmy. He didn't even want to be there. If I had listened and respected what he wanted, instead of once again bulldozing through my agenda, he would be okay today.

I was listening now. Jimmy needed me to save him from this marriage. He deserved more than a mediocre, at best, life with a woman who would soon abandon him, and who took it upon herself to ask me to be his best man.

I sat on the bed next to Mommy, and with her hand still in mine, asked, "Can we talk?"

"I'm not exactly dressed for it." She looked down at her half-naked self.

I reached over to pick up my suitcase and put it on the bed between us. I waited for her to reprimand me for putting a dirty suitcase on a clean bedspread, but she didn't say a word. It wasn't until I opened it that I realized I had no idea what was inside. I'd waited to the very last minute to pack. I was hoping for a miracle, an earthquake, any excuse not to go. The miracle once again didn't come. Half asleep, the shuttle bus to the airport beeping outside, I'd grabbed and shoved whatever clothing was near the top of my drawers into the suitcase.

There was a beige bra and two pairs of underwear – one pink, originally white until I washed it with a red sock, and the other, white with a tiny brown stain, which I quickly shoved under the suitcase to avoid a lecture on stain removal. Mommy believed the damage bleach caused to the environment was a price worth paying for sparkling panties. A toothbrush, a hairbrush, half a bottle of shampoo, two stale fig bars . . . "You packed garbage." Mommy shook an empty container of vanilla soy milk, which I think was there from my trip a year earlier where we marched on Sacramento to protest the governor's proposed student fee hike. It was the end of a three-day conference where student organizers and non-student organizers participated in seminars on educational equity, student housing, AIDS awareness, and a lot of other stuff. Those three days were the closest I ever came to considering going to college. I figured if you get to organize and protest for what you believe in and earn a degree, why not? I was going to enroll in summer classes at a local community college, when, well, Saddam invaded Kuwait and there was more important work that had to be done.

"Here." I handed Mommy the red silk blouse she had sent me for Christmas. I hated this blouse, but was glad I packed it and thought it would win me points, but the only thing I won was more criticism.

"This color is all wrong for you."

"It was a gift from you."

She lifted the fabric against my cheek. "Your coloring changed."

"You take it," I said.

She pushed it away. "It's too small for me."

I went back through my stuff and found a T-shirt that had belonged to a linebacker-size activist.

"Wear this," I said. Mommy lifted it in the air. "Your boyfriend's?" The hope sprayed from her mouth onto my face.

"Just a friend." He had spent a few nights at my place making calls and flyers and writing press releases with me. When we finally did fuck, it was clear he was a fighter and not a lover, so I told him we made better comrades than we would a couple. I think he understood.

"No Blood." She pulled at the red lettering below her chest. "For Oil." She read the black lettering that wrapped around her belly.

I waited for her to ask what it meant but instead she said, "If you don't unpack all your clothes, they're going to get wrinkled." And she unzipped an inside flap of the suitcase that I hadn't noticed was there. Next to several crumpled black long-sleeve T-shirts was a VHS tape.

I reached for it. Mommy got to it first. "Porn?"

"It's not porn," I said, not sure what it was, but I was almost positive it wasn't porn. "Can I have it, please?"

She twisted away, giving me her back. "'12/10/90. Interview/lead organizer CAIME.' What's a CAIME? Another game show?"

"Give it back," I said.

She bent forward but before she could stick it into the VCR attached to the TV, I grabbed onto the back of her head, and a large chunk of platinum blond hair came off. "You wear a wig?"

She turned to me, took her hair from my hand, and shrugged. "Extensions. Side effect of my meds, thinning hair." She dropped the tape onto the bed. "Secrets are destroying this family." I didn't disagree, but I wondered if we were thinking of the same secrets.

"Are you in a cult?" she asked.

"That's why I wear the weird shoes," I said.

She glanced over at my Birkenstocks. She finally had an explanation for my choice of footwear.

"Ma, it's not a cult. It's the acronym for Coalition Against US Intervention in the Middle East."

"That's a mouthful."

"It's forty community groups that have been working for months to try and educate people, and to stop Bush—"

"President Bush!"

"*President Bush* from going to war with Saddam Hussein."

"Hussein is a madman."

"I know, Ma, but going to war will only mean a whole lot of innocent people dying," I said. "Children, Ma."

"You work with this coalition?"

"I'm one of the lead organizers."

"Are you a Communist?"

"Unfortunately, this world had never had a true Communist country."

"What about Russia?"

"The former Soviet Union claimed to be Communist, but they were a corrupt bureaucracy."

"Our countries have a few things in common, then."

My heart fluttered. I had never before heard my mother criticize our government.

"We're a mess. Maybe a better mess than most."

"Ma, this war would be the biggest mess."

She stared at the portrait of her and her brother for what was only a few seconds, but seemed an eternity. "Most wars are a fucking mess." She made the sign of the cross. "Plain stupid."

"You miss him?"

"Uncle Richie?"

I nodded.

"He was an asshole." She turned to me. "He was my brother. Of course, I miss him. The kick in the ass was he died in *friendly fire*."

"He was shot by US soldiers?"

"Your uncle never made it to Vietnam. Basic training. Some young recruit freaked out and shot him. Right in the face."

"How? Why?"

"They were never clear about the details. The army never is, but the kid that made the mistake came to the house to tell your grandmother how sorry he was. Your grandmother, true to form, told him to tell it to the priest and slammed the door in his face."

"You never told me that story," I said.

"What was there to say? Your grandmother didn't believe in accidents. She thought there was no such thing as a mistake, only unconscious intentions."

I almost choked on the tears I was holding in the back of my throat.

"I was there when that kid came to our door." Mommy rubbed her nose. "Dust," she said. Women have time for allergies, but not for tears. "He never had any intention of killing Richie. He was broken. My mother could have given him some peace, and she knew that. But she didn't."

"She must have been so heartbroken over her son—"

"She was a tough bitch."

"Life was hard for women, especially single mothers . . ."

Mommy took the tape back from me. "You were on television?"

"Cable."

"That's still television."

"It's not what you think."

"I think my daughter who said she left home to be an actress was on television."

"I wasn't acting. It was a news show. Only local cable-access, but we needed all the media coverage we could get."

"They wanted to hear your opinion about this whole thing?"

"They did."

"So, go ahead," she said.

"Go ahead and what?" I said.

"Convince me why I shouldn't support this war."

Before I had a chance to ask if she was serious, she said, "Yes, I want to know what you think."

I took a deep breath. I had been on television, cable, talked in front of thousands, and had run more teach-ins than I could count over the past six months, but I never felt more nervous than I did in that moment sitting next to my mother, who was holding my tape in one hand and an extension of hair in the other.

"Get on with it."

"When Hussein gassed his own people and killed a million Kurds, we didn't do anything. But because he goes into some country ruled by billionaires, we're going to declare war? If Kuwait weren't a wealthy nation that sold us oil cheap, we would probably look the other way again. We're going to let millions of innocent people die for an emir who's spending hundreds of thousands a day gallivanting around Europe."

"How much?"

"Hundreds of thousands a day."

She reached behind her head and reattached the hair extension. "You're passionate about this?"

"Very."

"Julie is passionate too."

"But she's wrong, Ma."

"When they came back from Vietnam, people, protestors spit on them and called them baby killers—"

"This is not that. We, I, don't blame those who are sent to fight these wars. Many join the military because it's their only option. They don't have access to college or jobs. They think this will give them a better life. . . ."

"You certainly were pointing the shame finger at Julie." It was a kick in the throat to admit it, but she was right.

"I owe her an apology. But you know this wedding is wrong."

"You think I don't know what's best for my family?"

"You mean for Jimmy."

"I mean the family, the whole fucking bunch."

"Look, Ma, I get that Jimmy marrying a nurse would make life easier—"

"Is that why you think I want your brother to marry Julie?"

"I am not judging you—"

"Fuck you're not," she said. "Your brother is anything but a burden on this family. At least I know where I stand with your brother. He doesn't try to pretend he's something he's not. He knows who the fuck he is."

Before I could respond, though I don't know if I would have known what to say, she pressed the corner of the tape against my lips.

"I don't want to hear the bullshit. You're an actress, a Communist, a fucking cult leader, whatever the fuck. I may not agree or be happy with your choices, but I'd respect you for having the balls to tell the truth."

She stood up. "You know what breaks my heart?"

I knew she didn't expect a response. "You are almost thirty and you still haven't got a clue as to who you are, and that is on me. My mother was a hard-ass bitch who even whipped me with my dead father's belt, but when I left home, I knew who I was and what I wanted. She didn't give me a choice."

She took another deep breath, and when she let out a longer wheeze, I started to lift my arms to shield myself from whatever she would say next. Mike walked into the room and saved me.

He walked over to us, bent down, and from under Jimmy's bed pulled out the third saint. He scraped the edges of its golden wings against the palm of his hand and then, with his finger, touched the point of his sword. Mommy took the saint from Mike and lined him up between Saint Anthony and Saint Genesius. "He doesn't look happy." I assumed she was referring to the man-monster under the saint's foot.

"Who is he?" I asked.

Mommy shrugged.

"I thought you went to Catholic school?" Mike smiled.

"You went to public school. Can you name every president?"

"As a matter of fact, I can. Vice presidents, too."

"Show off." Mommy flashed him the smile that reminded me of how much she loved Mike, and how she had never loved my father the same way.

"Saint Michael, the archangel," Mike said. "The patron saint of soldiers. Battles."

"It's not a very good rendition of him," Mommy said.

"He's the one who leads God's army against Satan's forces," I said. "During the war in heaven he defeats Satan."

"Someone was paying attention in catechism class," Mike laughed.

"You see?" Mommy said. "Your brother is praying for the president to defeat that madman. Then Julie will come home soon."

"It's getting late." Mike extended his elbow as if he were asking Mommy to honor him with the last dance. She nodded, and he led her out into the hall. As the door closed behind them, Mike asked, "No Blood for Oil?"

"I think it's some rock band," Mommy said.

I changed out of my clothes and climbed back into the hospital bed. The air conditioning was turned on, and as I drifted, as I closed both eyes, the last thing I saw was the saints lined up on the nightstand. Though it was nearly impossible to grow up in Pelham Bay without avoiding sidewalk cracks or warding off the evil eye, I didn't consider myself superstitious. But Jimmy was. And though I wasn't sure exactly how these plastic saints would lead me to him, somehow, I knew they would. I thought about how Mommy believed Saint Michael was a sign that Jimmy wanted Bush to kick ass. I knew different. I was sure Jimmy was praying to Saint Michael for this war to not happen. If the war was canceled, he could call off the wedding.

I fell asleep praying to Saint Anthony, patron saint of the lost, and Saint Michael, the archangel, the patron saint of soldiers and battles.

CHAPTER 10

"Spread your legs," demanded the short gray-haired woman dressed in a purple velour tracksuit that clashed with the decade. She stretched her tape measure from the floor to the inside of my crotch.

"Thirty-eight," Carmela announced to the empty tuxedo shop she and her late husband, Luigi, opened in 1968, and she wrapped the yellow tape tight around my chest. Dad and I used to exterminate this store twice a month, but after Luigi died Carmela cut us down to once every other month. She said her husband might have been afraid of creepy-crawlies, but she'd survived Mussolini. I imagined Mussolini would have been a lot like Carmela had he been a tailor, only a little less patient and a lot less interested in state-sponsored social programs.

Not knowing where to look as she put her tape measure in places even I didn't touch, I kept my focus on the plastic statue of Jesus affixed to the top of Carmela's cash register, trying not to think about what was in the pocket of the coat Mommy had insisted I wear, which was currently hanging on a hook near the entrance. Jimmy would be pissed if he were to ever find out that I'd taken his saints, Anthony and Michael. Saints were never to leave the apartment, especially not the ones he had on the nightstand. You can take the girl out of Pelham Bay, but you can't take Pelham Bay superstitions out of the girl, and the voice in my head told me Saint Anthony would help me find Jimmy, and Archangel Michael gave me hope the war wouldn't start.

"Your father, he's late." Carmela's tape snapped back against her hand. She didn't even flinch. Dad had told me to meet him here at noon. It was almost one. He was never late for an appointment. If anything, Dad was early, too early. Then again, he always said, *There's a reason it's the only borough with a grammatical article in front of its name. Never underestimate The Bronx, especially its size.*

"Dad isn't coming," I said. "Don't know what could have happened."

Carmela raised her left eyebrow, and I inadvertently looked across the street to Fogerty's, formerly one of Dad's favorite pubs. *Traitor,* I scolded myself. "I have to go."

"Hollywood, you like?"

"Excuse me?"

"The stars on the ground and the big sign, Hollywood, you live there."

"I actually live in Venice," I said.

"Italia?"

"Venice Beach."

Now she raised both eyebrows.

"It's in Los Angeles. There're canals. No gondolas."

She nodded, but I couldn't tell if this was her way of saying she understood, or she didn't care.

"Venice, Italy, must be beautiful." I couldn't think of anything else to say.

"It smells in the heat," she said. "But you know, the water much-a more clean than people think." She reached out and grabbed a tux from the rack. "Try on." She shoved it in my direction.

I put my hands up.

"No problema. I give you a good deal."

If *no problema* followed by *a good deal* meant what it had always meant, Carmela was giving me the outsider treatment, and for sure there would be no good deal in my future. "I really appreciate it, but I'm not sure I'm going to need a tux," I said.

"You the best man." Again, she pushed the tux at me, and again, I waved no.

"You do the right thing. Don't be your father," she said.

"I don't drink, much, anymore," I said.

"I no care if your father drinks. His wife sleep-a with another man, his son can'ta walk, and his daughter live on the stars—"

"The beach," I said.

"You father, he drink because he not crazy."

"Then what did my father do wrong?" I asked, thinking of her good deal. "Are you seeing roaches?"

"You father not come for years. Billy, he comes."

"Is Billy not doing a good job?"

"Billy the best," she said.

"Then what did he do?"

"It's what he won't do." Carmela turned her back to me and went through the motions of looking for other formalwear options.

"Tell me." I reached out and put my hand on her right shoulder, frail enough to crush with one squeeze.

"Last week your father and brother come to my store."

"Jimmy was here?" My voice rose sharply.

"Where else?" She cupped my chin and shook my head back and forth. "This is the best place. I make the best fit." She let go of my cheeks. My head felt heavy, heavier than it had ever felt.

"Fa bene." She smiled. "I finish my story?"

"Okay," I said. Nodding would have taken more energy than I had.

"Your father and fratello come here, and I go get something from the back. People in this place, they speak the Italian, eat the Italian food, but they not like-a the Italians in Italy. You see, here people only care about what's in here." She tapped the side of my head with her forefinger. "When they describe a person, they no say 'You lookin' for Joe. He's the tall black with rosso hair.' Or 'Tony, he the short white guy with the shaved head.' Always, they say, 'Joey, tall black guy, real intelligent' or 'Tony, the short white guy with the shaved head, a real schmuck, idiot, stupido.' You know why this is?"

I shrugged.

"Because we think the world thinks we Italians stupid."

"My father called Jimmy stupid? Jimmy called my father stupid?"

"You no ask-a me the most important question," she said.

"Why were they calling each other stupid to begin with?"

"Good. The California sun no hurt your brain too much." She smiled so widely I could see the gold fillings in her back molars.

"Your father, no support his son."

There was no hiding the what-the-fuck expression on my face.

"I no talk about the TV things. I talk about the heart."

"My father loves Jimmy."

"You no listen." She reached out and squeezed my cheeks again.

"When I come out from back, Jimmy no here and your father face wanna cry. I ask him what happened. He ask me if I think it's-a wrong to ask his son if this marriage a good idea. He say it's not too late for his dream."

Dad doesn't think Jimmy wants to get married either, I translated to myself. I had one family member on my side.

"I tell your father what I tell you now. Dreams not real. They happen when you sleep. You wake up and you face the real life. You have one brother only. You do the right thing."

"You tellin' me," I said, sounding more like Carmela than I'd intended, "my brother should give up on his life?"

She shook both fists in the direction of her husband's portrait. "What I do to make them understand?"

She took the tape measure resting on her shoulder and pulled tight around the circumference of my hips. I felt bruised. "Thirty-six," she said. "Nice, you measure very nice."

I felt oddly relieved that she approved. "You not too thin," she declared in the Southern Italian–Bronx accent that surfaced only when she smiled. "Best man for your fratello's wedding," she sighed. "Today everything different. What you do?" She slapped my butt. "At least it's-a good for business." She held up a black tux that was taller than the length of her body.

"Fine," I said.

"No like?" She dropped the tux over the top of a long rack of other black tuxes cloned from the same piece of cloth. "Look here." She ran her fingers through the rack. "Top of the lines. See what feels right. I get some shirts."

Pushing through the rack, searching for a tux I would never wear was a waste of what little time I had left to keep this wedding from happening.

A bell tinkled. I looked over at the entrance, but instead of Dad, there were two men who, with the exception of their different lengths and widths, were similar to the rack of tuxes – not at all distinctive in style.

Right behind them, wearing the same Members Only jacket I was sure he had bought or "borrowed" in 1981, was the one person

I hated more than I had ever hated anyone, including Ollie North, the Contras, and the Republicans. This wasn't political. It was cut-gut personal. It was Fat Freddy Fungol.

Guys in the neighborhood often gave each other nicknames that were contrary to what they were. Shorty had been close to six foot seven, and Slim was over three hundred pounds, but the only part of Fat Freddy that wasn't fat was his face. His sunken cheeks matched his sunken eyes, which left little doubt that he was among the haunted. Fat Freddy was fat and he was the meanest fungol in the neighborhood. He was the kind of asshole who should have been dead by now.

"If it isn't the Exterminator's Daughter." He pushed through Wide and Long, who I assumed were his hench-boys. They had that *almost thirty, but lived at home with Mom, who cooked their meals and reminded them to wear clean underwear in case they got into a car accident* vibe. Fat Freddy Fungol got close enough for me to smell the peppers and onions on his breath, which still, after all these years, made my throat close.

"Looking good." He circled me, and I could have sworn I heard him sniffing. "Word has it you're a big star?" I would have assumed he was fucking with me, but Fat Freddy Fungol was too dumb for sarcasm. The only person I could imagine telling him this bullshit story about my rise to stardom was Billy, who had never turned away from an opportunity to mess with Fat Freddy, not after he discovered what had happened to me. I decided to have Billy's back and enjoy fucking with fungol-brains.

"*Goodfellas Part II.* That's huge." *Goodfellas?* I hadn't seen that one. Yet I knew it was one of the umpteenth Mafia-wiseguys movies revered and idolized by so many in the neighborhood. The movies were brutal and violent and often ended badly for the protagonists, or in the case of *Godfather III,* simply ended badly. Those who were wannabe wiseguys wanted to believe the lives of bookies and number runners were filled with tough-guy panache, and not the backbreaking, penny wise–pound stupid, risky work they did because they were undereducated and had few options to feed their families.

"That's fucking cool." The one who was longer in length stepped over to us.

Fat Freddy whacked him in the chest. "Shut the fuck up, Shorts. It's hush-hush until the studio releases the news."

"Fuck off," Shorts said under his breath.

"Excuse me?" Fat Freddy asked through a gust of pepper-and-onions breath.

"Fine. I said *fine*."

The wide one moved closer to me and whispered, "A real guy."

I had no idea who *he* was, but since Robert De Niro had been in every wiseguy film I knew of, and I did know most of them, I figured the probability of him starring in the film was high. "Robert, great guy."

"Everyone knows De Niro is the best," Shorts said. "Lip, tell her about the time you saw him in the city."

Lip shrugged, and I assumed his nickname came from how tight-lipped he was.

"Go ahead." Fat Freddy stared down at him. "Tell her."

Lip shook his head, and Shorts jumped in. "He was crossing Lexington and De Niro walked right by him and he said, 'Hey.'"

"Guess what De Niro said?" Fat Freddy jumped in.

"'Hey'?" I made an educated guess.

"You heard the story?" Fat Freddy said.

"Who hasn't?" I almost felt sorry for how clueless he was about my mocking him.

"Is Ray Liotta as cool as he looks?" Lip whispered.

I didn't know Ray Liotta, so I said what I knew they wanted to hear. "Cool. Very cool."

"I knew it!" Shorts and Lip high-fived each other.

"Carmel, she here?" Fat Freddy Fungol asked.

"She's in the back," I said.

"Good. Better she stays out of this." He stepped as close to me as his protruding belly would allow. I opened my mouth to scream. Carmela pushed her way through the orange curtain and stepped right between Fat Freddy Fungol's belly and me. "What you want here?"

"Hey, I gotta use the john," Shorts said.

"Me too," Lip mumbled.

"White Castle down the block." Carmela pointed toward the door.

"Carmela, that's cold. I'm a good customer." Shorts widened his eyes, as if this was a look that had worked for him before. "Please." He stuck his hands between his legs.

"Fast." Carmela shook her hand in the air. "Don't tell nobody! All the neighborhood want to use-a my bathroom," she yelled as Shorts and Lip rushed through the curtain.

I wasn't sure if Carmela was softer-hearted than her first impression implied, or if she was protecting her showroom floor from an accidental urine spill. Probably a little bit of both. "Still love the pasta too much." She patted Fat Freddy's belly. He blushed and stepped over to the mannequin in the corner of the store.

"Can you believe this?" He touched the sleeve of the powder blue tux with elephant ear–size lapels, probably the same one Billy had rented for our prom over a decade earlier.

Carmela rushed over to him and slapped his hand. "It's classical."

"That's one way to describe crap." His laugh reminded me of the chirp of a wounded bird.

"You try this." Carmela raised a black tux as high as she could.

"The pants look a little small," I said.

"You suppose to wear tight." She flung the black tux over my right shoulder and cupped her hands in front of my crotch. "It gives you nice shape. And make you look full, not-a so much bones." She grabbed the butt of my jeans. I thought she had said my measurements were good.

"A true Siciliano. No ass," she smiled.

Fat Freddy snorted.

"You too much ass." She whacked his butt so hard his eyes welled with tears.

She pointed to the back. "Go try, now." As I walked through the orange curtain with the black tux I could hear Carmela talking in Italian. The only word I understood was *basta*. Enough.

In the dressing room, a tiny closet with a long wall mirror, I changed out of my jeans and black tee, jumped into the tuxedo pants, but I was only halfway through the buttons on the shirt when the door opened. "Carmela?" I turned to face her.

"Still hot." It was Fat Freddy Fungol.

"Get the fuck out of here." He stepped inside and slammed the door behind him, but before I could scream his hand was pressed hard against my mouth and his over-three-hundred-pound body had me pinned against the glass.

I was fourteen again.

Fat Freddy had wanted to show me something in the alley between Joe's Candy Store and Dominick's Bakery. "It's cool," he had said.

"Not interested," I said.

"Chicken," he said. "Such a girl."

I followed him and he told me to turn around because he didn't want me to see his hiding place, and I did. "Okay, you can look."

There he stood with his dick hanging out of his pants.

"Asshole," I said. He wouldn't let me pass by until I touched it.

"Fuck you," I said.

He pushed me so hard I cracked my head on the pavement. I didn't lose consciousness, though I prayed I would.

"Get the fuck off," I screamed. He covered my mouth with his right hand, and he used his left to rub his dick against the inner thigh of my jeans. He leaned all of his body weight down on me. I couldn't breathe, but inside my head I prayed to Jesus for my lungs to crush. I wanted to die. Jesus wasn't listening. Fat Freddy lifted himself up enough to lower his pants and in one swift movement pulled my jeans and period-stained panties down to my knees. I looked right into his eyes. I wanted him to see the hate, to know I would kill him one day.

The tip of his penis touched strands of my pubic hairs, and he went flying into the air and landed smack against the side of the metal dumpster.

Anthony, one of the teens in the neighborhood and the only Anthony who didn't have a nickname, and half the size of Fat Freddy, saved me. He had an older brother who was doing time for stabbing his business partner into a coma, so not even fucking idiots messed with him.

"Where's Jimmy?" He asked me now. Dropped his hand from my mouth.

"Get the fuck off of me." I slammed my forehead against the bottom of his chin.

He backed off, shouting, "Fucking bitch." I kneed him in the groin, he went down, and I ran through the orange curtain.

Shorts and Lip were standing at Carmela's side.

"What take you so long?"

"The pig in the back."

"He's smelling my bathroom?"

Before I could tell her what happened, Fat Freddy Fungol rushed through the orange curtain. His face was red and strained. He was still hurting.

Carmela picked up the plastic Jesus near the register and threw it at Fat Freddy Fungol, who ducked, so Jesus slammed into the portrait of her late husband. The glass cracked and Jesus's head snapped off.

"You go now." Carmela's tone was even but her pupils darted back and forth.

"Tell Jimmy he better find me before it's too late."

"Before what's too late?" I asked, but I was almost grateful he didn't answer me. I wasn't ready to know.

Keeping a slapping distance from Carmela, Fat Freddy Fungol limped out of the shop. Shorts and Lip trailed behind. "We should have used White Castle's john," Lip said.

"Grazie," I said to Carmela.

"Fa bene?" she asked.

I nodded. We didn't need to talk about what happened, it was clear she knew. Carmela, the short lady with the round face, was a very wise woman.

"You like?" She pulled at my shoulders. "I take it in only a little."

"Actually, I have a different look in mind." I walked over to the powder blue tux on the mannequin. "That one."

Carmela took a step back. "The blue very nice on you. But your mama, she kill you."

"At least I'll die in style."

CHAPTER 11

The whole bus ride home, I rubbed Saint Anthony's bald spot in my pocket. I don't know if I believed for a second he would help me find Jimmy, and I didn't believe Archangel Michael would stop this war, but both chunks of plastic gave me hope. False hope was better than no hope.

The Don C and Son van was parked in front of the apartment. I expected to find Dad home, but no one was there. I figured he was in his office, which was the section of the basement that Sal, the landlord, hadn't converted to an illegal studio, or used to store his hundreds of jars of tomatoes and bottles of homemade wine. It was also not where Antoinette, the wife, hid to smoke her Virginia Slims, the cigarette with the slogan "You've come a long way, baby." The longest Antoinette had come was from a small town outside of Naples, Italy. She spat the word *feminist* with the same enthusiasm she used when she spat *fascist*. I had thought "the wife" title was some old-school misogynist custom, but now I wondered if it was old-school street smarts. She knew her husband was up to shady shit. We all did. The illegal basement studio was only the foam at the top of a blended tomato jar.

In exchange for spraying our building and the three others Sal owned, Dad was permitted to store his chemicals and other exterminating paraphernalia on the shelves with the jarred tomatoes and homemade wine, which I was sure Dad helped himself to on occasion. Dad never ratted out Antoinette for her smoking, and she apparently never told Sal where the bottles of missing wine went.

The door to the office was open, so I walked inside. Sitting at the makeshift desk, a card table that Sal let Dad use until he needed it for jarring season in August, was Billy, talking on the blue rotary phone and flipping through a Rolodex. I peeked over his shoulder at the wall calendar to see if there was any mention of Jimmy, any clue as to where he had gone. But other than the tux appointment that Carmela had told me about, the only things on the calendar were stops: when, where, and a note indicating whether a side or back entrance had to be used. Restaurant owners were especially uptight about an exterminator walking through the front door with a tank in hand.

"It's still there," Billy said to me, without looking up. Right on the shelf between a bottle of wine and a plastic container of pesticide was the empty glass jar we had used so many years ago to catch the moth we had thought was holy.

Billy hung up the phone and swung around. "What's up?"

"I went to Carmela's—"

"Shit." He smacked his forehead. "She's going to kill me. I was supposed to pick up my tux and have her check the fit today."

"Fat Freddy showed up."

Billy looked at me. "You okay?" Billy was the only one I had ever told about that day in the alley. I made him cross his heart and swear to die if he told anyone, even Jimmy. I understood now that what happened wasn't my fault, and my training as a rape intervention advocate taught me how victims blamed themselves, which was why so many rapes and sexual assaults went unreported. I had blamed myself. And maybe I still did. I knew Fat Freddy was an asshole and still I followed him into the alley.

"You okay?" he repeated.

I nodded, but we both knew I wasn't.

"What did the fat fuck want?"

"Jimmy."

"Oh." Billy swung back to the Rolodex.

"He said Jimmy better show before it 'was too late.' Does Jimmy owe him money? Is Jimmy in trouble? Is that why Jimmy ran away?" I swung Billy's chair around to me and knelt in front of him. "Please, talk to me."

Billy stood, pulled me to my feet, and hugged me. If I weren't shaking so hard and afraid that if he let go, I would crack into a trillion tiny pieces, I would have pushed him off and demanded he tell me what kind of trouble Jimmy was in.

"Don't worry. Jimmy knows what he's doing, trust me," he whispered in my ear, and to the rhythm of the steam radiator Billy held on to me, swaying side to side, until he knew I could stand on my own. When he stepped back, he took one of the metal tanks from the shelf, and to test the hose he sprayed into a corner. The smell of a skunk farting rotten eggs brought back memories of the days Dad and I exterminated together. When we were working stops it was about the job – killing roaches, setting mouse- or rattraps; it was about us.

Billy slipped into the gray overalls with DON C AND SON embroidered in red on the back. *Exterminating* had too many letters to fit; besides, it also cost five dollars a letter.

I insisted he let me help him lift the green camping-size pack with the filled tank over his shoulders and onto his back.

"Who ya gonna call?" I asked.

"I ain't afraid of no ghost." He smiled, but it was clear he was working hard at it. "Catch you later."

I pulled his strap. "Let me come."

"I got this," he said.

"I know you do, but it would be fun."

"LA has warped your idea of a good time."

I smiled, and I was sure he could see I was working hard at it too.

"You can tell me you don't want to be alone. It's okay."

"Thanks," I said, but for the first time in all the years that Billy, Jimmy, and I had been friends, nothing felt okay between us, not the way it had been when we hid in this basement so Dad wouldn't find Jimmy and force him to go on another audition, or played stickball on the street until one of the spaldeens hit a Beach Chair Lady in the leg, or hung out in the park drinking and laughing our asses off. We were inseparable. We finished each other's sentences. We started each other's sentences too. "Conjoined at the soul," the BCs would say, only it sounded better in Italian.

The van was gone.

"Fuck, I can't believe it," Billy said.

"You think it was stolen?"

"Fuck, fuck, fuck," he shouted.

"Watch the mouth," Mrs. Bellini called down from her window. Billy waved her an apology. I held back from giving her the finger. Everyone always cussed but it was only Billy, Jimmy, and I who were called out for it. *The Americans* and their wayward friend.

"Excuse me, Mrs. Bellini!" I called up to her.

"Is that Ms. Hollywood?"

"It's me, Angela."

"You got so skinny?" This was both an insult and a compliment.

"How are you?" If I didn't ask, it would be written on my gravestone: *Here lies Theresa Angela Campanosi. On that fateful day she didn't ask Mrs. Bellini how she was. May her soul burn for all eternity.*

"My bunions are Florida grapefruits."

"Sorry to hear that."

"What can you do?"

"Did you see the van?"

"Your father. Drove off. Ten minutes maybe."

"Thank you," I shouted.

"See, Billy, it's okay."

Billy took hold of my shoulders. "It's anything but okay."

"What are you talking about?"

"Not near elephant ears." He mouthed to me. Billy waved goodbye to Mrs. Bellini and I followed him in silence the seven blocks to the train.

Depending on which direction you were traveling, Pelham Bay Station was the first or the last stop on the 6 line. The real star of the blockbuster hit movie *The Taking of Pelham One Two Three,* featuring Walter Matthau, was the 6 train, the local to and from the city. Technically, Pelham Bay was in the Bronx, and the Bronx was part of New York City. Still, when Bronx natives referred to "the city," we meant Manhattan, New York, the city that never sleeps, the city that Frank Sinatra from Hoboken, New Jersey, sang on and on about.

On the 6 train now, Billy sat a few seats away from me. He claimed he needed the extra room for the tank, but he never took off the backpack. I thought about pushing to find out what was really going on with him. That had always been my role with Billy and Jimmy – I pushed and they sometimes pushed back, but usually they relented and told me everything. As much as Billy had changed on the outside, he was still Billy. And he was hiding something from me. I knew it, and he knew I knew it. It wasn't until the Parkchester stop, when I stood up to transfer to the express train, that he moved to the seat next to me and said, "Let's stay on here."

I assumed he wanted to take the local because he wanted to talk, but for the hour and five minutes that it took the local to get from way above ground to the bowels of the city, Billy kept his eyes straight ahead, making eye contact with no one, which was what we were all trained to do as kids; only people looking for trouble made eye contact on the subway. He didn't say a word to me, and whenever I tried to say anything, he pressed his index finger against his lips. Billy was withholding something, a lot of things, but I knew he was desperate to tell me. Every time his eye twitched or the middle finger of his left hand jerked slightly, it was clear to me that he was using every muscle in his body to keep the muscles in his mouth shut.

When we surfaced from the subway, the wind slapped my face. I was surprised that I was confused as to which way was east or which way was west, so I let Billy lead.

He walked over to a guy standing near a red bucket, wearing a sweatshirt with SALVATION ARMY imprinted on it. He had a bell, but he wasn't ringing it.

Billy stuck his black wool–gloved hand into his pocket, pulled out a dollar, and dropped it into the bucket. "Bless you," the man said. Billy turned and kept walking.

Salvation Man stared at me. I knew there was something only he could see. Wishing I could give him something, I put my hand in my pocket but all I had was a subway token for the return trip, and Archangel Michael.

"You're ready to fight?"

"Excuse me?"

"Michael, he's the one you want on your side."

I put the token back into my pocket. "Sorry, I don't have any money."

"Next time," he said. And I remembered what season it was; the after-Christmas season, when people cursed their credit card bills and the spirit of giving was officially on hold. Here we both stood, shortly before this country planned to bomb Iraq and my brother planned to blow up his dreams. I felt in solidarity with this man in the ugly sweatshirt. He, too, was on a futile mission, as futile as stopping a war or a wedding.

There may not be a next time, I thought, as I dropped the archangel into the bucket.

He handed me his bell. The handle was freezing. "Ring it," he said. I rang it hard and fast, and for a moment all was right in this small corner of the world.

"Are you coming?" Billy called out to me.

"Thank you," I said, handing the man his bell.

"Don't mention it." I thought of Mommy. *You never thank family.*

It took every bit of the New Yorker that hadn't yet been La-La'd out of me to catch up to Billy, and when I finally did, matching his pace was near impossible. We were moving so fast that when Billy stopped, I bumped into the tank on his back, and that's when I heard the roar.

"NO BLOOD FOR OIL! NO BLOOD FOR OIL!"

I looked up. There were hundreds, maybe thousands, of people chanting and marching down Park Avenue in the direction of the United Nations.

"What the hell is happening?" Billy shouted, and before I had a chance to tell him we were trying to stop a war, a woman in a mink coat looked at him and sneered, "Protestors."

"Move it along, please," said an NYPD officer.

"We have to keep moving," I said to Billy. I was very well versed in demonstration law. Also, I was feeling the cold. As I rubbed the head of the now lone saint, hands in my pockets to keep them from frostbite, I thought I should have listened to my mother and borrowed a pair of gloves.

"I'd be happy to," said the woman, "but I live over there." She lifted her right arm in the direction of one of the doorman buildings on the other side of the street. The same building we had to exterminate.

"Officer, I need to get to work," Billy said.

"You can go up and around," the officer said. Somehow, we all understood those directions.

"How far up does this thing go?" the woman asked.

"They're still gathering in Central Park, so I assume a long ways."

"What about going down and around?" Billy asked.

"It ends at the UN."

"This is outrageous." She clicked her heels and pivoted in the direction we had come from. Billy and I stood there on the sidelines as people marched by holding signs: AMERICANS FOR PEACE; NO WAR FOR OIL PROFITS; US OUT OF THE MIDDLE EAST; MONEY FOR HUMAN NEEDS, NOT WAR; DROP BUSH, NOT BOMBS; MONEY FOR AIDS, NOT WAR.

"Money for AIDS," Billy said.

"Thousands are dying from AIDS and there isn't enough money going to research. This war will only take more funding away."

"I know about the health crisis," Billy said. "I was questioning the wording. It reads like they want to fund AIDS. They need to add *research*."

"Oh." I felt a little foolish for not seeing that myself, but I was glad Billy understood the consequences of us going to war.

"How many do you estimate are here?" I asked the officer.

"Too many." He blew his whistle and waved over a guy probably no older than sixteen, wearing a green parka zipped above his chin and carrying a sign that read: SEND QUAYLE.

"No sticks." The officer reached for the sign.

"You kidding me?"

"Will a five-hundred-dollar fine show you how funny I am?"

The guy ripped the poster board off the wooden stick. "Here," he said. The cop took the stick and waved him on.

Billy squinted across the street. "We can't afford to lose this job. After what your father pulled last month, we're on thin ice."

I wanted to know what Dad had done but it wasn't the time or place to push. I pulled Billy by the strap of his backpack. "Come on."

"Where are you going?"

"To the other side," I said.

"I can't take the risk," Billy said.

Risk? What risk? The streets were packed, but the people were marching and chanting peacefully. I knew this scene. I was comfortable with it. The only things that felt different from LA were the skyscraper backdrop and the fact that everyone was wearing coats and hats and scarves instead of T-shirts and shorts and there wasn't a Frisbee or Hacky Sack in sight.

"We can go around," Billy said.

"You heard the cop. That will take forever. The customer has already been waiting for hours. They must be in full-blown roach-sighting panic by now."

Billy glanced down at his watch and then adjusted the backpack. "This is getting heavy. But how do you suggest we get through the police barricade?"

I had no idea what he was talking about. A police barricade in LA was a big moving wall of officers in riot gear. Here, there were only blue wooden hobbyhorses that the police used to keep people from getting too close to the floats during the Thanksgiving Day Parade.

"Under." We bent our knees, lowered our heads, took a step, and suddenly we were in the middle of the most congested demonstration I had ever experienced. The police had us packed tighter than a can of sardines, but at least folks were moving, and all the body heat created a warmish feeling. Too bad the crowd was moving in the opposite direction of the way Billy and I needed to go.

"Now what?" Billy shouted.

"Pretend we're on the subway during rush hour," I said.

"Gotcha," Billy said, and we wove in and out of protestors chanting, "Get the troops out now!" "The people, united, will never be defeated!" and of course, "No blood for oil!"

We maneuvered our way past three, maybe four hundred protestors, maybe a thousand (I wanted to believe), to the meridian, the divider between uptown traffic and downtown, when the march stopped. No one was moving, and there was no place for Billy and me to go. Subway tactics weren't going to work.

"I gotta get out of here," Billy shouted into my ear. When I heard his breathing, fast and erratic, I shouted back, "Take slow, deep breaths," watching my own breath become visible in the cold air.

"Ange, you got to get me out of here now." Billy sounded panicked now.

"What's going on?" I asked a woman to my left with red teardrops painted down her cheeks.

"The rally must be starting."

"We're avenues away from the UN," I said.

"This is the closest we're going to get. There are so many of us. We have to be at least fifty thousand."

"Billy did you hear that? Fifty thousand people!"

"Get me out of here, now," Billy said, and the strain in his voice snapped me right back to the present. I had to get him through this crowd.

"It's too tight." We were sardines in a tin can with a broken pull tab: there was nowhere to go and no way out. Billy shifted to his left and his backpack brushed against my arm. I had an idea.

"Exterminator coming through," I shouted. Anyone in the business knew yelling "exterminator" in a crowded area was as dangerous as yelling "fire."

"You're carrying toxic chemicals?" Teardrop Woman repeated, alarmed.

"They're safer than the stuff that's sprayed on your food," Billy said.

"Still toxic," I said, and as I had hoped she would do, she shouted, "This guy's carrying poison!"

The crowd parted. Billy and I dashed to the other side of Park Avenue, and with no police in sight, we crawled under the barricade, and we were now on the right side of Park.

"You good?" I asked. Before Billy could respond, a Channel 4 news reporter shoved her microphone in my face. "Do you support the war?"

"We're not at war yet," I said.

"You support the protesters here today?"

"I don't want anyone dying in my name in Iraq or here in this country, because the money spent on this war won't be spent on health care, AIDS research, cancer research, education. We have the highest illiteracy rate of any developed nation. We need more books, not bombs—"

Before I could say anything else, someone yanked me away. It was Billy. "We have to go."

"Finally, I have a chance to tell people how fucked up this war would be, and you pull me away to kill roaches?"

"Killing those roaches for those fucking rich-ass people is what pays the bills."

"Give me a break. Five minutes wasn't going to lose you the account. Dad's had this building for twenty years."

"That's why when he was so pissed drunk and he dropped a bag of half-dead mice still in their traps in the middle of the lobby, they didn't fire our ass."

"I didn't know."

"There's a lot you don't know."

"Maybe if someone told me what the fuck was going on—"

"What the hell would you do about it?"

"I could try to help."

"Three thousand miles away?"

"You sound like fucking Mommy."

"She's not always wrong."

"Why are you being such an asshole?"

He walked away, even faster than he had earlier. I wasn't going to let him get away with not talking to me. I had to run to keep up but I did.

Billy halted in front of the building I remembered spraying with my dad starting back in junior high school. Jerry, the doorman, always had a pocket filled with butterscotch candy. He gave me two, sometimes three, every time. I hated butterscotch but it was Jimmy's favorite, so I brought them home for him.

There was a new doorman now. I wondered if he had candy in his pockets.

"Hey, Ralph."

"Glad you're here, Mr. Billy."

"Peters not doing so well?"

"Thought he was going to have a stroke."

"We better get started before he does have that stroke."

"Burns no longer the manager?" I asked.

"Retired." Ralph smiled.

"Ralph, this is my associate. Angela," Billy hesitated, "Campanosi."

"Mr. Campanosi is actually here already," Ralph said.

"James is here." Billy's tone sounded more panicked than it had been when we were trapped among the protesters. "Mr. Peters knows?"

"You know how a roach sighting causes havoc. Desperation."

"Dad must have taken the van," I said.

"You think?" Billy rolled his eyes at me. "God help him," he mumbled.

"He's probably halfway through the building," Ralph said.

"I'm going to lend a hand," said Billy.

"Of course, Mr. Billy." Ralph held open the front door and waved his white-gloved hand for us to enter. Mr. Billy made a dash to the elevator.

"Nice to meet you, Ralph," I said, and I was again running to catch up.

"Pleasure" was the last thing I heard Ralph say before I jumped into the elevator as the doors were closing.

Billy pressed 15, the highest floor with the exception of the penthouse, and I reached around him and pressed 7. Billy yelled, "What the fuck?" and this time when he turned around, the tank hit the soft bridge of my nose. The pain was so intense I had no idea about anything until I heard Billy's voice. "Oh God."

When I looked down, the front of Mommy's beige coat was now a rich dark brown. I touched my nose. I was bleeding.

"Hold your head back." Billy put a wad of white paper napkins he pulled from his pocket, probably taken from one of the diner stops, against my nose. I jumped back. "That hurts."

"Then you do it," he said. "Keep the pressure on."

The blood was pouring too furiously for me to argue. I pressed the napkins against my nose and tilted my head back. The elevator stopped. The doors opened. I took a step forward, and Billy pulled me to him. "Wrong floor."

"Ralph said Dad would be halfway done by now." When I lowered my gaze to make eye contact, blood rushed out of my nostrils.

"Back." Billy lifted my chin up until I was again staring at the brown-paneled elevator ceiling. I remembered the time the elevator had gotten stuck between floors. The power had gone out, and Dad, who always carried a flashlight on his belt, instructed me to point it up at the elevator ceiling, while he, Spiderman-style, climbed up and out. He reached down to hoist me up. It was dark – maybe I dropped the flashlight or the battery died, I don't remember – but Dad felt so out of my reach, and I was sure it was hopeless. But somehow, he convinced me he could grab on to me if I jumped, and I did. I wasn't sure if my memory of what happened was even close to reality, but the feeling that he'd always kept me safe was more real to me than my bloody nose.

". . . let me do all the talking," Billy said.

Before I could tell him that I hadn't heard most of what he'd said, the elevator stopped. Billy guided me onto the fifteenth floor. "Still bleeding?"

I lowered my head and moved the blob of bloody napkins away from my face. "I think it stopped," I said.

Billy stepped in closer. I was ready for him to kiss me, but instead he pinched my nose between his thumb and finger and asked, "Hurt?"

I shook my head, relieved that the pain was gone.

"Good. Not broken." He dropped his hand. "Maybe we should put you in a cab and get you home." It was clear from the expression on his face that I looked a lot worse than I felt. Or he wanted me anywhere but here with him. A cab would cost a small fortune. I didn't feel comfortable borrowing that from him. More than that, I had to find out what Billy wasn't telling me. My leaving for ten years and not coming back, even when he needed me the most, would have been reason enough for him to resent me, but my gut, and my sore nose, told me there was more to it. This wasn't about Dad, or Jimmy. It was about Billy and me.

"I'm staying," I said.

He didn't argue, and the two of us walked down the long corridor to apartment 1524.

Before he rang the bell, he repeated, "Let me do all the talking." Only this time he added, "One wrong word can set her off."

CHAPTER 12

Billy leaned on the doorbell, but no one came. "Nobody's home," I said.

"She's home," said Billy, who was now banging on the door with his fist.

"What is wrong with you?" I asked.

"Maybe you should be asking yourself that question." He banged harder.

"What's that supposed to mean?" I said.

"This isn't the time," he said.

"When is the time?"

The door cracked open. "Who's there?" a voice asked.

"It's Billy. Open up."

"I didn't call for an exterminator."

"Margaret, stop fooling around and open the door." Billy had never sounded angrier.

"This is a very bad time right now."

"Margaret, cut the shit and open up!" Billy shoved his foot in the crack so she couldn't close the door even if she wanted to.

"Who are you with?" she demanded, and I forced a smile, assuming she was looking at me. "Angela," I said.

The chain rattled and dropped. The door opened wide to a woman who looked starved enough to be a model, but it was hard to tell whether she looked old or young for her age; the brown, torn-at-the-edges terrycloth robe she wore looked ancient.

"James's daughter!" She hugged me like I was her long-lost something-or-other.

"Let her breathe," Billy said, prying Margaret from my body.

She stepped back, looked me up and down, and said, "You're a beauty. Striking. She brushed my face with the back of her hand.

"Those eyes. I bet you get whatever you want."

I had no idea who this Margaret was, but I thought that maybe for a white woman of privilege she might be okay.

"Please come in." She waved us into her apartment.

"Eclectic filth" was what Mommy would have called the style of the apartment. It had been some time since anyone cleaned the place, and nothing matched or coordinated with anything else. It was a tribute to the United Nations: a mixture of Japanese minimalism, lots of stones and water; and Moroccan ornate, low-to-the-floor brass tables, and rugs, too expensive for the floor, hanging on the walls. Except for the empty Chinese food cartoons, which Dad called "roach airlines," and the thick layer of dust on all the surfaces, I liked it.

I'd had time to learn from Mommy. After my parents divorced, there was a period of about a year when Dad went full throttle in his quest to help Jimmy's career take off. The only thing my parents had resembling a custody settlement was a verbal agreement that if Jimmy didn't get some substantial work, a national commercial or Broadway play, within a year, Dad would let the whole showbiz thing go.

With Dad needing to spend all his free time with Jimmy and his career, Mommy and I had mother-daughter time, which meant I stayed out of the way and kept myself busy when she had an open house, but when she was staging a house, she would show me all the secrets to interior decorating, and by default, geography. It was important to know the country of origin and time period of the piece purchased, even if the piece was a knockoff made in Taiwan. These were some of my best memories with my mother. I not only got to share something she was passionate about with her, but we laughed more than we ever had before or since, especially when Mommy's suppliers, guys who had extra inventory, would try and pass off what was a fake Chippendale for what was clearly a fake Queen Anne. There were even times when Mommy not only asked for my opinion, she actually took it.

Eventually, Dad's relentlessness paid off when Jimmy got his first national commercial – sniffing clothes with a talking teddy bear, and Mommy insisted I spend my weekends with Dad and Jimmy, as I heard her telling Mike she needed me to be a buffer between Jimmy's and Dad's insanity.

"Where is he?" Without waiting for Margaret to answer, Billy walked off to another room.

"He was here, but he's gone now," she called after him. To me, she said, "Your father has told me so much about you."

"You're friends with my father?"

Margaret lay down on a futon, twice the thickness of the "special"-priced sciatica-triggering one I slept on in LA.

"We're much more than friends," she smiled.

"They're drinking buddies." Billy was back. My eyes went to the half bottle of cognac resting on the blue wool rug by Margaret's right leg. Cognac had been Dad's drink of choice. If you drink sophisticated, you will never be a drunk. That's what he had always said right before he passed out.

"Billy, Billy. Always so dramatic." She sat up, her back and neck in perfect alignment. "A few celebratory drinks don't make us drunks."

"You've been celebrating for two months now."

It wasn't a surprise to hear Dad had been drinking and his AA chip a farce, but Dad always said "You don't drink where you pee."

"He doesn't go to meetings?"

Billy kept his eyes on Margaret and said, "Court-mandated."

"Dad was arrested?"

Margaret reached up, grabbed the bottom of my coat, and pulled me down next to her. Her pupils were dilated, and I wondered if cognac was her only vice. "Your father is a hero."

I tried to stand, but she pulled me closer. "A hero," she said. Then she peered at me and said, "You have his eyes."

"Okay," I said, not knowing what else to say.

"Billy, doesn't she have his eyes?"

Billy took a step closer to us, and I was hoping he would help me up, but his arms stiffened at his sides, the tank still on his back. I had never seen him look so disgusted, but in the last ten years there were a lot of Billy's faces that I had skipped: the face of someone strung out on heroin; the face of withdrawal; the face of someone crawling his way back from hell. I was glad I hadn't been around for any of that, but the Billy who'd gone out and saved Dad's business, the Billy who'd stuck by Jimmy no matter how much shit Jimmy (I imagined) threw at him, the Billy who'd discovered he was an artist – those faces, yes, those faces, I would have wanted to see.

"Oh God," Margaret cried, staring at me.

"What is it?" I said.

"Blood." She started to wipe her hands furiously up and down the front of my coat.

"It's okay," I said.

But she wouldn't stop. Finally, Billy ripped her away from me. She sobbed into his shoulder.

"It's okay," he whispered as he patted her matted hair. "It's okay. Angela is okay." He mouthed to me, "Off." I took the coat off.

"See, look, Angela's fine," he said.

Margaret broke away from Billy, and with tears still streaming down her face, smiled at me. I looked around for a tissue, paper towel, anything she could wipe her eyes with, but I only could find a crumpled bed sheet, which I handed to her. With precision, she dabbed her eyes.

"Margaret." Billy wiped the remaining tears with the sleeve of his coat. "Did you eat today?" He held her chin in the palm of his hand and I felt a twinge of jealousy, which I pushed down fast.

"I can make you something," I said.

"No, no, I'm not hungry," she said.

Billy kicked one of the empty Chinese food containers and said, "I'm going to spray."

She nodded and Billy got up and left the room. I stood there making what Jimmy had always called my clown smile. Jimmy said he always knew when I was feeling tortured by the Bozo the Clown expression on my face.

"Your father is a great man," Margaret said.

My cheeks were starting to hurt, but I was afraid to change the expression on my face because any sudden move might set her off.

Without warning or a word said, she pulled a page from the *Times* entertainment section resting underneath the carton with the half-eaten contents of a shrimp dish and covered her face with it.

"Margaret," I asked. "Are you okay?"

She sat with perfect posture, her face covered with ads for *Three Men and a Little Lady*, the sequel to *Three Men and a Baby*, another dull comedy stolen from the French, and a movie with a wide-eyed, wide-mouthed boy: HOME ALONE. NOW PLAYING AT THEATERS NEAR YOU. AL SHARPTON SHOT, read a headline.

My face was aching. "Margaret, I'm going to go help Billy, okay?"

She nodded. At least I thought she did.

I found Billy in the kitchen.

"You want to spray?" Billy handed me his can.

"That's okay."

"Go ahead, it won't kill you . . . not for at least twenty years anyway."

"Very funny." I took the can and the hose from him, placed my finger on the trigger device, and squeezed.

"Still fun?"

I didn't answer him. Besides, it was never fun for me. It was therapy.

After one of those days or weeks when everything went wrong, making a fist so tight around the handle of the gun that it made my hand hurt, squirting into cracks and corners and sometimes directly into the eye of a roach too tough to hide dissipated all my frustrations.

I took a deep breath and inhaled the smell of Combat. Squeezing the trigger didn't feel as good as it used to. Maybe because I now knew too much about the chemicals, how detrimental they were to the environment, and to my dad's, and now Billy's, health.

Billy pointed the spray gun at a four-by-six-inch framed sketch that hung over the kitchen sink. "Picasso," he said.

"A copy," I said.

"Original," he said.

"Tell me she has a Rembrandt hanging in her bathroom."

"There's a lot of Picasso's work out there—"

"You're telling me it's not valuable?"

"It is, but I think it's more personal."

I stepped closer. It was a profile of a young woman, but it wasn't the disjointed, grotesque style I associated with Picasso. The sketch was simple, but there was something about this girl that made me feel hopeful. "Margaret," I said.

"She was a photographer. *Life* magazine. *New York Times* front page kind of thing. She knew a lot of famous people, but she had some special relationships with them too."

"What does this have to do with my father?"

"I was in bed with the flu, and we got one of those emergency beeps from the building manager—"

"The new Mr. Burns," I said.

"New guy's not as uptight, but the stick is still pretty far up his ass. Well, there was no way I could do the stop, and your dad said he couldn't handle it."

"Why would Dad not be able to handle a stop?"

"For him, doing stops, exterminating, is more challenging to his sobriety than walking into a bar."

"Killing bugs and rodents causes Dad to drink?"

Billy opened a cabinet – empty – and squirted inside. "The work, the people, I don't know, but it's a trigger."

"That makes no sense," I said, but if I had been willing to think about it, I would have seen how it made perfect sense. The only time Dad didn't drink was when he was taking Jimmy to auditions, or rehearsing with him, or fighting with Mommy, which he only did when it was about Jimmy's career.

Then Jimmy got the first commercial, and the second, and all those years when Jimmy was working regularly, Dad never had so much as a liqueur-filled chocolate. But during the lulls, when Dad had to do more exterminating, the drinking would start up again.

"Addiction isn't a math equation. There's no logic you can apply to solve it."

I took back the gun and pressed the trigger so hard my knuckles went white. Chemicals sprayed all over the stove.

"Ange, you have to aim."

I squirted again with less enthusiasm.

Billy shut the nozzle on the top of the tank. There was nothing coming out, but I couldn't release my grip.

He stepped in front of the gun and said, "It sucks. I know." I dropped the gun.

"That lush in there" – I was shouting, but Billy didn't insist I lower my voice; I didn't know if it was because he didn't think she was listening or because he didn't think it would make any difference – "is the reason my father is drinking again?"

"She's not the reason and she is the reason, and everything and nothing is the reason, Angela."

"I guess you would know how this all works." As soon as I said it, I wanted to take it back.

"I'm an addict. And yes, I'm ashamed of a lot of the shit I've done, but I'm also grateful because my addiction is the reason I was finally able to stop mourning the past – fucked-up childhood, Jimmy, all the years you were gone, the phone calls with all the empty promises on both sides. Dysfunctional us. And I loved us."

"I still love us," I said, and maybe I should have taken it back or at least wanted to, but I didn't. "Billy, why was Dad arrested? Drunk driving?"

Billy turned the nozzle on, picked the gun up off the floor, and with his back to me continued to spray. "That and driving right through a wall into a family's living room."

"Did anyone . . ." I paused.

"Die?" He turned to face me. "Your dad's not in prison, is he? Luck. No one got hurt. There was a lot of property damage, though. Three-year probation and AA."

"And they took his license away," I said.

"For good," he said. "I bought the van from him to get it insured."

"Thank you," I said.

"You don't thank family." He continued spraying, only now he was covering the areas he already did. "I know he took the van today." He lowered his voice. "He better pray to fucking God I don't catch him driving."

"Why? You're going to call the cops?" I asked with more than a hint of sarcasm.

Billy continued to spray in silence. The third time he sprayed under the fridge, I couldn't keep quiet any longer.

"You wouldn't," I said.

"There has to be consequences."

"Consequences?" I stepped in front of him and got chemicals sprayed on the thighs of my jeans.

"Are you crazy?"

"How could you turn Dad over to the police?"

"I don't expect you to understand."

"Understand? He treats you like a son."

"Better than a son," he said. We both knew he was referring to how hard Dad pushed Jimmy. *"Greatness comes at a price,"* he always said. For Jimmy, the price was childhood, but everyone grew up fast in our neighborhood. If you weren't smoking cigarettes by eleven, pot by thirteen, and making-out before junior high school, you were considered developmentally challenged, though the words used were "Fucking retarded." What did Jimmy miss when he couldn't hang out after school and most weekends because he was working? I often thought I would have been more than happy to make the sacrifices Jimmy had made, if given the chance he had at greatness.

"Actions have consequences," Billy said. "They have to."

"Is that why you were upset when I was talking to that reporter? You believe Saddam Hussein's actions should have consequences? Those consequences are blowing up Iraq."

"Fuck this war. I have to keep this business running. We can't afford to lose another client."

"You're losing clients?"

"It's fine now." Billy shoved his tank into the backpack, zipped it, and without my help hoisted it over his shoulders and onto his back. "There are still several floors left to do."

"I'm here to help."

"I'll move faster on my own." Billy looked at me, and I squinted so my eyes wouldn't give away my hurt.

"There's only one tank." He forced a smile. "You head home. I'll catch up with you later."

CHAPTER 13

There was so much more to say, too much. I would have caught up to Billy before he walked out the front door and insisted we talk, if Margaret hadn't jumped up and said, "Hang up the damn phone!"

Until she mentioned it, I hadn't noticed the incessantly droning dial tone.

"I must have forgot to hang it up," she said.

I followed the sound to the futon, where she was now at least sitting and not lying flat. I couldn't find the damn phone. Cordless phones. No wire to follow. I got down on my hands and knees and felt around under the futon, but no phone. The sound was now driving me mad. I crawled over a pile of newspapers, around to the back of the futon, and peering at the floor, the headlines stopped me. BORN IN THE USA: ARAB VISITOR GIVES BIRTH TO '91'S FIRST BABY. The top newspaper on the pile was dated January 2, 1991. The irony was that in a few days, the headlines would read, FIRST ARAB KILLED.

"Where is the damn thing?" I said.

"Got it," Margaret said. "I must have been sitting on it." I took a deep breath, and the smell of sweat and stale sweet-and-sour pork almost made me barf. I got back on my feet.

"I will be going, then."

"Please." She extended the phone to me. "Would you put it on its base to charge? It's in the bedroom."

She looked as though she might cry again if I said no. I took the phone from her and went to the bedroom, which was surprisingly neat. The bed was made and she had an extraordinary number of perfectly placed show pillows for a woman who gave the impression she hadn't taken the time to wash her hair in weeks.

I returned the phone to its base on the nightstand, and there was a black-and-white photo, eight and a half by eleven, of John Lennon kneeling next to his younger son, Sean, who was four, maybe five.

Billy was the same age as Sean when his father was shot. Only they never arrested Billy's dad's killer. He was buying a pack of Camel no filters when something went down. The something was never discussed, except to say it wasn't personal. The wrong place at the wrong time.

The day John Lennon died was the only day Dad had ever insisted Jimmy skip an audition without him having a fever of 101 or higher. Dad showed up at our high school and told us to get in the car. He didn't say a word until we reached the Triborough Bridge and he asked me to get the coin purse from the glove compartment for the toll. When we got on the FDR, he told us an important man died last night. I thought he was talking about some politician, the mayor or president.

He told us one of the Beatles had been shot in front of his building. We got as close as we could and Dad parked the car in a No Standing zone. We got out of the car and into a crowd of thousands holding lit candles. A woman offered us candles. Dad said "No thank you" and then the three of us joined hands, while Dad said a prayer for John Lennon's family, and for our family, and for a world that would take, in front of his home, someone who had as much heart and talent as John Lennon.

"You get lost?" Margaret called out. "Do I need to send Saint Anthony in to find you?"

I took the photo and went back to her. She peered over her glasses at me. My coat was on the floor next to her, and she was rubbing the plastic statue of Saint Anthony between her palms. "Not the best rendition, but I guess there's only so much you can do with plastic."

"You went through my coat pockets?"

"You snooped a bit yourself." She glanced down at the photo in my hand.

"Did you take this?" I said.

The muscles in her face went up and then down, making it seem as if she was smiling and frowning. "You know Cartier-Bresson?"

"The watch?"

She let out what was most definitely a giggle. "He was a genius photographer. He described the unexpected and spontaneous moments when you capture what could not have been captured at any other moment in time. The decisive moment."

"Moments that make history," I said. "The picture you took of John Lennon and his son."

"That was my intention, but to tell you the truth, I think John was indulging me. He knew I was taking his picture. Sean for sure did."

"You should frame it," I said.

"Caging my photos would make them seem too finite. Besides, I promised Yoko the photo years ago. Couldn't find the damn thing. Never had much of a filing system. If Billy hadn't helped me clean, it would still be in the back of the closet under all those stupid throw pillows."

"There are a lot of them," I said.

"My ex was so obsessive-compulsive he couldn't take a shit in the morning until the bed was made and all twenty-two pillows were perfectly arranged. I told Billy to burn all but two."

"The photo is extraordinary."

She took it from me and studied it. "They were good people. A little too peacenik for me."

"You don't think peace is a good thing?"

"Let's say in my twenty years working as a photojournalist, I saw a lot of crap, and peace didn't always come with a lot of justice." I wanted to ask her more about places she had been and the things she had seen, but the bottle of cognac had diminished several inches since I first got there, so I decided against it. She dropped the photo, her not-so-decisive moment, on the floor next to my blood-stained coat. I bent to pick up the photo, but she blocked me with her hand. "Please. Leave it for now."

"Okay, but promise me you won't spill takeout on it."

"I'll try not to," she laughed. I surprised myself and laughed too.

"Your smile isn't his," she said, looking at me. "But your eyes, distant, faraway, are your father's."

I never thought of myself as sharing this trait with my father, but maybe there were some things so out of reach for me that self-imposed distance was my way of protecting myself from the disappointment; the pain, I was sure would follow.

"I hope you find your way." This time she rubbed Saint Anthony between her palms. "Patron saint of lost souls." She handed the plastic statue back to me. "I'm sure you'll find your way."

"It's not mine," I said. "He belongs to my brother."

"The one who's getting married?"

"I know he doesn't want to get married. I want him to know he doesn't have to." I had no idea why I was baring my soul to a stranger, who was most likely not going to remember any of our conversation, or maybe that's exactly why.

She put on a pair of pink cat-shaped framed reading glasses and looked me up and down.

"Are you telling me I'm an open book?"

"Wanted to get a better look at the bullshit you're telling me."

"Bullshit? If Jimmy wanted to get married, why would he take off days before the wedding? Not tell anyone where he was going?"

"I don't know your brother, and maybe you're right and he doesn't want to get married, but I wonder if you're the one who isn't ready for him to get married."

This was more than I could wrap my head around at the moment.

"It's been good talking to you." I meant it. Her eccentricity attracted me to her. I could have talked with her for the rest of the afternoon, but I had to find Billy. I had to find Dad before Billy found him driving the van.

I thought I would put the coat on outside so the dried bloodstains wouldn't freak Margaret out again, though there was something different about her since I had first walked into the apartment less than an hour ago. I wasn't worried that a wrong word would cause her to fall into an emotional abyss, or she'd try to fly away, a wounded bird with a broken wing.

"Thanks," I said. This time when I looked over at her, I could see that she was an older woman who looked young for her age and knew a lot more than I did about life.

"Maybe I'll see you again someday." She extended her hand to me, but instead of a handshake goodbye, she pulled me to her until I was sitting on the futon at her side, with the bloody coat resting on my lap.

"Did he tell you?" she asked.

"Tell me?"

"Billy, did he tell you how your father saved my life?"

I shook my head.

"You want to know?" After everything Billy had told me, I needed to hear something Dad did right. Sitting next to Margaret, I thought of my mother. They couldn't have looked more different from each other, and it didn't appear they had anything in common, though Mommy would love the throw pillows. Margaret seemed to idolize my father, and I wanted to believe my mother once did too.

Margaret pulled up her bathrobe sleeve and tapped her finger against her vein. "See this?" she asked. I didn't want to see her track marks or hear some story about how my father found her lying on the floor with a needle still stuck in her arm and how he gave her mouth-to-mouth or called 911. But I could never look away from a car crash. . . . There were no track marks, only a few scars from what were probably persistent scratching from eczema or – "You had bedbugs."

"You are your father's daughter," she said.

"Dad discovered you had bedbugs."

"That's right," she said, and I would have said "Bedbugs aren't life-threatening" if she hadn't first said, "I know, bedbugs don't kill people."

"They don't," I agreed.

"But pills do," she said.

Now she'd lost me.

"Your dad knocked on my door and said he was there to exterminate. I almost didn't let him in, but when he explained that if he didn't, all the bugs would flee from the exterminated apartments to mine, I opened the door. Funny how the image of a roach scampering around your apartment is so disturbing, even at a time when you're minutes away from committing suicide."

"The pills," I said, starting to understand.

She nodded. "For months, I'd had these red itchy spots all over my body. I couldn't sleep, stopped eating. I saw doctor after doctor and they could find nothing wrong. Right before your father came to the door, I received a call, the results of a test I thought was my last hope.

If this one didn't find something physically wrong with me, then I had to accept that what was happening was in my head and I had lost my mind. And if that was the case, then after the months of no sleep and constant itching, I didn't want to live. I have to say, it was comforting to feel certain about something, even if it was the decision to take my own life. I guess it was almost my decisive moment."

"Dad saw your arm and asked to see your bed."

She laughed. "Were you here?"

"I know the protocol. You got rid of your bed and couch. That explains the futon. Of course, your doctors would have never even thought someone of your—"

"I know. I'm a rich bitch."

This time I smiled comfortably. "Bedbugs are associated with poverty. You traveled."

"For work. All the time. As your dad explained, I brought them back with me. If it wasn't for your father, I wouldn't be here right now."

"You've been seeing my father since then."

"Pretty much," she said.

"You know my father is an alcoholic."

"We have that in common."

"Margaret, I like you. If it weren't for the—"

She took a swig of cognac. "Then you'd approve of your father seeing me?"

"I wouldn't disapprove."

"You know your father makes his own decisions."

"I don't know if addicts are capable of making their own decisions."

"You think the alcohol and drugs are deciding for us?"

"Aren't they?"

"That's one way of seeing it."

"How do you see it?"

"It's my life and your father's life, and we can live it as we fucking please." She picked up my coat from the floor and handed it to me. "You don't want to forget this. I hear it's cold out."

Then she added, "There could be another interpretation. One might pray to Saint Michael for the strength to fight one's demons. Too bad I'm not the praying type." She smiled.

As I opened the door to let myself out, Margaret said, "Congratulate your brother for me."

I checked a few of the floors, hoping to find Billy. There was more we needed to talk about, even if I wasn't sure if I was up to it. Billy, the patron saint of brutal honesty. Then a woman threatened to call the police on me after I'd knocked on her door and said I was looking for the exterminator, and I thought better of continuing my search. When I got to the lobby, the doorman on duty told me I was the only person he'd seen come off the elevator since he started his shift.

The demonstration had passed, and the police barricades were moved to the side. I walked as fast as I could down to Grand Central station and got on the express train, which I rode as far as I could, and then I switched to the local to Pelham Bay.

The Don C and Son van was there. Billy must have caught up with Dad and they drove back together – without me.

CHAPTER 14

The Don C and Son van was parked across the street, inches away from blocking Mrs. Bellini's driveway. All I could do was pray that Billy didn't catch Dad driving the van. I stuck my hand in my pocket and gripped Saint Anthony so tight he cracked. I couldn't look, but the sound of breaking plastic was clear; I broke him. I don't know what that meant according to Jimmy's saint rules book, but it couldn't be good.

I could hear Mike and Mommy shouting. I didn't give it a second thought. But as I ascended the staircase, I realized this wasn't Mommy and Mike communicating as usual. They were fighting the way Mommy and Dad had at the beginning of their end. I couldn't make out most of the words, but I heard Mommy shout "You know why" and "You promised" and "You traitor." Mike's response was loud and clear. "Enough."

Three steps before I reached our apartment, Mike burst out of the front door and pushed past me, knocking me against the wall.

"Mike!" I called to him, but he didn't stop. He was wearing a blue sharkskin suit, which either meant someone had died, or his lottery number hit. He was way too upset to have won the lottery.

Inside the apartment, Mommy was wiping her face with a paper towel, which she believed was the equivalent of rubbing sandpaper across the face's delicate skin. Something was indeed very wrong.

"Who died?" I asked.

"I have no time or patience for guessing games," she said, turning on the kitchen sink and splashing water on her face. Another anti-aging taboo.

"Paper towels and water?" I said.

Mommy gripped the edge of the counter, her back to me. "This is not your concern."

"Mike rushed by me without as much as a hello, and you're committing facial suicide. I think this is very much my concern."

"If you really want to know," she said, and flipped around to face me, then frowned. "Your face is filthy." She stepped closer and sniffed. "That's blood."

There was a crash.

"Jimmy's room," Mommy said.

We rushed there to find Dad lying on his stomach, swallowed up by the airless air mattress, the wheelchair turned on its side, and the glass-framed portrait of Mommy and her brother shattered on the floor. Surrounded by broken glass was the VHS tape of my cable interview.

Mommy bent down and picked the tape up and tossed it into my open suitcase, now on the floor, and then she picked up the portrait.

"I painted this from memory," she said. "Years after he was gone."

I took the piece from her and for the first time in my life I understood there was more to my mother than I had known or would ever know. "You're an artist."

"I'm a mother and wife and realtor." She contorted her face in a way I had never seen before. By the time I could figure out what was happening, my mother was crying. This unfamiliar scene both blew my mind and broke my heart.

I touched the slight hump she now had on her upper back and said, "We can get another frame."

Mommy raised her eyes and when they met mine, I saw she needed me to soak in all the pain she was feeling before she spoke. We were sharing a genuine tender moment. She opened her mouth and said, "Your father's a fuckin' moron."

"He's drunk," I sighed.

"What clued you in?" She walked over to the side of the bed. "One thing about your dad, no matter how pissed he is, he always manages to find his way home – to my home."

"Billy," I said. "Was he here?"

"Why?"

"The van is outside now, but earlier it wasn't, and Billy . . ." I paused.

Mommy waited for me to continue, but I was sure she knew what I was going to say next. "He said if it was Dad who took the van, he would—"

"Call the fucking police." She reached down and slapped the back of Dad's head. "The van?" Dad grumbled something intelligible. "James, did you drive the van?"

This time there was no reaction.

Mommy put her hands into Dad's pants. I had never seen them this physical when they were married. "Idiot," she said, coming up with a set of keys on a silver rat-shaped key chain I had found on Venice Beach and sent to him for one of his birthdays.

"Hold on to these." She forced the keys into my hand. "If Billy asks, you say that you borrowed the van."

"I was with Billy. He knows it wasn't me."

"What were you doing with Billy? Don't tell me you were having sex?"

"Why would you even ask me that?"

"Save it. I knew you and Billy were intimate since you were fourteen."

I didn't bother to deny it. "And you never said anything?"

"I didn't want you growing up the way I did."

"What way was that?"

She glared over at Dad, still out cold. "When I met your father, I was still wearing undershirts under my dresses because your grandmother was fearful that I'd catch a cold. I was sixteen."

"You never even talked about sex with me."

"I figured you and Billy had a better chance learning from each other, and I found the book." She tipped her head toward the closet where Jimmy kept his saints and I kept a copy of Our Bodies, Ourselves.

"After I got over my disgust – do they really need so many graphic pictures? – I knew it was a better source than I could be." Mommy had never before admitted to being less than an expert on anything. Could this be a major breakthrough? Not likely.

She squinted her eyes at me. "Did you have sex today?"

"Yay, that's right Ma, we fucked. Billy and I fucked all afternoon."

"Watch your mouth."

"Calm down, Ma."

"Don't tell me to be calm." She dropped her hand to her side.

"We didn't have sex, Ma."

"Then why did you say you did?"

"Sarcasm, Ma."

"There's too much going on around here for you to be funny. Where is Billy now?"

"We had a fight about Dad and he took off."

"There's a good chance he doesn't know the van is back?"

"Probably," I said.

"That means the van could have been stolen or taken for a joy ride."

"Ma, it wasn't stolen."

"Do you want your father to go to jail? He's on probation. We're talking time. Serious time." I had only heard her so frantic when she convinced herself I was hiding cocaine inside a baby powder container. Jimmy and I found her on my bed covered in white powder. All she had to say for herself was "A mother does what she needs to do to protect her children."

"You can talk to Billy," I said. "He listens to you."

"He didn't even invite me to his show."

"What show?"

"Will you please focus? We need to get the van out of here."

"And do what with it?"

"Break a few windows, spray-paint some tag on its side, take the hubcaps and a few other parts, leave it in Queens by the bridge, so when the police find it, they'll assume it's a stolen, abandoned vehicle. The insurance company will cover the damages and your father won't get his ass raped in jail."

That image I refused to let linger. "Ma, you're talking about committing fraud—"

"*I'm* not going to do this."

"You expect me to?"

She laughed and didn't stop, until I threw the keys and they ricocheted off the empty wall and fell at her feet.

"Pick them up," she said.

"You can't even trust me with vandalism?"

She raised her arms and, expecting to be hit, I closed my eyes. When I opened them, my mother was hugging me. I wasn't sure what this meant. Maybe this was her showing me I wasn't useless and she loved me. Right then, I didn't care. It felt good, and I needed it.

"Let's go." She stepped back and glanced down at her feet.

I picked up the keys. She took them from me and dropped them into the pocket of her raggedy housecoat.

"Where are we going?"

"To see the only person I know who can handle this situation without a hitch, or" – she smiled – "should I say stitch?" I didn't get the joke but there was no time for explanations. Besides, I didn't care. I wanted to help Dad out of this mess.

"Ma, you think it's okay to leave him like this?"

She looked down at my father and said, "He's on his stomach. If he vomits, he won't choke." She walked to the front door, which was still wide open. "You can't wear that coat," she said. "It's disgusting."

I looked down at the beige coat she had lent me, stained from my bloody nose. I knew it had been an accident but I couldn't help feeling Billy was angry and there was a lot he wasn't telling me. "What do you expect me to wear?" I asked.

She took her inhaler from her pocket and sucked, and never in my life had I seen Mommy run, and I wasn't seeing her run now, but she was moving down the stairs faster than I had imagined possible for her. The screen door crashed into my face, just missing my sore nose.

From the middle of the street she yelled, "Theresa Angela, get out here!"

This was serious. I stepped outside. The sun had set, and in the windows of the buildings on the block were the shadows of our nosy neighbors. The nosiest of all, Mrs. Bellini, was in full silhouette.

I went to Mommy's side and whispered, "Everybody's watching."

"Mind your freakin' business, old lady," Mommy shouted, and Mrs. Bellini, a few years younger than Mommy, slammed her window shut.

"Where is the van?" She was still shouting.

"Turn around, Ma. Right in front of you."

"It's dark out," she said, and I resisted the urge to point out the huge painted rat glowing on the side panel.

Mommy unlocked the passenger door, took a flashlight from the glove compartment, and threw me the keys.

"You drive. I can't handle this monster."

I climbed in, and through the windshield I watched Mommy inspect the front of the car. She shut off the flashlight and climbed up into the passenger seat. "Start the car." I put the key in the ignition.

"No damage. Pray your father didn't hit anything."

"You think he could have hit something?"

"The LA air is making your brain slow."

"Insult away." I folded my arms. "We can sit here all night."

"He was wasted, Angela. I'd be shocked if he didn't hit something. I'm praying that something wasn't a person." Mommy let out a deep breath, no wheeze; maybe the new meds were working. Then she moved the gearshift into drive.

The van jolted forward. I hit the brake and shifted back into park. "You're out of your mind."

"We need to get this van out of here before Billy shows up."

"Billy loves Dad. Why would he want to hurt him?"

"That cult he's in—"

"AA?"

"AA, NA, how many goddam *A*'s do you need?"

"They help a lot of people, Ma."

"All I know is that they were the ones who brainwashed him. 'You can't help someone who won't help themself'? What kind of bullshit is that? If someone could help themself, why would they need your help?"

"I think it's more complicated than that."

"I'll tell you what's fucking complicated. Billy believes if your father breaks the law, the only way to help him is to have him locked up."

"What if Billy's right? What if we're hurting Dad by protecting him?"

"Don't you start giving me that AA mumbo jumbo."

I needed air. I rolled down the window and stuck my head out.

"Did I call the police on his junkie ass when Billy robbed the money I won at the casino? No, I did not. Why? Because Billy's family, and you protect family. Standing by family is not enabling them. Tough-love, bullshit – It's freezing. You're going to make yourself sick, both of us sick."

I tried to take a deep breath but could only manage to pant.

"This is why we don't tell you things."

I swung my head back inside the car so fast I could have got whiplash. "Every week you call, and you spend most of the conversation telling me about the weather in LA – *I LIVE IN LA*. I *know* the forecast. SUNNY AND MORE SUN."

"It does rain, and you have to be prepared for the Niños."

"El Niño, Ma."

"They create havoc. The weather patterns change."

"Please stop talking about the weather." I hit my forehead against the steering wheel.

"You're going to hurt yourself." She slipped her hand between the steering wheel and my forehead, and the next time my forehead landed hard in her palm. She made this strange sound, more squeak then wail, and withdrew her hand to her lap. I could see how much pain she was in from how relaxed the muscles in her face were. Letting her face go limp was Mommy's way of holding back tears.

"Are you okay?"

She wouldn't answer me.

"Ma, please say something."

"The headlights, please."

I turned the lever on the steering wheel and the windshield wipers flapped back and forth.

"You forgot how to drive?" Mommy said.

"Give me a break. It's been years since I drove this thing."

Mommy opened the door and climbed out. I found the right switch and turned on the headlights in time to spotlight Mommy's body lying on the street in front of the van.

I opened my door and jumped out. As I stood over her, the lights were blinding. I shielded my eyes. "The street is filthy. Germs."

"You have been away for how long?"

"I don't know."

"How long?"

"Ten years, Ma, ten years." I took her hand and tried to pull her up but I couldn't get her to budge.

"You're telling me in ten years you forgot where you came from? No memory of how your mother takes care of her own shit?"

I stood behind her and tried to lift her up by her shoulders, but her body was limp and unmovable, like she had been trained in nonviolent resistance.

"What do you want from me?"

"Run her over!" Mrs. Bellini yelled from her window.

"Shut up, old woman!" Mommy yelled back. Then out of nowhere she asked, "Saddam Hussein, you're taking his side?"

"He's a monster," I said.

"Why shouldn't we bomb him? Consequences of his actions?"

"It's not about him. If we go to war, innocent people, hundreds of thousands, will die."

"And this is not about your father. This is about our family."

"Ma, please, let's get back in the van, and I'll drive you wherever you want to go."

"You know we never were accepted by the people here, if you can call the witch in the window a person. We were the outsiders. Never invited to backyard barbecues. No one ever gave us a freaking jar of tomatoes or figs from their trees. You know why I'm okay with that?"

I thought it was a rhetorical question, but when I didn't respond she repeated, "Do you know why?"

"Why, Ma?"

"It meant we were on the outside of all the shit that went down here. It meant my children, my husbands, first and second, with all their flaws, never went to jail. My children didn't hate a person because of the color of their skin or the pronunciation of their last name. That's something I am proud of."

She shut her eyes and crossed her arms over her chest. "You can drive over me now."

"Okay, I get it, Ma."

She opened one eye. "You will drive without questioning me?"

"Yes."

"Yes, what?"

"Yes, Ma, I will drive without questioning you."

"Help me up." She raised her arm and this time I got her on her feet. The back of her yellow housecoat and her platinum blond hair were filthy. I tried using the sleeves of my coat to wipe the dirt off. She shrugged me away.

We climbed into the van. I put the gearshift in drive. Mommy rolled down her window and yelled, "Good night, old woman." I hit the gas, and we were off, to where or to whom I wasn't sure, but Mommy was convinced they would help save Dad from prison.

CHAPTER 15

The clock on the dashboard had stopped at 2 p.m.; on what day I had no idea. Mommy wasn't wearing a watch, but she was sure it was 6:45 p.m. I didn't argue. Her internal clock was always spot-on. She was wrong about me. I hadn't forgotten everything from my life before LA. I was maneuvering in and out of traffic, and around pedestrians; no time had passed since I was last behind the wheel of this van. I even braked twice for stray cats (one may have been a large rat), and we only came close to tipping over once, on a very sharp turn. Even Mommy said I handled the van well, after she had crossed herself and asked God for his mercy.

It wasn't until Mommy said, "Double park here," that I realized we were at Carmela's tuxedo shop. Is she the one who was going to "handle this situation"? The stitch joke, because Carmela does alterations. I got it, but I still didn't think it was funny.

The gate was down on the front of the shop, but Mommy said she knew where to find Carmela, and I resisted the urge to ask any questions. I knew Mommy would only tell me what she wanted me to know when she wanted me to know it.

She said she would be back in five minutes, which in Mommy time meant twenty, twenty-five. The gas gauge was inching toward the red, so I turned off the engine. The street was quiet. I imagined families eating dinner and watching television. We always watched television while we ate, and if it was past *Jeopardy!*, but too early for one of Mommy's night shows, *Dallas* or *Dynasty,* she would let the children decide. Jimmy and I fought over who would be the master of the remote even when we wanted the same program, but Billy, who was with us most nights, never cared what we watched. His answer to everything was "Doesn't matter to me." It seemed that a lot mattered to him now.

Six minutes had passed and no Mommy. I wanted to listen to the news to see if there was anything about the demonstration today. Would the news here report there had been fifty thousand people marching in the streets of New York City to tell the president, the UN, and Congress that the answer to going to war with Iraq was "NO"? Or would they say five thousand? Would they not report the demonstration at all? "No blood for oil," I chanted under my breath. A police siren wailed, and I jerked forward and hit my chest against the steering wheel. A photo-booth strip fell from the visor facedown onto my lap. *Rye Playland, summer 1978* was written on the back. I flipped it over; the top two pictures were of Billy and Jimmy and me with our tongues stuck out and our eyelids flipped inside out. In the bottom photos Billy and Jimmy and I had our arms wrapped around each other, flashing our best on-camera smiles. We looked happy, and normal, the way I remembered us before—

The police sirens were getting louder, and I remembered how I'd cried for them to stop that night. I didn't know if I was more drunk or in shock, but Billy was shouting for help and then he ran off and I could see Jimmy's limp body at the bottom of the six-stories-of-concrete stadium. I didn't rush down the stairs to be at his side. Instead, I hid behind the seven-foot statue of the naked boy with the blue-spray-painted balls, screaming "Shut up!" until a police officer found me and took me to the hospital. Mommy, Dad, and Mike were already there. I supposed it was Billy who had called them. I never asked.

I later discovered Billy had called 911 and said, "Officer Down." He knew it was illegal, but Jimmy was lying at the bottom of the stadium stairs unconscious, or possibly dead.

I touched both faces on the Rye Playland photo and felt a twinge behind my rib cage. I missed the three of us, together.

I slipped the picture back into the visor and thought how Billy and Mommy both loved this family with their own unique ways of showing it.

I must have fallen asleep, because a thud woke me up, and a face pressed against the windshield startled me.

"What you do?" It was Carmela.

I rolled down my window. "You almost gave me a heart attack."

"Lucky I come before you die from-a the cold."

It was above freezing, but questioning Carmela's authority was a risk I wasn't willing to take.

"Get out," she said.

I turned the ignition halfway and dialed the heat to max. "It's okay. It will be warm soon."

"Get out," she repeated. "Mama has a surprise for you inside." The gate was now up and the lights were on in the shop. I got out of the van and the top of Carmela's head was level with my nipples. Could she have shrunk since this afternoon?

She tried climbing up into the driver's seat on her own, but soon gave up and asked me to give her a little push, and I did. Behind the wheel she looked even smaller.

"You ever drive a van before?"

"Can't be harder than driving my papa's milk truck." She pulled the door shut, adjusted the seat as close as possible to the wheel, and drove off. From behind, it appeared the van was driving itself.

I walked inside the shop and the bell tinkled. "An angel got its wings." Mommy called out from behind the orange curtain.

"Carmela is parking the van," I said. "I hope she can handle it."

"She used to drive a milk truck," Mommy said.

"So I hear." I wondered how big the milk truck was.

"Ta-da." Mommy pushed the orange curtain open. There she was, sporting tails and a top hat. The star of a 1930s' big-screen musical. She looked amazing.

"Wow," I said.

She stepped into the room. "Too much of a *Victor Victoria* feel?"

"You're beautiful." I shifted the full-length mirror so she could get a full view of herself.

She spun around and tilted her top hat at me. "Hides the matted mess on my head."

"It works well," I said.

"Nobody does alterations as quickly, and as well, as Carmela. Not even her late husband. She's a witch with a needle." I glanced over at the photo of Luigi. Carmela had already replaced the broken glass. Two framed pictures of dead people, Carmela's husband and Mommy's brother, had shattered today, and one plastic saint cracked, and if I were superstitious, I would have seen this as a bad omen.

"It will have to do," Mommy said.

"Ma, you do look wonderful, but this wedding is wrong."

"First of all, you're wrong, and second of all, you really think I would wear a man's tuxedo to my son's wedding? Even though I am the best mother." She grinned.

"Then what are we doing here, playing dress-up?"

"I certainly can't go into the city wearing bag lady chic."

"You're going to the city tonight?" I asked.

"We are going to the city."

"You hate the city."

"Despise it, but we want to find Jimmy, right?"

"Jimmy's in the city?" I felt as if I could breathe again.

"Julie, is she perfect? No. Does she wear the ugliest old-lady, sensible shoes you've ever seen? Yes. But you haven't seen your brother with Julie. Around her, well, he's the old Jimmy, no, even better than who he was before the accident."

"If he wants to get married, why did he take off?"

Mommy leaned back against the cash register and covered her face with her hands.

She was crying. "Whatever it is, we can fix it," I said. I wanted her to stop crying.

Mommy dropped her hands, and of course her mascara wasn't smeared. Waterproof. "I went too far," she said.

"Ma, what did you do?" I took hold of her shoulders.

Her eyes widened, and I would have sworn there was a bright yellow aura around her. Did she have some kind of spiritual awakening?

"That's it," she said. "You, Theresa Angela. You are the answer."

I was sure I didn't want to know the question.

"Jimmy will listen to you." With the energy of someone with the lungs of a marathon runner, she marched over to the phone near the register.

I went to her side. "Ma, Jimmy hates me."

She put the receiver down. "Your brother loves you."

"The accident, Ma."

"Your only crime was that you wanted to celebrate with your brother. Did you both drink too much? A couple of idiots. But the accident was not your fault."

Secrets were destroying this family – Mommy had said so herself. It was time for me to come clean. I had to finally say it out loud, the truth, "Listen to me, Ma—"

"Carmela has something for you to wear in the back." She picked up the receiver again.

I had to keep talking. I had to tell her the truth. It wasn't only that I got Jimmy drunk and dragged him to park that night. I had to finally come out and say it. "Ma, on the stadium stairs, I was the one—"

She slapped me.

I touched my cheek, feeling the heat on my skin. I closed my eyes tight. I couldn't cry. If I started, I wouldn't be able to stop.

Mommy grabbed my shoulders and shook me. "What happened, happened, and it was an accident. Do you understand me?"

I opened my eyes.

"Tell me you understand." Her fleshy fingers pressed against my clavicle.

"I understand." I understood that the truth would kill her. For the first time in my life, I was able to see life from my mother's point of view. To live with her paralyzed child had to be difficult beyond belief, but if her other child were to tell her how it was her fault, that she was the reason her brother would never walk again, it would kill her.

"Go in the back and change out of the crime scene you're wearing." She lifted her chin at my stained jacket.

"Okay," I said.

I needed her to lead me to Jimmy. I went behind the orange curtain. There were two dressing rooms. The one on the right was empty. But the image of Fat Freddy pressing against me, earlier this morning as well as all those years ago, suddenly flooded my brain, and I had to run to the bathroom to avoid vomiting in the dressing room.

"You're sick?" Mommy stood in the bathroom doorway. I rinsed my mouth with water, looking at my mother's reflection. I thought I should tell her that Fat Freddy was looking for Jimmy, but she had enough to deal with right now. I never told her about what almost happened in the alley. I had tried to make myself believe that *almost* didn't count, and with all that she had to deal with, between working full time and managing my father from over-managing my brother, there was no time to worry about *almost*.

"Something I ate."

"I bet the damn butcher is selling horse meat again."

"Again?" I turned to her.

"It was one time. It actually was tasty."

"I had a hot dog in the city," I said.

"Are you crazy? You don't know what's in those things."

Before letting me pass, she asked me to lower my head toward her, and she put her lips to my forehead the way she used to, to see if I had a temperature. "You do feel warm."

"I'm fine. Where's the surprise?"

Mommy pointed to the other dressing room. "You want my help?"

Mommy had never asked if I, or anyone, wanted her help. She gave it whether you wanted it or not. I wasn't sure if this meant I was growing up or if she was growing up; maybe it was both of us.

"I'm okay," I said.

Hanging on the wall hook was the powder-blue tux. Carmela had already altered it. I took off my coat and then my tee and jeans and slipped into the pants and ruffled shirt. I thought I'd never get every button done, but I did. After having a moment of *what the hell do I do with this?*, I picked up the cummerbund and, remembering Billy wearing his, clipped it around my waist. I put on the jacket with the wide lapels, and I was surprised: I looked good. The fit was perfect. The only thing left was the white bow tie. I couldn't get it around my collar, so I walked onto the showroom floor. Mommy was sitting in a folding chair.

"Powder blue," she smiled. "It's a choice." She circled her pointer finger in the air and I turned around. "Your ass looks great in those pants." She stood, walked around to face me, tied my bow tie, and said, "You look good."

"Carmela will need to hem the length a few inches." I lifted my leg to show the pants dangling over my toes.

"Or you can try these." She waved a pair of heels in front of my face. They weren't dyed to match, but they might as well have been.

"Where did you get those?"

"Carmela's cousin sells wholesale. She has a closet filled with shoes. You're lucky she had a pair in your size."

She stuck out her leg to show me one of the four-inch sling-back heels she was wearing. "Isn't this a beauty?"

"I can wear the shoes I have on."

She sucked her cheek at my choice in footwear. "You don't want to be dragging the hems all over the place. The pants will be ruined. You should know these things at your age."

I kicked off my shoes, and with Mommy's help and her shoulder to lean on, I slipped into the heels. They weren't as uncomfortable as they looked, but I doubted I could run in them.

"Are we taking the van?"

"Of course not."

"Going back home and getting your car?"

"Not enough time."

"You in tails and top hat, and me from the set of *Saturday Night Fever*. We're going to get some attention on the subway."

"The subway." Mommy rolled her eyes so far back I was relieved when they didn't get stuck. "Our ride will be here any minute." She stood on her tippy toes to see over the heads of the mannequins in the store window.

"I'm glad Mike's cooled down."

"Mike? After tonight I may be in search of husband number three."

"Why would you say that?" I stepped right behind her, and when she turned to me, her face was so close to mine the tip of my tongue could have reached the tip of her nose.

"Get a sense of humor."

"There's nothing funny about family." I sounded more Mommy than Mommy, and, of course, this brought a wide smile to her face.

"You were fighting about Jimmy," I said.

"Mike has no idea about what happened between your brother and me. And you don't say a word."

"I don't even know what happened."

"That makes it easy to keep your mouth shut."

"If you weren't fighting about Jimmy, what?"

She turned back toward the window. "He didn't want me going to Billy's art opening tonight."

"Billy's art opening?"

She turned to me again, and slowly enunciated, "That means his art is hanging in a gallery."

"I know what an opening is; I didn't know Billy was that serious."

"I didn't know he was that good," she said.

"Why wouldn't Mike want to go? He loves Billy."

"He's going, and your father, if he gets his drunken ass out of bed, and I'm assuming Jimmy will be there. He has to be. How could he not show up?" She waited for me to answer, which meant she really did want my opinion on this one.

"I don't know, Ma."

"It's for Billy." The desperation in her voice scared me.

I put my arm around her shoulders; the pads felt thicker than they looked. "I'm sure he'll be there, Mom."

She shrugged me off. "Mike gave me some horseshit about my opinion meaning too much to Billy." I wondered if that was why I hadn't been invited – or was it that he didn't care enough about me to want me there? "Do you know in all the years Mike and I have been together, this was the first time he ever kept anything from me?"

"He did tell you, Ma."

She reached into her pleated pants pocket. "I found this in your father's pocket when I was doing laundry." She handed me a flattened origami beetle. Written on its legs was: *Opening of William Benetti's Creepy-Crawlies and Other Such Things. January 14, 8 p.m. The Tribeca Gallery. By invitation only.*

"William?"

"Pretentious."

"I never thought about his name being anything other than Billy."

"It's not. His birth certificate says Billy."

"You've seen his birth certificate?" I laughed.

"Billy may have his shit together now, but he was a mess forever. I was there for that kid. I was the one who cleaned up his vomit and drove him to rehab. I've been more of a mother to him than his own mother ever was."

"You think he invited his mom?"

"Sweetie, Billy's mother died five years ago. You didn't know?"

"Why would you think I knew?"

"I figured Billy would have told you."

"He didn't."

"It was fine. We didn't need you to be there. I made all the arrangements. Only a few people came from the neighborhood, thank God, the old ladies who never miss a funeral."

"I would have come."

Mommy raised her penciled-in eyebrows. We both knew that I wouldn't have come.

"She checked out long ago. You know that. At least Billy was finally able to say goodbye and mourn."

My heart was cracking, but it wasn't for Billy losing his mom, it was for all the years I'd let him down. I left without telling him. Every time he called me, I listened, but not really, and I always cut him off and told him I'd call him right back, which sometimes meant days or not at all.

The door tinkled. Carmela was back. "All done." She wiped her hands together.

"I owe you," Mommy said.

"You owe me nothing," Carmela said.

"What did you do with the van?" I asked.

Carmela and Mommy shook their heads and sucked their teeth in unison.

"What is it?" I said.

"No more questions," Mommy said to me. This I didn't question.

Carmela took her husband's picture off the wall, kissed it, and hung it back on the hook. "He was good man, my Luigi." She crossed herself and went through the curtain.

A horn beeped. I looked over the mannequin's head and saw a black car with CALL HOBART FOR THE RIDE OF YOUR LIFE stenciled on the driver's-side door. The neighborhood cab company was a family-run business. I didn't know how many nights Hobart cabs had gotten my drunk ass home safe after I had ditched Jimmy and Billy at some club, but I did know how many drivers I had fucked in the front and back seats of their cars in the months after the accident: seven. All seven brothers. The only reason I hadn't slept with their father, the dispatcher, was because their mother never let him out of her sight.

"Ma, I'm going to meet you at the gallery."

Mommy opened the front door and yelled, "One minute." She turned to me. "I asked for the new guy. He's no relation, not even from the neighborhood."

I wasn't surprised she knew about my past with the seven brothers, but I was thankful that I didn't feel judged.

"Let's go," Mommy said. "Carmela, we're heading out."

"Aspet." Wait up. Carmela ran out to us holding, with the tips of her fingers, the blood-stained beige coat. "You want to take?"

"Burn it," Mommy said.

"Wait," I said, taking the coat from Carmela.

"Please, Angela, it's ruined."

I went into the left pocket and retrieved Saint Anthony, who wasn't broken after all. "Now you can burn it."

CHAPTER 16

Mommy handed the driver a ten on a nine-dollar-and-fifty-cents fare. "Next time, cut the 'ma'am' crap, and maybe you'll get a better tip." She exited the cab.

I wish I had something more to give him. The statute of Saint Anthony, resting in the inside pocket of my powder-blue tux jacket, didn't feel as appropriate a gift as the Archangel Michael had with Salvation Man.

"Sorry," I told him.

"Don't sweat it." His resignation made it clear he had dealt with Mommy before.

I nodded to his rearview mirror and got out.

There, in front of an abandoned warehouse, Mommy kissed Julie on both cheeks, which was something I had never seen Mommy do, except for a brief phase after she first saw *The Godfather.*

Julie was dressed all in black – an unbuttoned black coat exposing the front of a black cocktail dress – and smoking a cigarette. She really did have a death wish, I thought.

"Angela!" Julie stepped around Mommy and hugged me tight, a little too tight. Saint Anthony pressed into my rib. "That color looks great on you." She blew smoke out of the side of her mouth.

"You smoke?" I said.

"Maybe you could not tell Jimmy?" She dropped her cigarette, and with the toe of her (even I had to say) ugly shoe, she stomped it out. "He thinks I quit."

"There's something you need to know about my son." Mommy moved in close and let out a deep wheeze. This was it, I thought, the moment Mommy would tell Julie her son didn't want to marry her.

"I'm listening." She sounded afraid. I almost felt sorry for her.

"He has a keen sense of smell. You're going to have to get that Binaca stuff, mints won't do it, and a stronger perfume." Unbelievable. What kind of hold did Julie have on my mother? This family?

"I should quit," Julie said.

"He's inside?" Mommy asked.

"Not even superstition could keep him away," Julie said.

Mommy scrunched her face. She didn't know what Julie was referring to.

"Or it's worse luck to not attend your best friend's art opening." I figured I owed Mommy something for helping Dad tonight and not freaking out over my choice in formalwear.

"Oh, yes, bad luck to see the bride!" Mommy screeched like a winning contestant on a game show.

Julie took a moment before she smiled, but it was so forced, it had to hurt to hold her face in that position. She was clearly on edge. Again, I almost felt sorry for her.

"These stairs." Mommy raised her chin to the ten wide steps leading to the entrance.

"There's a ramp around the back," Julie said.

"Unacceptable." Mommy climbed the ten steps, and before walking inside, looked over her shoulder and said, "Angela, you coming?"

I wanted to see Mommy bawl out some landlord or building manager for their lack of sensitivity to appropriate accessibility, but I needed a few more minutes to grow a pair. I was now *almost* sure I could deal with Jimmy telling me to go fuck myself, but what if he didn't say anything? *In silence there was no hope for forgiveness.*

And Mommy was through the doors before I could answer her.

"I hope she doesn't get upset." Julie took a pack of Marlboro Lights from her black shoulder bag, the same brand I had smoked before I quit. "The sculpture is the size of David."

"I think she can handle a naked statue." After the last few hours, I was starting to believe my mother could probably handle most anything.

"You haven't seen it?"

"Haven't seen any of Billy's art."

"You've been away," she said. I was starting to get tired of people reminding me of that.

"It's of your mom."

"A nude of my mom?" I didn't know whether to laugh or cringe and run.

"Not a nude." Julie smiled. I was sure she wanted to cringe. "I still haven't seen the finished piece, but the work in progress was extraordinary." I had long ago given up any right to expect Billy to share his life with me, but it still hurt to know he was sharing it with someone else.

"What, then?"

"She may not see it as flattering." Julie fumbled around in her purse. "My lighter. It has to be here somewhere." She pulled out a brush, lipstick, and keys, and then asked, "Could you hold this?" When I had the entire contents of her purse in my hands and there was still no lighter, she plopped down onto the stoop clutching the pack of cigarettes, the only thing between her and happiness. "You know I had quit, but with everything that's happening . . ."

I sat down next to her. "I smoked. I get it. It's hard. But, you're a nurse—"

"Yes, and as a nurse I know smoking will, at best, leather my skin, and at worst kill me, slowly and painfully."

"Or you'll get your head blown off." I regretted the words as soon as they left my mouth.

She stared at me.

"That was fucked of me to say."

She let loose an airless laugh. "Very fucked." I couldn't tell if she sounded amused, insulted, or pissed off, and the streetlight was too dim for me to see the full expression on her face. She glanced down at her watch. "Where is my damn lighter?"

A man and a woman, both with their hair cut short enough for them to be mistaken for terminally ill, and dressed in identical black leather motorcycle jackets, stood in front of us.

We were blocking the entrance. I grabbed the pack of cigarettes from Julie's lap and jumped up. "You have a light?"

The man walked past me, but the woman took out a red Bic lighter, lit my cigarette, and said, "He's such a dick."

"Thanks," I said.

"Nice threads," she winked, and followed the dick inside. I sat back down, took another cigarette from Julie's pack, stuck it between my teeth, lit it from the other one, and passed it to her. She took a long deep drag, and on the exhale said, "You're a lifesaver."

"The surgeon general may disagree." I took a drag and was saddened by how good it tasted. I had believed I would never smoke again. Never say never, I thought. There were several drags between us before I said, "You can be a conscientious objector. They can't make you go."

"No one is making me go. Not yet anyway."

"You're not in the reserves?"

She took a drag. "Reservists have already been deployed." She exhaled a stream of smoke close to my face. "They're waiting in Saudi, on the borders right now." I knew that, but until right then I hadn't connected the dots. It was already too late.

"My tour was over two years ago. They wouldn't deploy me unless we were long into the war."

"You don't have to go?"

"For so many, joining the reserves was their only choice."

"To go to school."

"Or, in my case, not go to jail."

"Jail?"

"An asshole I was dating." The fingers she used to hold her cigarette trembled. "Let's say I got caught up in his shit and the judge gave me the choice of jail or the reserves. . . . I almost chose prison." She smiled as her eyes welled up with tears. "Listen, I got it together and got my ass in school."

"You don't owe this government anything."

"In my work, every day I watch people die because they don't have the health insurance to get the treatment they need, or they waited too long to come in, or they were pushed aside in the ER because they weren't bleeding out. . . . Do you know how few medical personnel they will have over there?"

I had no idea.

"Do you know how many people will die?"

"Too many," I said.

"Too many," she repeated. "I don't support this war." She coughed. "I will do whatever I can to support the troops." She coughed harder.

"You want me to get you water?" I asked. "Mommy's inhaler?"

She shook her head and waved me off. After a few more coughs she flicked her cigarette into the street, got on her feet, brushed off the back of her coat, and said, "Let's go see some art."

I stood now and took hold of her black wool–clad forearm. "Did you have a chance to talk to Jimmy about me being his best man?"

"I haven't seen him yet," she said. "I arrived only a few minutes before you and your mother. Now we can tell Jimmy together."

I wanted another cigarette, but we didn't have a light, so I blurted out, "Do you really think he's ready to get married?"

She smiled. This looked genuine. "You remember your teenage brother, but he's grown up." I couldn't remember Jimmy ever being anything but grown up. He was younger, but always the mature, serious, responsible one.

"I don't think Jimmy would get married this way, you know?"

"You mean half-assed?"

She said it, not me. I nodded.

"It's not my dream wedding either, but you know your brother." Right then, I believed I did.

"Getting married now, well, it's his way of trying to control what is out of our hands."

"Influence fate," I said.

"That's Jimmy," she said. I didn't tell her it was Dad who had said this. It felt good to have someone believe I still knew what my brother would say, or want.

"I'm not superstitious," she said. "Well, maybe a little. You can't grow up Bronx-Catholic without some of that crap getting into your head." This time the worry broke through her smile. "Maybe letting Jimmy lead this one, right now, well, helps me keep the faith. It's going to be okay."

I pressed against my chest and felt Saint Anthony's outline. Jimmy's steadfast beliefs, even when they did seem wonky to most, did have the power to comfort. Still, facts were facts. Even if Jimmy was upstairs right now, a few days ago he had run away. He wasn't sure about this wedding. If I knew my brother the way Julie thought I did, the way I believed I did, he would still go through with it because it was the *right* thing, not because he wanted to. How could I let that happen?

"Julie," I started, but she was scissoring the pointer and middle fingers of her right hand, the ones that had held her cigarette minutes ago, and I couldn't bring myself to continue. She was on edge, and I felt sorry for her, and I felt sorry for Jimmy. I felt sorry for all three of us. I didn't have the heart to tell her this marriage would be a huge mistake and she had to call it off, but there was one thing I could do for my brother. "I can't be the best man."

"Are you kidding me?"

"I haven't been Jimmy's best anything in a long time."

"Since the day we met, everything has been 'Angela did this,' and 'you should have seen when Angela did that,' and 'no one does it better than my sister.'" She dragged in the air around her, and I could almost see a cigarette reappear between her fingers. "Okay, so the best man thing was my idea, but I would never have suggested it if I didn't think it's what he wanted."

I wished she was right, but she didn't know my brother.

"Even Billy thought it should be you," she said. "That's why he said no to Jimmy. It wasn't the Opening."

"We should go inside," I said.

"Lead the way," Julie said.

She followed me up the stairs, through a huge and empty lobby, to an eight-and-a-half-by-eleven-inch sign electrical-taped to a rusted metal freight elevator door: *Opening of Creepy-Crawlies and Other Such Things, Second Floor.* The same name on the invitation but instead of elegant calligraphy it was written in messy black marker.

Why didn't he use a crayon? Even the anti-war movement, as disenfranchised and underfunded as it was, made better flyers. At least we used computers. I shook my head, disappointed at how judgmental I sounded, even if it was in my head. I was more Mommy than I thought.

Julie pressed both the up and the down buttons of the freight elevator and I thought about what a difference a day really did make. Last night I was determined to find my brother and help him get away from this marriage and a family that was forcing him into it. Now, I was letting Julie lead me to Jimmy, so I could be there when she would tell him "Surprise, honey, guess who's your best man?"

The elevator door opened to a man sitting on a metal stool wearing a black turtleneck that emphasized his wide chin. "Second floor?" he asked.

"Please," Julie said.

We entered the elevator, almost the size of my studio back in LA. The man pushed a lever down and the doors closed, and I was cloaked in remorse. I wanted to help my brother. I wanted to help Julie understand. The wedding wasn't what Jimmy wanted. Once again, I'd chickened out. I ran away. Only this time I didn't need to take a plane three thousand miles. This time it was a freight elevator two floors up.

The wide-chinned elevator operator pulled the lever up and announced, "Welcome to Creepy-Crawlies and Other Such Things." The doors opened. Julie walked into the darkness.

I hesitated until I heard, at least I thought I heard, the operator say, "Time to step up."

CHAPTER 17

I exited the elevator, a big powder-blue polyester puff, and in a sea of slick black leather hip I lost Julie. I couldn't find her anywhere. But I had to find her before she got to Jimmy.

"What doesn't kill us makes us stronger," I murmured to myself, not believing a word, and then I stepped into the darkness.

There was a flash of white. I'd walked right into a very tall waiter's chest.

"Sorry," I said as I grabbed two glasses from the tray of champagne he managed to prevent from crashing to the floor.

"Two hands. Two glasses." I faked a laugh. He snickered and walked away.

Using the glow-in-the-dark paintings as a guide, I moved my way through the dark gallery, managing not to stumble in the heels Mommy had insisted I wear. I could hear but couldn't see the other people who were mingling; then I bumped into a woman wearing night vision goggles. I clearly was missing an important element of the experience. Finally, I saw the light, and it was coming from a room up ahead. Maybe Julie was in there.

I found myself in a replica of my family's kitchen, on steroids. The stove, the refrigerator, every appliance was the same as the ones in my family's apartment; only they were a foot and a half taller than I was. The aroma of garlic and oil was in the air. Mike's gravy. At first, I thought artificial scents were being pumped into the room, but when I looked up and saw what had to be at least a thirty-quart pot on the front burner of the stove, I knew the heavenly scent was for real. I was starting to salivate. I hadn't eaten since breakfast, and all I'd had then was a buttered roll and coffee.

In front of the stove was a many-stepped stepladder. CLIMB AT YOUR OWN RISK was painted on the bottom step. I'll play Alice in Wonderland, I said to myself. I rested the empty champagne glasses on the same black and white floor tiles as in my family's apartment and started my ascent. When I reached the top step, I was waist level with the top of the stove, with the kitchen counter adjacent, which was covered with large, long loaves of Dominick's bread. It was obvious what the artist wanted me to do: I ripped off the end of one of the loaves. Then, using the bath towel–size potholder hanging on a hook above the stove, I lifted the pot's lid and dipped the bread into the gravy, then brought it to my open mouth. I was about to bite when I realized that something was twitching – a leg – a roach – and now I saw that the whole top layer of the gravy was covered in roaches. I threw the bread into the pot and closed the lid. There was a flash. By the time I reached the floor, there had been three more consecutive flashes. For several seconds, all I could see were white spots.

When my vision finally cleared, standing in front of me was a tall, slender man wearing a banana-yellow suit with a purple polka-dotted bow tie, with very even, clearly salon-tanned skin. He was a stereotype of something, but what that something was I wasn't exactly sure.

He thrust his hand at me, but when I took it, he kept it still and waited for me to initiate the shake. "The Decisive Moment."

"Cartier-Bresson," I said.

The muscles in his face went up and then down, making it seem as if he was smiling and frowning. "You know Cartier-Bresson?"

"The photographer. I heard of him." This afternoon, I didn't say.

"Most people think I'm talking about a watch." He let out what was most definitely a giggle. He pointed to the corners of the ceiling, showing me where the cameras were stationed. "We are capturing those spontaneous moments that make history."

"My discovering the roaches in the gravy was a decisive moment?"

"Precisely, but I must say you have been the only participant not to panic. Two fell off the ladder."

"Were they hurt?"

"Please step back." I wasn't sure why, but I did, and he rattled the ladder slightly. A trampoline popped out of the broiler. "It's designed to detect any irregular movement."

"Sorry my moment in history wasn't a very interesting photo op," I said.

"It's not about interesting; it's about what is in the moment it happens, whatever that is."

I wasn't sure I had any idea what he was talking about, but I didn't have the time to find out. "Nice meeting you," I said. The trampoline was blocking me from getting out of there. "Could you please?"

"Of course." He pressed the oven handle and the trampoline slid back into the broiler.

"Can I tell you a secret?" He didn't wait for my response. "There's been several inquiries on this piece, so if you're interested, you should move on it."

"There are people who want to buy a pot of boiling cockroaches?" I didn't mean to dis Billy's art, but this I found unbelievable even for the pretentious rich.

"The whole installation."

"The Jolly Green Giant kitchen?"

"The tile work alone is extraordinary."

"They're the same black and white kitchen floor tiles my mom bought off the back of some guy's truck."

"Bend," he said, pulling me with him to the floor. Close up, what I had thought were square black tiles were actually collages of miniature paintings, all of roaches.

"There must be thousands."

"Forty-five hundred, to be exact," he said.

"One for every species of cockroach," I said. "Each with its unique personality."

"You know your bugs."

"Exterminator's daughter," I said.

"Angela?" he said.

"That's me," I said, wondering if I had ever exterminated this guy's place.

He took my hand and helped us both to our feet. "You are as gorgeous as Billy described." It was hard for me to believe Billy had called me gorgeous. *Pretty, cute* maybe, but *gorgeous* wasn't a word

Billy would have used. I had a strong feeling this guy was trying to sell me something.

"You're a friend of Billy's?"

"Better than a friend. I'm Eric, his manager." Now this made total sense. If managers of visual artists were akin to managers who represented actors, they were always selling something you couldn't live without. Activists often sounded this way too, only what they were selling was often matters of life and death.

"It's so gratifying" – Eric took a deep breath – "when one of my clients has success after years of dedicating themselves to their work. But then, I don't need to tell you about Billy's work."

Yes, yes, you do, I thought. "It must have taken him years to do this one floor," I said, hoping to glean something about this version of Billy I had never known.

"This piece, as I'm sure you know, he started in high school," Eric said.

"Of course," I said, acting as if I had always known this but wondering where I had been when this was happening. Billy had never shown any interest in art, and I couldn't even remember him doodling in his notebook in class the way Jimmy and I had.

"I'm so glad to finally meet the woman who inspired Billy's masterpiece—"

"That's my mother—"

"Not *Ode to Rose,* although it *is* a masterpiece. I'm talking about the piece that you and Wheelchair Guy inspired."

"Jimmy," I said. "His name is *Jimmy.*"

"He insists I call him Wheelchair Guy. I assume it's his way of reappropriating . . ." He leaned in closer. "The resemblance between you and Wheel – Jimmy . . . remarkable."

"People usually tell us we don't look related."

"On the surface. I'm talking about an ethereal beauty."

It was nice to think Jimmy and I still shared something, even if that something was *ethereal.*

"But if we are talking about the surface, this . . ." He circled his finger at me. "Love what you have going on here." He pulled on his polka-dotted bow tie. "A lot more interesting than the basic black tux your brother is wearing." It was confirmed. Jimmy was in the house. "Where did you last see him?"

"I think it was *The Termite* . . . or maybe *The Roulette.* . . . Sweetie, it was at the beginning of the night, so much going on. I can't remember. You'll find him."

There was a scream followed by a flash. Eric pulled me out of the way as the trampoline popped out, and a man, dressed in black, of course, bounced onto it, exclaiming, "I must have this!"

"Another decisive moment," Eric said.

CHAPTER 18

Before I took another step, I heard, "His choice of silver and gold in this piece is quite extraordinary." Two women, maybe Mommy's age, with wide smiles and white fur coats fluorescent under the black light, stood in front of a six-by-eight-foot image of a glow-in-the-dark termite. Unlike Mommy's painting, this wasn't made using a sophisticated technique a child's untrained eye might mistake for a kit with an easy-to-follow chart creation. This was a genuine paint-by-numbers work of art. Several of the sections were left without color, exposing the numbers, and to the side of the painting, behind a piece of Plexiglas, was the key that showed what numbers matched what colors.

"Yes, one might have gone with only the red and blue to signify the indigestible American dream," said the woman to my right.

"But silver and gold represent what? Our monetary system," said the woman to my left.

The pretense level was off the Richter scale, and if art was anything like theater, the smarter the piece made the audience feel, the more money it would be worth.

"Actually, I think both your observations are on the money," Julie said, emerging from the shadows. "Don't you agree?" Julie raised her eyebrows in my direction. "Or does LA have a different sensibility?"

"Actually," I said, "I think the painting is making a statement about how our society is both literally and figuratively being eaten out of our homes, as you both keenly observed." I was surprised by how well I could sling shit with the smell of pretense. "However, one must ask oneself if the artist's choice to use a black light for the glow-in-the-dark effect is a broader statement on the state of human nature." The two women nodded. I was on a roll. "After all, the luminescence of the piece, which also causes your furs to glow, is a result of layers upon layers of radiation. I would think the piece is a reminder of how we are eradicating our very existence, the way someone eradicated the animals to make your furs. The artist is clearly saying, 'Shame, shame on you.'"

The whites of their teeth where no longer showing.

I'd gone too far.

"I wonder if the artist used whatever glow-in-the-dark paints he found on sale," Julie added, and both women nodded. "Brilliant,"

Julie rested her chin in her hand, hummed and sighed, and then said, "Yes, I am going to buy this piece."

"Not if I buy it first." I let out a fake laugh.

The women whispered into each other's ears – probably something about how they had to buy the piece before we could. Without bidding us farewell, they took off and disappeared into the darkness.

"You saved that," I said.

Julie grabbed two glasses of champagne from a passing waiter's tray. She handed me a glass and we clinked.

"To Billy," Julie said.

"To Billy," I repeated.

We both chugged.

"The look on their faces when you not so subtly called them murderers was priceless."

"I didn't really call them murderers."

"You implied it."

"I didn't throw red paint on their furs."

"That would have been performance art." We both laughed, and then Julie went silent. The only sound between us was the faint thumping of – techno? I wondered if this piece was homage to the underground club scene, when Julie banged the rim of her empty glass against her fluorescent teeth and said, "Do you really think Jimmy doesn't want to marry me?"

It was as if she'd turned on the kitchen light and I wanted to go full-out water bug on her. Scamper and hide. I wasn't a creepy-crawly. I was an activist. This was my chance to stand up and do right by Jimmy.

I opened my mouth wide, but before I formed the words *I know Jimmy doesn't want to get married,* Julie's *tap, tap, tap* of her glass against the whites of her teeth to the aggressive distorted beat of terrible techno crap stopped me. She was vulnerable and scared. If she needed to ask me what Jimmy wanted, it was clear she already knew. For me to declare war would be redundant. "It doesn't matter what I think," I said.

"You think he doesn't want to marry me?" She wasn't letting this go. "That the only reason he's marrying me is because I might . . ." She paused and this time tapped her glass against her chin. "Get my head blown off."

"I didn't say that."

"Not with words."

"You said yourself this wasn't your dream. So why go through with it? Why not wait?"

"That's what people do for love," she said.

"They abandon them?" slipped out, and before Julie could respond, I beat her to the punch in the gut: "That's something I know. Unfortunately, all too well."

"How is anyone supposed to see a damn thing?"

"Ma?" I said.

"I've been looking for you everywhere." She showed the whites of her teeth, but no smile.

"I was talking with Julie," I said.

Mommy glanced over my shoulder. I knew from her expression Julie was gone.

"She must have moved on," I said. "Lots to see."

From everything Mommy didn't say, it was clear she didn't believe me, but she didn't push, not about Julie anyway. "Did you see Jimmy?" she asked.

"I haven't."

"Thank God." She crossed herself.

"What's going on?"

"For once in your life, please, follow my lead, and don't fucking question me."

CHAPTER 19

Mommy dragged me to a room where there was a fifteen-foot-tall sculpture of a rat wearing high heels and a feather-cut hairstyle. Julie had called it Billy's *David*. Inspired by Michelangelo's masterpiece, Billy had sculpted it from a single piece of marble; I was awestruck by how well he captured my mother's essence as the alpha, the leader of the pack.

At her base were four smaller marble rat statues, all identical. It was clear these were the beta rats, the ones that followed the alpha wherever she went. If the alpha was Mommy, the four rats at her feet were the four of us, but which four? It was pretty much a given that two of the four were Mike and Dad, but who were the remaining two? Jimmy and Billy, Jimmy and me, or Billy and me? Or was it Jimmy and Julie?

"Here's my star." Stepping out from behind the mother rat was the fattest rat of all the rats, Fat Freddy, the fuck. He was sandwiched in between Lip and Shorts, the two beta rats I met at Carmela's that morning. Between them they wore enough hair product to lacquer Alpha Rat's ass, which had to be at least four feet wide. Instead of their Members Only jackets, they sported cheap leather motorcycle ones the type the guys from the neighborhood would wear to look tough, though none of them had the guts to ride anything with two wheels, motorized or not.

"Twice in one day." Fat Freddy walked up to me, the two beta rats right behind him. "It's my lucky day."

Mommy pushed herself in between us, and he looked as if he wanted to bite her head off, literally. "What does he mean 'twice'?"

"He was at Carmela's this morning." I took a breath. "Looking for Jimmy."

Mommy's top hat tipped in Freddy's direction. She was ready to go for his jugular. "I told you to keep Jimmy out of this."

"And I told you, no can do!"

"Angela." She gripped my forearm. "Did you tell Freddy about your movie?"

My movie? Mommy concocting the bullshit story would have made sense if Fat Freddy were someone she had wanted to impress, but I knew she couldn't care less what he thought. He was feared by some, respected by none. Mommy dug her nails into my arm. I had no clue what my mother was up to, but I figured the safest bet was to play along with her.

"We were sadly interrupted." He smiled with his mouth open, again exposing the gaps where teeth should have been. "I'd love to hear more about it."

"Us too," Shorts and Lip said in unison with the same enthusiasm as mice running toward a piece of cheese.

I didn't know anything more about *Goodfellas* than I had that morning: a Mafia movie with De Niro and Ray something or other. I walked over to the sculpture of Alpha, her mouth opened, fangs exposed.

Freddy stayed close to me. He wasn't taking any chances that I might disappear into thin air. If only I could, I thought. "Billy's really got a lot of talent," I said.

"You really a big deal in this movie?" Freddy said. "Or you only got a few lines before you get whacked?" He laughed, and Shorts and Lip howled along with him.

"Do you know that a rat can jump six feet into the air and bite you right in the neck?" I asked.

"Thanks for that image," he said.

"Did you also know that a rat, even a rat as fat as a cat, can squeeze through a pipe with an opening as small as this?" I peered through the quarter-size circle I made with my thumb and pointer at Freddy's small nose, so much smaller than every other feature on his face. Big eyes, wide mouth. "They will swim up through your toilet and bite your ass."

"What is this crap?" Freddy said to Mommy. "She going to tell me about the movie or blabber about rats?" It was clear he was feeling uneasy, and it felt good to have the tables turned, even if only a few inches.

"Angela, don't you want to tell Freddy about playing Ray Liotta's grown daughter who's a hippie and wants to save the world?"

Liotta, I thought. That's his name.

"No shit?" Freddy said.

I strolled around the beta sculptures with Mommy on my arm, and Freddy on my ass.

Petting the head of the middle rat and smiling at Freddy, I said, "My character is not so much a hippie." I glared at Mommy. "She's an anti-war activist."

"Don't tell me," Freddy interrupted. "Let me guess. She goes back to New York and finds everyone who would have any reason to take her father out and she kills them. The hippie chick goes ballistic. Do I know movies or what?" He raised the palm of his hand and Lip and Shorts each took a turn high-fiving him. "Tell me, am I right?"

It was as good a plot as any, but I wasn't going to give him anything I didn't have to. "Actually, she returns to New York and reunites with the family she never knew."

"She doesn't take out anyone?" Lip sounded disappointed.

"One guy." I stared directly into Fat Freddy's beady eyes, which were in fact wide and startling blue. "It's not for her father. It's revenge for what he did to her." Fat Freddy lowered his gaze.

"The torture scene is badass," I continued. "She gives him this paralyzing drug, where he can't move but he can feel, and she slices his penis with a butter knife." Freddy cringed.

"That's messed up," Shorts said.

"He must have done some really bad shit to go out that way," Lip said. "What's his backstory?"

"Shut the fuck up," Freddy shouted. I could see fear in Lip's eyes, and a chill ran down my spine. I was sure it was the same look I had all those years ago, but was it there this morning? Was it there now? The unpredictability in Freddy's behavior was his lethal weapon.

"I need to asks you something," Freddy said. "In private."

"Sure," I said, certain that I sounded calmer than I felt.

Mommy wasn't letting go of my arm. If I was going to find out why he was here and what he wanted with Jimmy, I had to talk to him alone, at least semi-alone.

"Hey, I'm going to walk over there with him." Her grip tightened, and her eyes stayed on Freddy. "You can see me the whole time." I couldn't remember my mother ever not being in control. Was Mommy afraid of Freddy too? The possibility scared me more than anything I could imagine him doing to me.

"In private," Freddy repeated.

"Ma," I put my hand over hers. "It's okay. Let go." She did, but her eyes never moved away from Freddy.

Freddy and I walked over to the far corner of the room. Far enough so Mommy and the betas couldn't hear us, but they could see us. I felt sweat rolling down my back. *You can handle this,* I told myself.

"What's up?" I said.

"So your mother says this role pays some good money."

I wanted to tell him it was none of his business, but then I thought, why get defensive about a part that I didn't have in a movie that wasn't real? "It's an equity role."

"What the hell is that?"

"Union job," I said.

"That's good. Very good." The closer he moved to me, the harder I had to fight my panic.

"The amount Jimmy owes is thirty thousand—"

"Jimmy owes you thirty thousand?" I almost choked on my saliva.

"My associate. Then there's the fifty percent interest."

"That's forty-five thousand dollars." Jimmy owed Fat Freddy Fungol forty-five thousand dollars? That Jimmy owed him anything was hard to believe.

I glanced over at my mother and she was biting her cuticles. That was something she had reprimanded me for my whole childhood – a disgusting habit she said – so either she had changed her views on the benefits of bacteria, or she was more nervous than I had ever seen her.

"It's clear your bro isn't able to come through with what he promised." He moved closer and whispered in my ear: "Time's about up."

"How much time are we talking about?"

"I know with the whole West Coast, East Coast time difference you'll need some time to get the money wired, so you can give me the money at the bachelor party tomorrow night."

"Bachelor party?"

"I hear you're the best man. Congratulations." He slapped me on the back. Mommy lunged forward. I raised my hand to signal her to stay back. "You and Jimmy were always tight. It's good he has you to help him with this situation."

I opened my mouth to tell him that I needed more time – I even was ready to go into all the details about how actors don't get paid upfront and most of the money I was getting was on the back end, and actors rarely get that good a deal but I helped write the script. . . . But if I was sure about anything since I got home, I was sure that this fat fuck had no interest in anything I had to say, and the only thing he would be willing to negotiate was which of Jimmy's arms he would break first.

"Tomorrow night," I said.

He looked into my eyes and for a moment I was afraid he was going to suck in my soul. "Great seeing you again." He cocked his head to the right, and he and the two betas were out of there.

Mommy scrunched her face and shook her head, and standing on her tippy toes she squinted up into the mouth of her doppelgänger. "Is this rat supposed to be me?"

There were so many questions flooding my brain, I didn't know where to begin. I started with the first question that came to mind:

"What the fuck?"

Mommy continued to stare into the big rat's mouth and remained silent. A moment of historical record, I thought.

"Rat got your tongue?"

"What do you want me to say?" Her tone made it clear that she was involved in this mess and felt guilty, though I was sure there would be no atoning for her sins.

"What the hell, Ma?"

She turned from the rat to me. "It's complicated."

"Forty-five thousand dollars?"

"Thirty thousand," she said. "Thirty was the deal."

"Is that why he took off? He doesn't have it?"

"Your brother doesn't run away from his problems." Mommy either didn't hear the irony, or this was a reminder of how I had committed sins of my own.

"How does Jimmy owe Fat Freddy forty-five thousand dollars?"

"It's thirty, thirty, and he owes Fat Freddy's boss."

"Fat Freddy is the one collecting, and if he doesn't get his money, Jimmy's in trouble."

"You bought us some time. I could hear you. Slicing a penis with a butter knife? You're definitely no hippie." Mommy smiled.

"Twenty-four hours, Ma, we have until tomorrow night."

"I heard him."

"There's a bachelor party?" I had never expected a bachelor party to be on the list of things for me to worry about.

"Everything's done."

"You planned Jimmy's bachelor party?"

"Someone had to do it."

"You're his mother." My voice so high I thought it might crack the marble.

"Yes, and you're his sister, and this whole wedding was dumped on this family two weeks ago, so there's nothing orthodox about any of this."

"Was it gambling?" I said. "There are programs."

"Your brother isn't a fucking addict." Mommy pivoted toward me on her four-inch heels.

"Forty-five thousand dollars," I said.

"Thirty thousand."

"Does Julie know?"

"I swear to fucking God, if you say anything to Julie, to Jimmy, or to anyone . . ." Mommy's face went from the color of her pale foundation to devil red. And there was the asthmatic wheeze. "You smell like cigarettes!"

"Do you need your inhaler?"

She pivoted away from me.

"Where are you going?"

"To congratulate the artist." She click-clacked away. I tried to follow her, but my feet were killing me. I would have taken off my shoes, but I didn't want to find myself walking barefoot over one of Billy's masterpieces, like *Ode to a Thousand Live Water Bugs.*

CHAPTER 20

I asked the first waiter I saw if he'd seen a woman in a top hat and tails. He said he hadn't, but much of the place was dark, so he could have missed her. However, he had spotted the artist walking into the gallery owner's office.

If I found Billy, I would find Mommy, and maybe Julie, and – God help him, Jimmy.

I knocked at a red door, but there was no answer. I turned the knob. The door opened but it wasn't an office. It was a large room with three bare walls, and on the fourth wall hung a painting of what looked to be the front of our building, stoop and all.

"Get closer."

I jumped.

It was Billy. "Didn't mean to startle you." In his white shirt and black jacket he blended in with the wait staff. One would never think he was the guest of honor. Still, he looked pretty wonderful.

"Hey," I said, wanting nothing more than to beg him to help me find Mommy, or Jimmy, even Julie. I knew Mommy would kill him for saying anything about the money, but Billy probably knew, and if he didn't maybe he could help. Maybe the show would do well enough tonight and he could lend Jimmy the money.

Billy smiled. The last time I remembered him looking this clean and confident was when he made his First Holy Communion.

Mike was right – this was Billy's night.

"Sorry I crashed your party," I said. I wasn't very good at hiding the hurt.

"I hear you didn't crash alone," he said.

I nodded. He knew she was there.

"I'm assuming she saw the work she inspired."

"She did. Spent a good deal of time—"

"Admiring it." He smiled.

"Tell you the truth, I think she loved it."

"It is a tribute to her."

"Then why didn't you want her to see it?"

"I did. I even had several cameras set up in strategic places to capture her reaction. . . ."

The decisive moment, I thought. *Why didn't you invite her?* And for that matter, *why didn't you invite me?* I wasn't ready to know.

"If I had formally invited her, she'd be so wrapped up in what she was going to wear and what was I going to wear and what food we were serving, and then the complaints about the city and why couldn't I do this at the Knights of Columbus . . . micromanaging."

"I get it."

"So I didn't invite her, knowing full well, one way or another, she'd find out and stomp her way down here."

"Mike and her got into it—"

"I heard. I didn't think Mike would insist she not come."

"Mike has your back."

"Our stomachs too." Billy smiled, and the sexy, bearded man who picked me up at the airport vanished. In his place stood the kid I grew up with, and too often fucked-up with. Billy, my brother from another mother and father, but who lived with me in that place from which we would forever be looking in from the outside.

"I'm sorry." The words felt hollow.

"I ran out on you today," he said.

"I ran first."

"You had no choice."

"Don't we always have a choice?"

"If I believed that," he waved his hand around the room, "none of this would have happened."

"You didn't choose art?"

"The self-blame game would have sucked up all of my energy."

"You had a disease."

"Have," he said.

"It wasn't your fault."

"Taking responsibility for my shit is different than blaming myself, or others, which is paralyzing."

"And self-absorbed," I said. Billy twitched his nose and his hazel eyes sparkled. He didn't need me to explain. He knew I was talking about myself.

"Speaking of self-absorbed, what do you think?" He opened his arms wide.

"Your work is extraordinary." It was the only thing I could think to say.

"Come on, if I wanted someone to blow smoke up my ass I would go talk to my manager."

"Nice guy," I said.

"You met him?"

"At *Mike's Gravy,*" I said.

Billy smiled.

"Does Mike know that you call it that?"

"He was flattered."

"Mike is cool," I said.

"He gets it," Billy said.

"Listen, I couldn't be happier for you."

"But you don't get it," he said.

I hesitated. What I said next was "It must have taken you years to do all of these pieces."

He nodded.

"You clearly have so much talent."

"So why would I make bug and vermin art?"

I shrugged.

"I started helping you and your dad when we were in high school, and there was always something about the exterminating that got under my skin."

"The killing of a living creature?"

He smiled. "Mike's right, your eyes are smart, but no, it wasn't the killing that got to me, it was the resilience. You know how hard the pests we exterminate fight to survive. Everybody talks about the cockroach and how it will survive a nuclear war, but a cockroach doesn't survive alone. They're part of a whole species that works together.

The alpha rat will sacrifice everything for her family, and her family, the beta rats, will do anything to find and bring back food to her—"

"All about sacrifice," I said.

"And love." He shrugged. "Maybe love isn't experienced the same way by these creatures, but it's still love."

"Your work is about family." I thought about Mommy and what a pain in the ass she could be, and how she judged us but would kill for us if she had to. I didn't know the details or the circumstances around Jimmy borrowing money from Fat Freddy's boss, who was probably even more dangerous than Fat Freddy. I was certain Mommy would do whatever she needed to do to protect her son. I needed to do what I could to protect them both.

"There you are." I turned around and saw the manager in the banana-yellow suit, and Billy – kissing. I stood and waited until Billy remembered my presence. When his and Eric's lips broke suction and my shock abated, I could see that they were in love, longing for each other. What they shared was real, something Billy and I never had.

"Eric, you met Angela."

"Yes, I had the pleasure earlier," he said. "My apologies," Eric said. "I know I gave you 'the manager shuffle.'"

He didn't need to explain. I knew, as Dad had long ago told me, the shuffle is when a client or a customer is the most important person in the world, until the next most important person comes onto the scene.

"You didn't!" Billy smiled.

"I get it. No worries."

Billy straightened Eric's tie and my left eye felt a tinge of jealousy, or was it envy? One meant you wanted what the person had but you were glad they had it. I wanted someone to fix my tie . . . and I was happy Billy and Eric had each other.

"She really is a beauty." Eric moved in for a kiss, and I gave him my cheek.

"That she is." Billy put his arm around my shoulders, and I felt the love of a brother. Now I laughed at how silly I was to think there was anything more than friendship between us, or anything more important than protecting that friendship.

"What's so funny?" Billy asked.

"Inside joke," I said.

"Speaking of inside," Eric said, "do you know who that is?" Eric was peering through the doorway. "He makes and breaks careers. We must catch him before he leaves." He took my hand into his. "You don't mind if I take Billy with me to kiss some huge ass?"

"Of course not," I said.

"It was great to meet you again." Eric shuffled out the door.

"Billy," I said.

He turned to me.

"I'm sorry about your mother. I wish I'd known."

"What could you have done?"

I didn't respond. I wanted to believe I could have done something, been there for Billy, my friend and brother, but I probably would have come up with an excuse as to why I couldn't go to New York. As much as I had complained about all the things my mother kept secret, because what could I do so far away, I was grateful for the protection. What could I have done?

"Coming?" Eric was in the doorway waving Billy to him.

"Give me a minute. I'll catch up."

"We can't keep the rich and entitled waiting too long." Eric split like the banana peel his attire mocked.

"Go," I said. "I'll see you at the bachelor party." I wanted to tell him about Fat Freddy and the money Jimmy owed, but this was his night. Besides, what could he do tonight?

"Not really my scene, but then again, your mom planned it, and you're the best man, so I don't know whose scene it would be. I'll try to get there."

"You and Eric?"

"It's new."

"Our kiss," I said.

"What kiss?" He grinned.

"The kiss when you dropped me off . . . You were messing with me?"

"Old times' sake," he said. "And maybe I was messing with you a little."

"You're happy?"

The hazel in his eyes smiled. "Come here," he said. "I want you to see this painting."

I joined him under a streetlight, an actual city streetlight. "Where did you get this?" I asked.

"I know someone who knows someone." He smiled.

Standing close to me, Billy's beard brushed against my cheek. "This is the perfect spot to get perspective."

All I saw was a gray blotch speckled with red.

"It's nice," I said.

"Look closer," he said.

"Billy, abstract art isn't really my thing."

"Look."

I looked. "It's the holy moth!" I said.

He moved behind me, put his hands on my shoulders, and guided me two steps backward.

Inside the holy moth was an enormous fig tree, and inside the tree, our childhood faces, Jimmy's, Billy's, and mine. Our faces reminded me of the painting of Mommy and her brother. Our expressions were stoic. No smiles.

"What do you call it?" I said.

"Miracles Happen, Some Days."

CHAPTER 21

I rushed to the freight elevator. I had to get out of there. I needed a cigarette. The door opened, the operator asked, "Getting in?"

"Yes," I said, and then I heard, "My best man is my choice!" *Jimmy!* I waved the operator away. The mature move would have been to walk up to my brother and hug him hello, but instead I hid in the shadow of an eight-foot sculpture made from Raid cans.

In clear view, under a bright spotlight, Julie, Mommy, Mike, Dad – who looked shockingly put together and awake – a vaguely familiar woman wearing a designer pantsuit that was not from off a truck, and Jimmy gathered around thirty-eight thumb-size beetles strapped to a roulette wheel.

Jimmy looked good. He had more gray than I would have expected. Then again, Mommy claimed she started showing gray at eighteen, though I had yet to ever see a gray strand or root. His baby face hadn't changed, small nose, big eyes, and a skewed smile that everyone loved and couldn't resist. As his agent used to say, "A face that could sell horseshit to Belmont."

The well-dressed stranger offered a wine glass to Dad, who shook his head, still playing the part of sober, then she offered the glass to Mommy, who I would have expected to say, "No thank you, darling," or "Lovely," or some other snooty phrase Mommy used when she was around anyone impeccably dressed, but instead she said, "Who the hell are you?"

"Margaret, a friend of James's, and a fan of Billy's." Brown terrycloth flashed before my eyes. It was Bedbug Woman. She did clean up well, I had to give her that. Her chic outfit now matched her starved older-model features.

"I thought it would make you happy." Julie knelt in front of Jimmy, showing no concern about the possible creepy-crawlies on the ground.

I hadn't noticed his wheelchair before then. I saw him first. He crinkled his nose the same way I remembered him doing when he was confused or pissed.

I missed him.

"Round and round it goes, where it stops, nobody knows," a recording played as the roulette wheel spun around. When it stopped at number 23, Margaret touched her glass against one of the beetles. "James, what is this?"

"It's a rare Australian beetle, only sighted in this city once in the last fifty years," Dad said, shaking his head. "But the eyes. All wrong."

"Magnificent."

"You like this?" Mommy asked, and it was clear to all of us what she was thinking: *This is crap. If you like crap, you are crap.* "I don't get it."

Margaret chugged her glass of champagne. "Art is subjective." Dad used to say the same thing when Jimmy got a bad review.

"It's a little fucking weird for my subjective taste," Margaret said.

I was expecting Mommy to attack but instead she snorted and howled. I couldn't remember her ever laughing that hard. I couldn't remember her laughing at all. She snickered but she never laughed. Dad joined in and then Mike and Julie; Jimmy was holding his side and saying, "It hurts, it hurts."

Like roach spray in the face, it hit me. All the years I had been away, I could only see the Jimmy from ten years ago, sad and hopeless. He'd moved on. He was able to express joy. He, my whole fucking family, was happy. *Happy without me.*

Mommy took two deep breaths from her inhaler and asked, "Where are we on this whole *best man* nonsense?"

The laughter stopped.

"I really thought this was what you wanted."

"My relationship with my sister is complicated."

He wasn't wrong. If our relationship were a surgery with complications, I would know the statistical probabilities of outcomes, the survival rate. All I knew was the ache in the pit of my stomach.

"You met her," Mommy said. "She's not exactly like the rest of the family." She offered Julie her hand and helped her to her feet. It appeared Julie was like the rest of the family, enough to be part of the inner circle.

"I knew the best man idea wouldn't fly," Dad said.

"How can I tell her?" Julie asked.

"I'll tell her for you," Mommy said.

"I don't want either of you telling her anything," Jimmy said. He didn't look happy now. I was pissed.

I emerged from the shadow but stood on the edge of their circle.

"You heard?" Julie covered her mouth.

"I heard," I said.

"I'm so sorry," Julie said.

"What are you apologizing for?" Mommy snapped. "Women are not *best mans*."

"Staying alive." Striking the iconic John Travolta pose, Margaret pointed her right index finger to the ceiling and her left one toward Dad's feet. It was a sweet gesture to try and break the tension, but a futile one.

"What the hell is she talking about?" Mommy asked.

"Angela's tux," Margaret said. "Straight out of *Saturday Night Fever*."

"Never heard of it." Mommy was fucking with her. She had taken me to see *Saturday Night Fever* nine and a half times in the movie theaters. The half was because after five minutes of brought-from-home potato chip bag ruffling, security escorted us out, and Mommy shouted, "I'm never coming to this theater again," and the audience applauded.

"Is that the same tux Billy wore for prom?" Jimmy asked.

"Carmela's," Mommy said.

I grabbed two champagne glasses from a passing waiter's tray and chugged one right after the other.

"Easy," Dad said to me.

"Are you kidding me?" If I gripped the empty champagne glass any tighter it would have shattered.

Before Dad and I had the chance to get into it, Jimmy said, "You're back. Long time."

"You're back too. Get in today?"

"Where were you?" Julie moved closer to Jimmy.

Jimmy took her hand in his. "I had some business to take care of."

"You promised me you were done with all that," she said.

"It's no big deal."

"It's a huge deal." She pulled her hand away.

"Business!" Dad was a puppy who'd heard the word *treat;* as always, he equated Jimmy's "business" with show business.

"Can we talk about this later?" Jimmy said, his eyes fixated on Julie.

"Commercial? TV? Movie?" Dad said.

"He wants to talk about this later," Mommy said. "Where is that artist anyway?"

"Rose, you need to go home. I'll take you," Mike said. "Let Billy have his night."

"I practically raised that boy," Mommy said.

"Rose, that boy is a man, and he doesn't want you here."

"Why is that?" To my shock, tears were streaming from her eyes. "All I do is sacrifice for this family." She glared at all of us – Mike, Dad, me, Jimmy, Julie, even Margaret.

"Billy expected Mike to tell you," I said. "He wanted you to come."

"He was counting on my not being able to keep a secret?" Mike said.

"You tell her everything," Dad said.

"I didn't tell her about this." He sounded as hurt as he did angry.

"Why didn't he invite me, then?" Mommy looked at me.

"He probably knew you'd make a huge fuss," Dad interjected.

"And control everything," Mike snapped.

"Now I really can't wait to congratulate the artist," Mommy said, with her jaw clenched so hard I was afraid we'd have to take her to the ER to get it released.

"We agreed you wouldn't do this again." Julie glared down at Jimmy. "And you went behind my back?"

"And you went behind mine, when you reenlisted, but we all do what we have to do."

"This is not the same thing," Julie said.

"What are we talking about?" Dad persisted.

"Shut up, James," Mom snapped.

"Don't tell him to shut up." Margaret stood up for Dad, and if I hadn't been so angry with him, I would have almost been happy.

"This is none of your business," Mommy said.

"James is my business."

"Really?"

"Really!"

"Jimmy owes forty-five thousand dollars to the Mafia," I blurted out.

"The Mafia?" Margaret said.

"Fat Freddy is looking for Jimmy," I said.

"This just got interesting," Margaret said.

The rest of the family froze – cornered cockroaches playing dead. Then Jimmy waved his hand at me. "Don't talk about me in the third person."

"I'm sorry," I said.

I expected Mommy to shout "You should be sorry for opening your big mouth" or "You should be sorry for sticking your nose where it doesn't belong," but she was silent. I couldn't even hear her wheeze. She had to be holding her breath.

"You told me it was thirty thousand," Julie said. I would have been surprised she knew about the money had it not been so clear she was now one of them.

"It is thirty thousand," Jimmy said.

"Interest," I said.

"What interest?" Jimmy pulled hard on Mommy's tux tail.

Mommy remained silent, and when she glared at me all I could see was the alpha rat sculpture that she inspired. She was going to attack.

I refused to let her distract me from what mattered. I lowered my gaze until it met Jimmy's. "Until something can be worked out, you can come and live with me in LA."

"LA!" Now Mommy shouted, and Julie joined in. "Did you say LA?!"

I ignored them and waited for Jimmy to respond. He was quiet and his expression was neutral. Maybe he liked the idea, I hoped.

"You really are trying to break us up?" Julie stepped out of the circle and got right into my face. I could see her tears. "Why do you hate me?"

"I don't hate you. I want what's best for my brother."

"What is best for Jimmy?" Julie's arms folded across her chest told me she didn't want to hear my answer.

I gave it to her anyway. "I want what Jimmy wants."

Jimmy rolled between Julie and me. "You think what I want is to move to LA to live with you?"

"My place is small, but we can make it work."

"The right place to ignite your career," Dad said.

Jimmy glared up at me. "What are you doing here?"

"She came for the wedding," Dad said.

"To destroy it?" Julie said.

"Jimmy, tell Julie, and Ma, please, the truth," I begged.

"I owe money to the Mafia? Or I don't want to get married?" Every syllable dripped with sarcasm.

"You *do* want to get married?"

"Angela, I proposed."

"She's going to war." It hurt to say those words, more than I could have imagined.

"I asked her to marry me on our second date. Do you know what she said?"

"Yes?"

"She thought I was crazy, and I was crazy over her—"

"Awww," Margaret said.

"Shush," Mommy said.

Margaret stuck the tip of her tongue out at Mommy, and Jimmy continued. "I asked her again on our third, and then on our fourth. On our twelfth date, she told me to not ask her again for a year. January second was a year. I asked and she said yes. Her going to Iraq pushed up the wedding."

"Your dream of the perfect wedding?"

"I got the perfect woman. That's my dream."

Julie bent down and kissed Jimmy on the lips. Now everyone, with the exception of me, went "Awww."

"What about the money you owe?" I grabbed the side of the wheelchair and swung Jimmy around to face me. "Please, let me help."

"I don't need your help." Jimmy took hold of his wheels and spun away from me. "Now please, get out of my way."

Mommy pulled me out of Jimmy's way. "Stay out of our business."

Instead of wheeling away, Jimmy wheeled closer to me. "Not a call, not a fucking postcard!"

"You refused to talk to me."

"That was right after you left. I was angry. You took off. What about the last nine years?"

"You didn't call me either."

"There she goes with those big *poor me* eyes. Pathetic. I feel sorry for you." Jimmy dropped the pity bomb on me, and I went ballistic.

"It's you I feel sorry for, all of you." I waved my finger at everyone in the circle.

Round and round it goes, where it stops, nobody knows.

"Julie, you think you're going to help the soldiers in this fucked-up war?"

Julie stepped behind Jimmy's wheelchair.

"Even if you manage to patch them together, do you know how many will be fucked up from the shit they'll see and do? Vietnam all over again."

Round and round it goes, where it stops, nobody knows.

I looked down to Jimmy. "Your stupid superstitions. You think getting married and some stupid plastic saint on your dresser is going to protect her from bombs and Scud missiles?"

"Archangel Michael," Jimmy and Julie said in unison.

"A piece of cheap plastic won't save her!" I shouted.

Round and round it goes, where it stops, nobody knows.

"Stop." Dad put his hand on my shoulder.

"Have a fucking drink!" I shrugged him off.

"Enough!" Mommy said.

"He gets hammered again and again, and you protect his loser ass."

"Don't call your father a loser." Margaret took a step toward me.

"A fucking placating drinking buddy is the last thing my father needs. If you gave a shit about him, you'd get lost." She stepped away.

I turned back to Mommy. "You've never hesitated to tell when I've messed up. Jimmy loses forty, thirty, whatever-the-fuck thousand dollars, and do you have anything to say?"

"Angela," Mike jumped in. "Don't talk to your mother—"

"Please, Mike, you let her walk all over you. Where's your self-respect?"

Mike looked more hurt than if I'd told him he was going bald. I wanted to shut up, to walk away, yet I couldn't move anything but my lips.

"I may be the biggest screwup here, but unlike every one of you, I'm not a fucking hypocrite. And yes, my shoes are ugly but they're comfortable!" I took off one of the heels and threw it into the darkness.

"What the fuck," someone shouted. "A flying stiletto?"

Someone responded. "The shoe represents our masochist culture, a swarm of bees, attacking women at the fundamental—"

"Stiletto, Palmetto. It's a fucking shoe!" I shouted.

Mommy took in a breath, let out a long wheeze, adjusted her top hat, walked away from us, and bumped into the woman who had lit my cigarette earlier.

"Don't you say *excuse me?*" Mommy pushed past her.

Mike, Dad, Julie, Jimmy, and even Margaret followed, and together, one happy family unit, they disappeared into the darkness.

"She bumped into me," the woman mumbled as she banged into the sculpture made of recycled Raid cans. The sculpture swayed, mimicking the sound of wind chimes, and then I saw it: a fly. It was a fly.

There was an old lady who swallowed a fly, I don't know why she swallowed a fly – perhaps she'll die!

CHAPTER 22

Grass didn't grow in the backyards of Pelham Bay.

Yards were concrete floors surrounded by dirt, two-to-three-feet wide. My second-grade teacher, who commuted from the city, told us fig trees couldn't grow in New York weather. She didn't know the men and woman in our neighborhood had magic fingers and could grow anything from the "old country," and there were rows of tomatoes and hanging vines with red and green grapes. And every yard had a fig tree.

It was the summer before third grade. On a day so hot we sweated in the shower. We were stand-swimming in the cool water gushing from the open fire hydrant. Most days the cops didn't care, but on some days, especially when it was so hot you could sweat in the shower, the cops came by and used their police wrenches to turn the water off.

Jimmy always defended them. "It's their job." I always blamed them. "They're jealous because they can't jump in front of the gushing water too." Billy, who never wanted to take sides, said we both were right.

With no A/C options but Mommy's room, which was locked when she went to work, we snuck into the landlord's basement. Before Dad rented the basement as an office, it was off-limits to us kids. The landlord thought we would sneak out with his homemade wine. We were only nine and ten back then. We didn't start drinking his wine until we were twelve and thirteen. We'd return the bottles to the shelves filled with grape juice and red vinegar; the landlord would simply think the wine went bad.

"The basement is cool," I said. Billy protested, worried we would get caught. Jimmy usually took Billy's side when it came to taking the righteous path. But he'd spent the last several weeks driving to the city with Dad in a car with no A/C – and a horn Dad leaned on whenever another driver did anything to offend him, which was all the time – auditioning for commercials: a rip-off of Matchbox cars, peanut butter and marshmallow spread that sounded yummy but tasted gross, frozen corn, laundry detergent, and a new cereal for kids, which had the taste of loose-leaf paper and no prizes. Jimmy came close, but no part. Jimmy wanted a break from all the acting stuff, the auditioning. Most of all he wanted to play in the block's All-Stars Stickball Tournament, umpired by the BCs from their chairs. They made calls by committee, which meant a lot of standing around and listening to them argue, except when it came to Jimmy the call was always unanimous. He was the best player on our block, in the whole neighborhood. The tournament was scheduled at the same time Jimmy had an audition. Even if we could get the BCs to change the day, Jimmy seemed to have auditions every day.

The basement would not only keep us cool, but it would hide Jimmy from Dad.

As we tiptoed by the landlord's first-floor apartment, Tony Bennett sang, "I left my . . ." We made it to the basement door and down the stairs before we heard where exactly he had left his heart.

The basement was cooler but still too hot to play the games we usually played. Our favorite was Dracula. The jars were not filled with the juices and pulp of tomatoes for gravy. That's what Dracula wanted people to believe. Each jar contained the blood and guts of a child who snuck down here and was captured. This game meant one of us, usually me, chasing the other two around the room and when finally catching them, wrapping my hands around their necks and biting, not too hard, but hard enough to look real.

We plopped ourselves down on the cool concrete floor, the panting dogs we would never have because the landlord didn't allow pets and Mommy was allergic to everything including goldfish in a bag.

We stared up at the single exposed fluorescent bulb until Billy said, "I'm bored."

"Me too," Jimmy said.

"We can help Jimmy with his speech lessons."

"No way," Jimmy said.

"No fun," Billy said.

I got up on my feet. "Class, rise." When neither of them moved,

I kicked them both in the thighs, until they got up too.

"The word we will learn to articulate and enunciate . . ." I repeated what thought I had heard Jimmy's speech teacher say the few times Dad made me tag along hoping I too would lose my Bronx accent. *We all need to speak good to support Jimmy,* Dad had said. Mom told him to go to hell, and after a dozen lessons, when the teacher said Dad was going to have to pay for me too, he let me stay home.

"FACK."

"Fack?" Billy and Jimmy repeated.

"The way you bad talkers would pronounce it would be FUCK."

The three of us laughed until Billy couldn't breathe and Jimmy's sides hurt.

"Now repeat after me," I said, trying to keep a straight face. "FACK."

"FACK."

"FACK."

"FACK YOU."

"FACK YOU."

"NO, FACK YOU."

"FACK YOU TOO."

And on the next FACK a big bug flew into my face, missing my open mouth by a pinky tip.

I waved it away.

"Don't kill it," Billy shouted.

"It's a stupid bug." I swatted the air.

"In Italy, they say there's a holy moth. That could be the one," Billy said.

"Who told you that?"

"I heard the BCs talking about it," Billy said.

"What does a holy moth do?" Jimmy asked, and he squinted his eyes the way he always did when he wanted to both know and not know something.

"If it's the holy moth and it dies in front of us, we will have bad luck forever," Billy screeched.

I punched him in the arm. "Why would you tell that to Jimmy, you know how he worries about bad luck," I said.

"It's the truth," Billy said.

"They were trying to scare you," I said.

"They didn't even know I was listening."

Jimmy jumped, trying to catch the moth in his hands. "We can't let it get burned by the bulb." Jimmy jumped and swooped his hands together, but no moth. "Ange, help me!"

"Let's get out of here," Billy said. "If we don't see it die, maybe we'll be okay."

"Ange," Jimmy said. "We can't leave it alone."

Jimmy looked so sad and worried, and I didn't know if I believed in any holy moth, but I did know Dad would be home soon, and if we went upstairs now Jimmy was going to another audition and he'd miss the game.

"Oh God, it's too close, too close to the bulb. It's gonna burn." Jimmy got on his knees and prayed, "Please, God, don't let the holy moth die."

Billy threw a jar of children's blood and guts, aka tomatoes, missed the holy moth, but hit the wall. The jar shattered.

"Why'd you do that?" I said.

"I was trying to scare it away."

"The wall is bleeding," Jimmy cried. "It's a sign."

"It's tomatoes," I said.

"Ange, you can get it," Billy said. He grabbed another jar of tomatoes and walked over to the big sink.

"The landlord is going to kill us," I said. After Dad kills us first, I thought.

"Better the landlord being mad for a few days than a dead holy moth giving us bad luck for life." Billy leaned into the jar, and his face grew redder the more he tried to twist. "I can't." He breathed out. "It won't open."

"Give me that," Jimmy said.

"Good luck," Billy said. Jimmy wasn't as strong as Billy and me. He never beat either of us, not once, in arm wrestling.

On the first try there was a *pop*. Jimmy dropped the contents of the jar into the sink, turned on the faucet, and rinsed the jar under the running water. He walked over to where I was standing by the shelves of homemade wine, and held out the dripping jar and said, "Catch it."

It was true, I was the best firefly catcher on the block but only because my best friend Cathy died. I shook my head and said, "No."

"Please, Ange. Please." Jimmy got down on his knees in front of me. "Please. Please."

"I can't hear you." I clamped my palms against my ears.

Cathy made me want nothing to do with anything holy.

"Please, Ange. You have to."

"I prayed every day for three months, all day," I said.

"I know," Jimmy rocked against my knees. "We can't let it die."

"God let Cathy die." I pushed Jimmy away. "I did everything right. When I took the Eucharist into my mouth it didn't even stick."

"Mine stuck to the roof of my mouth," Jimmy said.

"Mine too," Billy said.

"Mine didn't, but Cathy died anyway. I prayed to Saint Catherine to make Cathy's blood good again!"

"You prayed to the wrong saint!" Jimmy cried. "You have to pray to a saint for their job, not their name!"

"Ange," Billy said, "maybe the moth is a message, a sign, from Cathy."

"From heaven," Jimmy said.

"I don't believe it," I said, but I wanted to.

"My mother told me that sometimes after people die, they try to communicate by sending messages, signs."

"Did your dad ever send you a message?" Jimmy asked.

Billy wiped his eyes with the back of his hands before there were tears, his way of stopping them before they started. "Not yet," he said.

"Maybe the holy moth is your dad," Jimmy said. "Saying hello."

Billy looked up at the moth flickering around the lightbulb, considering this possibility. Then he said, "Not my dad. He hated insects. And he hated the heat."

"Cathy loved butterflies," I said.

"Moths are butterflies." Jimmy grabbed onto my calves. "Ange, please help, please," he cried. "I'll buy you Pop-Tarts."

I knew he could. Daddy had given Jimmy a hundred dollars in good faith that he would get a commercial soon, and he said he could spend it on whatever he wanted. I thought Jimmy was the luckiest kid on earth, but I wouldn't want to be driving into the city every day in a car with no A/C to talk to strangers who Jimmy said weren't nice, mostly.

I would have caught the moth and released it anyway, in case it was a message from Cathy telling me hello, but I loved Pop-Tarts. "Three boxes," I said, spreading my fingers apart.

"Deal." Jimmy released me. "Save it."

I dragged the landlord's ladder near the lightbulb and the holy moth.

"Climb slow, you'll scare it," Jimmy shouted.

I reached out my hand and caught it. The flapping tickled. Cathy had loved tickle-fights. I got spooked and released it.

"Ange!"

"It felt weird," I said.

"Try again," Billy said, holding the jar and cap near his chest.

I tried again, and this time when the moth tickled the palm of my hand, I felt happy. It was Cathy saying hi from heaven.

I stepped down the ladder, and Billy brought the jar close to me. I stuck my hand inside the jar and opened it as wide as I could, which was only halfway, but it was enough. I pulled my hand out and Billy popped the lid on and we all took turns tightening it.

"Who's down there?" It was the landlord. I hid the jar under my tank top, and the three of us ran up the stairs and out the building door.

"You kids! The landlord yelled after us. "What you do?"

"You're bleeding," Billy said.

I had scraped my knee, but I didn't remember when or how.

"We got to put holes in the jar," Billy said.

Jimmy and I nodded.

"We need a screwdriver or a nail," Billy said.

"There's both in the kitchen junk drawer," Jimmy said. "One of us has to run past the landlord and upstairs."

"Rock, Paper, Scissors," Billy said.

I knew if I won, they would call two out of three and three out of four, and we would be playing Rock, Paper, Scissors, until I gave up.

"Dad's going to be home soon. Billy, hide Jimmy."

They both nodded and with the holy moth flapping in the empty tomato jar under my tank top, I made a run for it – past the landlord, who was shouting about "the no good kids," up the stairs, into our apartment, and bang, right into Dad's chest.

"Where's the van?" I asked.

"What do you have under there?"

I took the jar out from under my shirt.

Dad took it from me and lifted it up to the light. "We better punch some holes in the top."

I followed Dad into the kitchen. He fumbled around the junk drawer.

"You making dinner?" Mommy pushed the kitchen door open.

"Where is the screwdriver?" Dad was now taking everything out of the drawer and putting it on the counter.

Mommy shoved Dad to the side. "It would have bit you." She handed the screwdriver to Dad.

Dad jammed it into the top. The lid dented, but no holes.

"A bug." Mommy jumped back.

Dad jammed the screwdriver into the top again.

"James, I don't want that bug in my kitchen."

"It's in a jar." Dad jammed the screwdriver again into the lid. "Is this made of lead?"

"I thought Jimmy had an audition," Mommy said.

"What time is it?" Dad turned to the clock on the stove. "Damn," he said. "Sorry, sweetie. This isn't going to do it." He handed the jar back to me. The moth was resting against the side.

"Dad, please," I said. I needed to buy Jimmy some time. "It's a holy moth. If it dies, we get bad luck. We have to save it."

"A holy what?" Mom looked closer at the jar.

"Angela, the screwdriver isn't doing it."

"Get that bug out of here." Mommy left the kitchen.

"We can find something else." I used my right arm to hug the jar to my chest and moved my free hand inside the open junk drawer. "Here's a nail."

"A thumbtack won't do it." Dad looked at his wristwatch. "Where is your brother?"

"Dad, please, you can't let it die." I raised the moth up to Dad's face.

Dad tapped the side of the jar. The moth flapped around. "Your brother has a good shot at this one. We have to leave now." Dad walked out of the kitchen. I rushed after him.

"Wait, Dad, don't go," I said.

"Come for a ride." Dad left the apartment.

"Mommy." I ran to her bedroom. She clicked off the TV. "What did I tell you about knocking?"

"I need your help," I said.

She pointed to the door. "Knock."

"Jimmy needs your help!"

Mommy got out of bed. "What happened? Where is he?"

"I don't know."

"What do you mean you don't know?"

"Billy's hiding him."

"Theresa Angela, what is going on?"

"The big stickball game is in less than an hour and Dad wants to take Jimmy to another audition."

Mommy looked down at me. She was doing this strange thing with her mouth. Her lips wiggled and opened a crack but then she shut them and her lips wiggled again. She walked past me. *Yay, Mommy,* I thought. *She's going to tell Dad Jimmy's staying home to play stickball.*

She stopped at the kitchen.

"Mom, Dad's not in the kitchen. He's downstairs." I took hold of her hand. "Come on, we have to get to him before he finds Jimmy."

"I have to cook dinner," she said. I thought she didn't hear what I said.

"You have to tell Dad to let Jimmy play." I tugged on her hand, again.

Mommy kissed the top of my head. "There's no talking to your father."

"You talk to him all the time. You always tell him what to do."

"Angela," she sounded sad. "This acting thing. There's no talking your father out of it." She took back her hand and circled her arms around the room. "Big star. Who knows, maybe he's right." She glanced down at the moth in the jar. "Get the bug out of the house."

Mommy didn't go into the kitchen. She went back to her room and closed the door behind her. This time I knocked but there was no answer. I turned the knob. The door was locked. Mommy never locked her door. I knocked again and again until I was pounding and pleading, "Please, Mommy, please open up. Dad listens to you. He always does."

"The tournament begins!" Mrs. Bellini was using the bullhorn Mr. Bellini gave her for Christmas.

I ran down the stairs. There was no sign of Dad, or Billy or Jimmy.

The block All-Stars were eating the ziti the BCs made for them. Something about pasta is good for endurance. "Did anyone see my father?"

That's when I heard him shouting, "Get down from that tree now."

I looked over the fence of the landlord's yard and there was Dad shouting up at the landlord's fig tree. The BCs said it was the tallest and widest fig tree in Pelham Bay, maybe in the world. Fig trees only grow twenty feet high, max. This tree was almost twenty-five feet. The gate was open, but on instinct I hopped the fence.

"This is the one, Jimmy, I know it!" Dad called up to him.

Jimmy and Billy didn't make a peep. They were so frozen Dad wouldn't have known they were there if it hadn't been for the figs falling to the ground and their Converse sneakers, which Mommy got from some guy Mrs. Bellini knew, dangling off the upper branches.

"Can Jimmy miss this audition, please, Dad, for the All-Star Stickball Tournament?"

Dad glanced down at me. I had never seen this look before. I couldn't tell if he was angry, or disappointed, or crazy. He grabbed the glass jar out of my hands and raised it in the air. "If you don't come down from there now, the holy moth gets it."

"Dad, no!" I jumped and tried to get the jar. He was holding it over his head and it was too high for me to reach.

"Please, Dad," I said. "He's the best player."

He turned to me again. "Do you care anything about your brother? Or this family?"

I didn't understand why he was asking me such a strange question, so I stood there and didn't say a word.

"Answer me!" he shouted. Dad never shouted.

"I care." I ignored the tears rushing down my face.

"Then stop getting in your brother's way from living his dream." I hadn't realized that helping Jimmy to play stickball was crushing his dreams.

"Okay, Jimmy," Dad shouted. "On the count of three, the moth gets it. One . . ."

"Don't!" Jimmy climbed part way down the tree and jumped the rest of the twelve and a half feet to the ground.

Billy came down after him. He only jumped the last three feet to the ground. I could see Billy was ignoring his own tears too.

Jimmy's face was dry.

Dad handed the jar back to me. "You want to come for a ride?" I shook my head no.

"Billy?"

"No thank you," Billy said.

Dad squatted in front of Jimmy. "If you don't get this one, we toss in the towel. Okay?"

"Whatever," Jimmy said.

Billy and I watched as Dad and Jimmy left the yard.

"Is he okay?" Billy asked.

"This could be Jimmy's big break," I said.

"The moth," he tapped the side of the jar. The moth didn't move.

"He's dead." Billy whispered. He was trying so hard not to cry again. I banged my hand against the side, and still no movement.

"The holes. There are no holes in the lid."

"We tried," I said. "The screwdriver didn't work."

Billy dropped his head and screamed, "FACK!"

"What you kids doing now!" The landlord walked out of the cellar door. "My tomatoes. All on the floor."

"Sorry." We ran out the gate and smack into the middle of the stickball game.

"STOP THE GAME!" Mrs. Bellini shouted into her bullhorn. "You want a ball to take your eye out?"

Billy and I shook our heads and walked off, and we kept walking until we could no longer hear Mrs. Bellini calling the plays on her bullhorn.

We sat on the curb of a block identical to ours; buildings with the same brick exteriors, two legal apartments, and one illegal basement apartment. Only there were no other people outside but us.

I held the dead holy moth in the jar tight against my chest, and we sat there without talking, because what was there to say?

The sun had now set, and streetlights turned on.

"We should go back," Billy said.

"Okay," I said.

"What are you going to do with it?" He lifted his chin to the jar.

"Dump it out," I said. "Mommy freaks about bugs, even dead ones."

The cap twisted off easily this time. I turned over the jar and banged the sides to get the moth to fall out, but it didn't fall, it flew. The holy moth flew out of the jar. "It's alive!" I shouted.

It was free.

"Look! Look!" Billy pointed to the streetlamp. Swarming around its light were maybe a hundred, maybe two hundred moths, holy moths, flapping their wings.

Billy and I had witnessed a miracle.

When I got home, Mommy took the jar to wash all the dirty bug stuff out of it. I would have told her what happened, but I knew she wouldn't care about a bug, even if it was a bug miracle.

She called me over to the sink. She filled the jar with water, and it seeped out of the bottom. "This jar is broken," she said. "It's no good."

The next day when Billy was sharing the miracle story with Jimmy, I almost told them both there was no miracle. The crack in the jar had let enough oxygen in for the moth to breathe. Then I figured it was good for them to believe in miracles, even if I no longer did.

Two days later Jimmy's agent called. He got the part.

CHAPTER 23

I got out of the Hobart Cab. For old times' sake the driver didn't charge me, which was good because I didn't have any money.

"Angela," Mrs. Bellini shouted down to me. It was almost midnight, but on this block, it was *silence* that people feared. It was a quiet night when Son of Sam murdered the young couple around the corner. It was a quiet night when the thirteen-year-old girl behind the wheel of her eighteen-year-old boyfriend's Mustang accidentally hit the gas pedal instead of the brake and ran over the landlord's four-year-old son. The only reason he lived was because he was small and the car dragged him underneath instead of cutting him in half. It was a quiet night when one of the guys hanging around the candy store was shot dead in a drive-by in front of my house; no one asked who or why; no noise was heard from the El train that was less than a block away, nor from a mother or father yelling for their kids to get inside. It was summer, late, and not a barking dog or a cat in heat was heard on the night Jimmy cracked his spine. Silence was not welcome here.

"Something wrong, Mrs. Bellini?" I called up to her.

"I saw you on television," she said. "The news."

I had forgotten about sticking my head in front of the camera today at the demonstration. I was exhausted now and the last thing I wanted to hear was Mrs. Bellini ranting about my anti-American crazy talking. Yes, we were outsiders because we were born American, but anyone born here or on the other side who criticized the government was branded a traitor.

I closed my eyes and waited. "You talk good," she said. My eyes popped open. "War only good for the rich. Make a lotta money and our children die."

"You're right, Mrs. Bellini," I said, stunned that she was against this war.

"You're a good girl. You keep speaking your mind."

"I will, Mrs. Bellini. Thank you." For the first time in days, I felt hopeful.

I waved good night, crossed the street. When I reached the top of my stoop, she called to me again. "Angela!"

"Yes, Mrs. Bellini?"

"Where your shoe go?"

"I lost it."

The door to the apartment was locked. It was never locked. I knocked, and when no one answered, I pounded until both fists were red and swollen.

"What's the matter up there?" It was the landlord.

I got to my feet.

"My apologies," I shouted down to him.

"Miss Angela, that you?"

Before I could respond he was in front of me. "Welcome home." He leaned in and hugged me and when he let go, his hand was red.

"I'm bleeding?"

He sniffed his fingers. "Gravy. Tomatoes. Olive oil."

Billy's art must have splattered on me.

"You come home for Mr. Jimmy's wedding. You a good sister." It was hard to hear sarcasm through his accent, but I couldn't imagine he meant it, though, but maybe. I forced a smile. "No one home?"

I shook my head.

"Your family, it never change," he smiled. "Never have keys." He took off downstairs. I could hear him talking in Italian to his wife. I didn't understand the words, but their tone and the laughter told me it was at my expense. I was glad they found my predicament amusing and not pathetic and sad, which was how I felt.

He handed me the spare key. I opened the door.

"Grazie," I said, handing the key back to him. He patted me on the back and said, "You keep it. I have another copy."

He turned and left. I flipped the hallway light switch on and walked to Jimmy's room. I couldn't remember a time when I was alone in this apartment. I was relieved. I hadn't the energy to face my mother or the heart to face Mike. He, of all people, didn't deserve the way I treated him tonight. All he had done was what he always did. He stepped in and came to Mommy's defense. But this time, for the first time, Mommy was okay with Mike taking her side against her child. Then again, I wasn't a child. I tightened my grip on the spare key, and inside the bathroom I dropped it in the decorative soap dish with the pink shell-shaped soap, there for show, not use, and removed all of my clothes, my pants and cummerbund, my ruffle shirt and bow tie, and my bra and panties, and stepped into the shower. It was nice not to have to wait ten minutes for the water to get warm. In my Venice apartment some days it didn't get warm at all. The water pressure massaged my head and then my breasts and back. It was a luxury to allow myself more than a minute to shower because this was the East Coast and not the West Coast where there was always a water shortage. I knew wasting water was wrong anywhere, but right now I needed to lie to myself. Not until my fingertips began to shrivel did I shut off the water and get out of the shower. I dripped onto the bathroom floor and opened the cabinet where the towels were kept. Empty. I lifted the lid on the hamper. Full. I had three options: use a dirty towel, or the tux, or, the most dangerous of all the options, the one that was sure to bring my mother to slam my knees with a baseball bat, the guest towel. There was a saying in Pelham Bay: *Why make matters worse, why not?*

I took the guest towel off the rack and dried every inch of my body and rubbed it hard over my head and then I wrung it out over the sink and put it back on the rack from which it came.

I picked up the pile of tux and went to Jimmy's room. Someone had cleaned. The extra wheelchair was folded in the corner of the room. There was no shattered glass from the picture frame, and no portrait of Mommy and her dead brother. My suitcase, which I had left on the canopy bed, was gone. I opened the top drawer of my old dresser and inside, my clothes: two pairs of jeans, T-shirts – three short-sleeved and one long-sleeved – and my underwear. A long flannel nightgown that I was certain I had left behind. Did Dad do all this after he sobered up?

I wondered if Dad was with Margaret right now. She clearly wasn't good for his sobriety, but she did seem to care about him. The way she came to his defense tonight made me think that maybe Dad had found his Mike.

I pulled the flannel over my head. The fit was loose, but familiar, and the material was more scratchy than soft, and almost, but not quite, comfortable.

I don't know if it was out of respect for, or fear of, Carmela, but I decided to hang up the tux. I didn't have the money to get the tux dry-cleaned, but I wouldn't have to worry about the express-cleaning fee because I wasn't going to the wedding. Jimmy didn't want me there. No one wanted me there, maybe Julie, but I blew that. All I wanted was to make things right with Jimmy, or as right as possible, and if there was any hope of making things right with him, I blew that, too. Who was I kidding? I blew any hope of forgiveness a long time ago. Forgiveness can't happen in silence. I waited too long to speak up, come home, say I was sorry.

I glanced over at the clock. Ten thirty-three. Do you know where your return airline ticket is? I no longer had to worry about Mommy not buying me a ticket back to LA. After my behavior tonight, especially confronting Jimmy about his gambling debt after she told me not to, I was sure she'd shove me in a Hobart Cab and send me to the airport.

I slid open the closet. The door came off the track and got stuck halfway. I kicked the damn thing and *pop, pop, pop* as rows of the bubble-wrapped saints fell from their shelves. Damn it. Jimmy's going to freak. I tried to push the door again, no luck.

Saint Anthony, I had to get him back on the dresser. I picked up the jacket and checked the inside pocket and he wasn't there. I checked the other front jacket pockets. Nothing. Maybe the pants? The pockets were empty. I lost Saint Anthony. How? Where? I rushed over to the nightstand. He wasn't there. I had hoped that maybe he had found his way home. The only saint left standing was Saint Genesius, the saint of actors. I got on my knees and prayed. I didn't know how the patron saint of actors would help or could help, but I was alone and lost. I was Saint Anthony.

I got off my knees, fell into Jimmy's bed, and was again sucked into it; the air pump was off. Yes, of course I lost the *saint of lost souls*. The irony made me laugh until I cried myself to sleep.

"GET UP!" Dad hovered over me. He flipped the mattress switch, and underneath me filled with air.

The digital clock on the nightstand, next to the lonesome saint, flashed six.

I put the pillow over my head. "Let me sleep."

"You've been sleeping all day!"

"It's only six," I said.

"At night." He tugged at my flannel-covered arm and tried to pull me out of bed, the way Jimmy and I had done to him when we were children. Only, back then the two of us, one on each arm, more times than not, triumphed. Dad wasn't having any success with his daughter, who had no desire to get out of bed until she had the airline ticket to get her out of this city and back to where she belonged. I sat up. "Dad, I need a loan."

Dad nodded his chin twice. "We'll talk." He left the room.

I got out of bed. Grabbed the remote resting on top of the television and clicked. There he was, President Bush on the news, the six o'clock news. I wasn't hungover but the sound of his voice banged against the inside of my head. I clicked off the television, and after a quick pee and splash of water on my face, I joined Dad at the dining room table. He was picking at the edges of Mike's renowned spaghetti pie.

He pushed a fork and plate in front of me. "For you." He handed me a yellow Post-it. Mike's chicken scratch: *Smart Eyes, we didn't want to wake you. Your mom thought you needed your rest. Here's some of my spaghetti pie. M.*

Mike making one of my favorite foods was a spatula through the heart. I turned the Post-it to the other side and then glanced around the table.

"Your mom didn't leave a note." Dad cut me a slice of spaghetti pie. "Give her time." I didn't have time. I needed to get my return ticket and go.

He pushed the pie in front of me. It smelled great, but guilt was the ultimate appetite suppressant. I pushed the plate away and dropped my head onto the table. "Why did I even come back?"

"Your brother."

"He didn't even want me here." I mumbled into the crease of my arm.

"You got a little carried away last night."

I lifted my head. "I called you a loser."

"You did."

"And I was awful to your friend."

"You were."

"And you're not pissed?"

"You were harsh, but you weren't wrong."

"You're not a loser." I meant it.

"The jury is out on that one. But I do understand regret. You can wallow in it, or you can try and make things right."

"You'll loan me the money for a ticket back to LA? I can't ask Mommy, not now."

"You think leaving will make things right?"

"If it wasn't clear before, it was crystal clear last night. I don't belong here. I don't know if I ever did. Jimmy was furious that Julie asked me to be the best man. He doesn't want me here."

"Did you ever think that he would have wanted to ask you himself?"

"You know that's not true."

"I don't know what's true. I certainly don't know what your brother wants. I never bothered to ask, and if he told me, I didn't listen." Dad paused, and this time when I stared into the gray area of his blue eyes, I didn't feel cold inside. There was no apparition between us, keeping us apart. His eyes were clear, and for the first time in a long time, Dad was not somewhere else. He was here, with me. This was our moment. The moment my father would tell me he was sorry. He did make it all about Jimmy, his career, his interests, his everything. I wasn't there for the ride, tagging along, and he never intended to leave me behind. This was the moment when my father would tell me I mattered.

Dad took the slice of pie he had cut for me. "If you don't want it." He stabbed his fork into it and started to eat. I sat there, watching his every bite. Needing him to say something to me. Something that would make me believe everything would be okay, or at the very least, that he wanted me to stay. That he didn't want me to go. After his last bite, he wiped his mouth on the edge of the tablecloth. "Don't tell your mom." He stood up from the table.

"Where are you going?"

"Watch a little TV."

"Fuck you, Dad. Go fuck yourself." I said it and I didn't regret it. "You don't give a shit about me!"

And he applauded.

"Go ahead. Mock me."

"Angela, I'm proud. Relieved, really. Finally, you're telling the truth."

"Been there, done that, last night."

"You were hurt. You felt left out. Lost. Your words last night, those weren't you. Telling me to go fuck myself. That's you, finally, speaking up for you. I'm proud."

"Stop, Dad. No more bullshit."

"You really don't think I love you?"

"I don't even think you like me."

"You were my partner."

"Your business partner. At sixteen the last thing I wanted was a business partner. I needed a father. The one thing I never understood was why Jimmy and not me? I had the looks, why didn't you try and make me a star?"

"Passion," Dad shouted. I jumped back. "You had the look. You didn't care."

"All I wanted was for you to pay attention to me." I said the sad truth I had never wanted to admit before. "I was jealous. Maybe if you had shown me half the attention you showed Jimmy, I would have—"

"Hated me. The way your brother hates me."

I wanted to tell him he was wrong. Jimmy didn't hate him. But I knew Jimmy even less than Dad did. Maybe Jimmy did hate him. Hated the both of us.

Dad walked into the kitchen and came back with two cans of beer. He offered me one. I took it and threw it down on the black-and-white linoleum. The can punctured and beer sprayed all over the floor. "This is why I never felt I could say anything or cause you any problems—"

"I'm a drunk. Yes, a fucking drunk. At times, and even for several years this last run, I was a sober drunk, but still a drunk, never stopped being a drunk. And a coward."

"Your beer is your liquid courage."

"I don't need courage with this." He lifted the other can of Bud to my face. I don't need anything or anyone when I have this." He put the beer to his lips and chugged. "I neglected you. I pushed your brother to the breaking point, more times than I can let myself remember. I can't argue any of that, but I never chose your brother over you. I chose beer, wine, cognac, off-brand crappy gin, vanilla extract." He smacked the can down into what was left of the spaghetti pie. "I chose anything that would give me a buzz or a blackout, over you, and, believe it or not, over your brother, too. It was Jimmy's career that got my attention, not Jimmy. In truth, the times you and I spent together on the job, spraying, setting traps, were some of the only times I felt close to anyone."

"Why, Dad?"

"Why do I drink?" He forced a laugh. "I wish I could tell you the reason I drink was because my father beat me, or my mother starved me, or I didn't get enough love, but your grandparents, though far from perfect, did their best. My father was a prick at times, but he tried."

"So there's no reason for your drinking?"

"There is every reason and no reason. Angela, I was drinking since elementary school. I would steal sips of beer from my dad when he wasn't looking. Or I'd offer to help my mom clean up after a party so I could drink whatever wine or beer or cheap shit people left behind in their glasses, cigarette butts and all. The times I got caught, my parents made light of it. Thought it was boys being boys. And I was a boy drunk who grew into a man drunk. And now you know my AA story." He paused and let out a deep breath. The familiar smell of Bud hit me in the face. "Angela, I wish I could point to the moment when tragedy struck and changed everything for me. But I can't."

My dad didn't tell me anything I didn't already know, but there were no longer all these unanswered questions. Maybe the apparition that stood between us my whole life had finally left.

"For the record, even if it is broken, I love you, which is why if I had the money to lend you for the ticket back to LA, I'd give it to you, if that would make you happy." Dad took the plate of spaghetti pie and went into the living room.

It may not have been a decisive moment, but Dad did help me to see the truth. The accident wasn't the reason I left. It was the excuse I needed to run. I was afraid Jimmy's shadow would eat me alive. Now I see I had no idea who Jimmy was or what he wanted because I never asked, and if had, I probably wouldn't have listened.

It was too late to make things right with Jimmy, but I could try to not make things worse. It was time to go. Get out of town, Pelham Bay, and back to LA, before I caused any more heartache for this family or myself.

I couldn't ask Mommy for the ticket. Who knew when she would talk to me again? There was no one I knew in LA who had three-hundred-plus dollars to spare. Activism wasn't financially lucrative work. There had to be someone. Of course. Billy.

I rushed to the wall phone and dialed his number.

"Hey, what's up?"

"Thank God, you're home—"

"Sorry, it's not me. If you leave a message, I'll call you back."

"Billy, it's Angela." Before I said another word, I heard the television. *"Families on both sides will be pulled apart and destroyed for what? Oil? Protecting the rich elite?"* It was me. I hung up and followed the sound of my voice to the living room. *"I don't want anyone's blood on my hands, not in my name."* Dad was sitting on the couch in front of the thirty-two-inch state-of-the-art color television watching the tape of my cable-access interview about the war.

Dad clicked the pause button. "You know, this woman . . ." He pointed the remote at my wrinkled brow and wide-eyed-means-business stare on the screen. "She has what casting agents are looking for but more importantly what we all need." He clicked the VCR back on. I could barely stand to watch myself. *"Children, families, our troops will die, and for what?"* He clicked the television off, looked up at me, and said, "Whatever you do in this world – and I don't care what it is, if it makes you money, or makes you happy – but do what makes you feel the way the woman on that screen feels. You care, it matters. Passion. Now that's what I'm talking about."

He stood. "I'm going to get out of here before your mother comes back and finds me here. She's adamant about my going to that bachelor party tonight at the Knights of Columbus. But the last thing Jimmy needs is *Dad* at his bachelor party."

"Or his sister," I said.

"He does need his best man," Dad said.

"If I see him, I will send him on over."

"Angela, it's your choice whether you go tonight or not, but don't let the reason you don't go be because you think Jimmy doesn't want you there."

"He doesn't," I said.

"You thought he didn't want to talk to you all these years and it turned out he was waiting for you to call."

Dad kissed me on the forehead and put twenty bucks in my hand. "It's not enough for a ticket to LA, but if you get hungry, it's enough for a pizza, or a cab ride."

"Thank you," I said.

"You don't thank family," he said.

"Maybe it's time we start," I said.

"You are as smart as you look."

I followed him to the front door and stood at the top of the stairs waiting to hear the outside door open and shut. When I didn't, I ran down to the next level and called out, "Dad?"

"For what it's worth," he called up to me. "I may not agree with you about this war, but I'm proud of you for standing up for what you believe."

I heard both doors slam shut.

The phone rang. It had to be Billy. Before I got to it, the machine picked up: "Leave a message, if you recognize my voice." It was Mommy. "If you don't, hang up. You have the wrong number. *Beep.*"

"Mrs. Marchesi? Or Campanosi? Mrs. Petrolli? I don't remember your last name, is it one or two or all three. . . ."

Fat Freddy Fungol.

"Would you tell Angela, I'll meet her in front of the Knights, so we could take care of business first thing. We don't want to put on the party a damp rag or a lit one." He snorted and hung up.

I had no choice. I may not be Jimmy's best man, or his best anything, but I had to get to the bachelor party and try to stop Fat Freddy from doing anything stupid. On second thought, stopping him from doing all things stupid would take an act of God. I narrowed my focus. I had to go to that bachelor party and stop Fat Freddy and associates from hurting Jimmy by any means necessary. I was the apparition, the activist, who would take a stand between Fat Freddy's fist and Jimmy's face.

The plan of action: save my brother and then figure out a way to get back to LA. I was still wearing the scratchy flannel nightgown. New plan of action: get dressed, save my brother, and then figure out a way to get back to LA.

CHAPTER 24

In Los Angeles, on the steps of the downtown federal building, the twenty-four-hour vigil, the countdown to the UN Security Council's deadline to Hussein, was well on its way. When we were organizing the vigil and debating the order of speakers (one hundred and twenty at last count), I still held out hope we could convince the coalition, led by the US, not to declare war on Iraq, even if Hussein didn't pull his troops out of Kuwait. Now I understood that millions of protesters weren't enough to stop this war from starting. Julie had said US troops were on the border waiting, so in a sense the war had already begun. *The line had been drawn in the sand.*

Sometime after midnight, Eastern Standard Time, the United States would officially declare war, Julie and Jimmy would get married, and Julie would be flying out. I didn't agree with her choice, but I understood it, and I admired her courage. She was a badass in the way only a woman from the Bronx could be.

I went into Jimmy's bedroom and this time I pushed the closet door open all the way. There wasn't enough room between Jimmy's bed and the closet to kneel, so I stood, hands clasped together, and prayed to the hundreds of plastic saints in bubble wrap, including, or especially to, the dozens that had fallen. "If I have any chance in hell, I mean heaven, of standing up to Fat Freddy, whose breath alone paralyzes me and I regress to the frightened fourteen-year-old girl he tried to rape, I will need at my side the combined powers of each and every one of you tonight. Amen." I crossed myself, not knowing any other way to formally end a prayer.

I had nothing to wear. The blue tux was out for several reasons. The T-shirts and jeans I had in the dresser drawer were all wrong. The flannel nightgown was the most appropriate item of clothing I had and it was not going to work.

For the performance of my lifetime, I needed a costume that shouted, "She's hot and don't you dare fuck with her."

I knew where to find it, way in the back of Mommy's closet. As I suspected, it was there she stored her sexy-skinny clothes. The clothes the mother I grew up with wore. There was the perfect dress for combat – the red strapless, slutty, fuck-me dress. The dress that made Jimmy flinch with shame whenever our mother had worn it, which was often for school events and neighborhood block parties.

With the red dress in one hand and the mauve six-inch stilettos she had bought me in the other, it was time to begin my countdown to saving Jimmy, my family, and somewhere in there, myself.

At nineteen hundred hours I opened my mother's makeup drawer, and I applied dark blue eye shadow and black eyeliner.

At nineteen hundred hours and ten minutes I smeared a blob of cold cream on my face and wiped off the eye makeup.

At nineteen hundred hours and twenty minutes I reapplied makeup. This time, shades of purple and mauve, with the same black eyeliner.

At twenty hundred hours and ten minutes, I gave up on thinking in military time, swapped the flannel for the polyester-blend silk-looking slutty red dress, slipped on the stilettos, hobbled to Jimmy's room, grabbed Saint Genesius, put him into my backpack (couldn't find where Mommy kept her clutches), went back to the closet and stuffed my backpack with all the bubble-wrapped plastic saints I could fit, and then I called Hobart Cabs.

At eight forty-five, give or take a few minutes, I made my grand entrance at the Knights of Columbus.

"Here she is! The best man!" Vinny, aka V, the oldest Hobart brother, greeted me at the entrance to the party room, smiling wide. His left incisor was long and sharp, hence his nickname, V, for Vampire. His right incisor was still missing. He'd lost it after Gina, his girlfriend of two years, heard that he was seen parked in the back of Casinelli's Funeral Home, fucking some girl. After he finished the dinner she made, steak pizzaiola, his favorite, she whacked him in the mouth with the cast iron frying pan. She broke his nose too, but it had been broken twice before, so there was no significant difference in his appearance. I was still thankful whenever I'd go to have my teeth cleaned that the puttana's identity had remained a mystery.

"All the way from Hollywood, and sizzling." I know he thought he thought he was paying me a compliment, but the idea that V or anyone found me attractive, with all the makeup and hairspray and heels, made me cringe. "For old times' sake," V said, and kissed me on the mouth.

I scrunched my face. His lips still felt as gritty as the sand in the Orchard Beach parking lot, and I wondered why I ever fucked him. I slept around, but there was always something I had found attractive about the person. Now I had more important things to focus on than my questionable past.

"Jimmy here?" I asked. My backpack dropped off my right shoulder.

"The guest of honor has yet to arrive." V helped me slip both arms through the straps so the backpack was secured on my back, and I thought maybe Jimmy wouldn't show.

"My mom?"

"She came in earlier to make sure everything was set up, then left. Thank God – a sister at your bachelor party is weird, but your mom, well, that's plain wrong."

"Thanks V," I said.

"Hey, Ange, you remember—"

"I gotta use the restroom." I didn't have to pee, but I needed an excuse to get away from V before he started going down *do-you-remember* lane.

"Thought you should know Fat Freddy was here asking for you, and I think he's coming back."

"Was he with anyone?"

"Naw, bozo one and two weren't with him."

"No one else, you sure?" No *associates*? I thought.

"He came in alone. Hey, you okay?" There they were, his droopy dog eyes that had made me pity him enough to fuck him back then.

"Nothing I can't take care of," I interrupted, pretending I wasn't scared shitless. I had no idea what I was going to say or do when Fat Freddy returned, but for my Jimmy's sake, I had to face him.

I tried to maneuver around him.

"Ange, you need my help, I'm here."

If it were only Fat Freddy, I would have taken him up on his offer. Fat Freddy was the muscle and flab of the operation. I was sure, compared to his, boss Freddy was an altar boy. I didn't want to get V hurt, again.

"You ever see Gina?" I asked.

"Married, five years." He lifted his wedding band to my face.

"Five years. Congrats." It was definitely time to pee. I knew wives and girlfriends didn't show at bachelor parties, but then again, neither did mothers and sisters. Keeping a distance between V and me was probably a smart move. True, Gina had never discovered I had been the one to fuck her boyfriend in the back seat of the cab, but she wasn't all brawn, she had a brain. If she saw V and me together, even if we weren't horizontal, two and two would equal a cast iron skillet to my face.

"I really gotta go," I said, hopping from one heel to the other for dramatic effect.

"Go! We can catch up later," he said.

The Knights of Columbus's party room remained trapped in an era when platform shoes and Nixon were good ideas to people. Same fake wood–paneled walls and the same rancid beer and stale cigarettes aroma that always reminded me of our First Holy Communion.

Jimmy and I had our Communion party here, and it was on the floor of the back room where I played strip poker with some boy, my cousin three or four times removed; I never did understand how that worked. After his mom caught us and gave us the "you're going to burn in hell" speech, I spent the rest of the night praying in the bathroom stall.

Looking up at the DAMES sign on the bathroom door, I considered doing the same thing now, until I flipped on the light and saw the place apparently hadn't been cleaned since then. I flipped off the light. There was so much I was unsure about, but I had never been more confident about needing a drink.

The bar was at the far end of the party room. Usually, spaces look smaller when you're grown up, but from where I stood it was a mile away.

In the center of the room stood a TV screen, not much smaller than the film screens in some of the multiplex theaters I've been to in LA. I didn't recognize all of the guys sitting at purple-cloth-covered tables, but a few childhood friends called out and waved to me. Johnny Barbecue Jr., whose father, Johnny Barbecue Sr., barbecued all year round, through rain, sleet, and ice. There was Sal, the first of our friends in high school to have a car. He drove a green Chevy Nova that comfortably fit four, but we uncomfortably shoved in ten, sometimes eleven, to drive two hours, with no A/C, in bumper-to-bumper traffic to Jones Beach. Others I didn't know, but from their business attire – Armani and Ralph Lauren – I had a feeling they weren't from around here, at least not anymore.

Billy wasn't here. This wasn't his scene. Still, it would have been nice to have someone around who had my back, without a wife or a girlfriend I had to worry about.

At the bar, I hopped up onto a stool and waited for the probably underage bartender who was stacking drinks onto a server's tray. The top of the bar was carved with a litany of coy phrases. *For a good time call . . . Bullshit . . . Fuck that shit,* and my personal favorite, *Life's a big joint so smoke one and live.* I couldn't find *A.C. loves God,* which I had carved in the hope of redemption after the strip-poker incident.

The liquor bottles on the shelves started to vibrate. Earthquake, I thought, before someone shouted, "Turn it down."

The bartender ran over and picked up the remote from under the bar and, pressing it in the direction of a football game playing on the television screen, turned down the volume. Joe Namath, the guy I recognized from those pantyhose and shaving cream commercials from when I was a kid, was throwing a pass in big-screen glory. It was probably a tape of the first game Jimmy had ever seen. Mommy had thought of everything.

"Can I get you a drink?" he asked, and up close I had no doubt he wasn't legal. But he was old enough to join the military. I was glad the smaller television over the bar wasn't turned on. I couldn't bear to watch the news countdown to the war.

"A screwdriver." I was feeling more nostalgic than I thought. OJ and vodka had been my beverage of choice in high school. I tilted my head toward Namath. "This the only videotape you have back there?"

"The lady dropped off a bunch." He pointed to a white plastic bag behind him.

"Mind if I take a look?"

"Knock yourself out." He dropped the bag in front of me. Inside were all of Jimmy's favorites: an assortment of sports classics, Jimmy's favorite movie of all time – *The Ten Commandments,* with Charlton Heston as Moses and Yul Brynner as Rameses – and about twenty episodes of Road Runner cartoons. There was also erotica – "Made for Women" videos; "Sex with a Story" was the promo line. Mommy may have thought of a little too much "everything."

"Do women really want that?" The minor handed me my drink. "I mean . . . I love a good love story myself, but when I want to . . . you know . . ." His face didn't blush, but his voice definitely did. "I don't need it getting in the way. You know?"

"I don't want a lot of plot with my porn either." I smiled.

"Do you enjoy your work?" He smiled back. "Performing in front of people takes guts."

Mommy had told him I was an actor, or God help me, Fat Freddy had. Did he tell him about *Goodfellas II*? I had this sudden urge to share with this bartender, underage or not, my woes.

"You look great in red," he interjected. When I looked down at my low-cut neckline, my boobs popping out of the red slut dress, I remembered this was a bachelor party, and I was a woman. He thought I was part of the entertainment.

"You don't," I started, "understand." I stopped. I no longer had the will to tell him my story, even if he was a bartender.

"I bet you'll be great tonight." He winked. Now the minor was flirting, and I felt illegal. I took a gulp and then another and finished off my vodka and OJ. On the big screen, Joe Namath was no longer throwing passes, and instead Moses was raising his staff at Rameses.

"Another?" The minor raised a bottle of what looked to be top-shelf vodka, which, if things were how they used to be, the only thing top shelf about it was the label; what was inside was rotgut.

The image of my head over the toilet in the Dames' room flashed before me. "Glass of water."

"You got it," he said.

"Let it be written! Let it be done!" *The Ten Commandments,* on the big screen, cued to Yul Brynner delivering Jimmy's favorite line, blared from the screen as my old dear friend, the guy who had saved me from Fat Freddy all those years ago, Anthony, made his entrance into the party room.

"Anthony's here!" V shouted, and all the guys from the neighborhood stood. The others followed, though from the expressions on their faces they weren't sure why. I wasn't positive myself, though if Anthony had taken over his brother's business, some of these guys were standing out of respect, and some out of fear, and some out of both. What his brother did, and how he did it and for whom, was never discussed, especially after he was put in jail, but I was sure the business wasn't listed in the Yellow Pages.

He walked into the room, and with a slight nod of his chin, everyone sat. There wasn't any muscle behind him or in front of him, or at his sides. His brother never walked the streets without at least three, most of the time five, guys forming a wall of men around him.

Onscreen, the Pharaoh Rameses pronounced and declared, at the moment Anthony took the stool at my right. I thought my prayers had been answered. Anthony was clearly connected, so it stood to reason he knew Fat Freddy's boss, and maybe he could help me get to him and work something out before Fat Freddy or his associates got to Jimmy.

"You haven't changed," he said. I couldn't say the same for him. He was only a few years older than I was, but the gray in his hair and the tiny lines around his eyes made him look much older. But also distinguished. He had that look of someone who has spiritually lived life hard.

"Did I really wear this much makeup before?" I said.

He took a monogrammed handkerchief from his suit pocket. Anthony always did have this old-fashioned but sweet way about him. "Close your eyes," I did, and he patted my eyelids and then my lips. "That's better." I opened my eyes to his sincere smile. "Word has it that you're going to be the star of *Goodfellas II.*"

I should have known that Fat Freddy would be blabbing it all over the neighborhood. Unless it was Mommy, who knew it didn't matter what was true, it only mattered what people believed. If you repeated a lie enough, it became an undisputed fact. I hated to deceive Anthony, especially with all he had done for me. No one but him would have stood up to Fat Freddy. But if Fat Freddy thought this was made up and I wasn't going to be in a big movie, then there was no way that I would be able to convince him to give me more time to get the forty-five thousand dollars Jimmy owed. Based on my current economic status I couldn't see how I would come up with that kind of money in forty-five thousand years; I needed the time to get Jimmy out of town.

"Lucky break," I finally said.

"I am sure luck had nothing to do with it."

"That's sweet," I said. "A roomful of men don't stand up when I enter," I said.

"They should."

"Excuse me?" I said.

"When a gorgeous woman enters a room, all should rise and show respect." He was flirting, big time. This felt uncomfortable, but if he thought I was hot, he'd probably listen to me, for a little while anyway. He gestured to the bartender. "What are you drinking?"

"Just water."

"Get us both water." He smiled.

"Right away, Mr. Capresi." The bartender's hand shook when he squirted water into two cups, and when he placed them in front of us, Anthony nodded and put a twenty down on the bar. "Thank you, Mr. Capresi." The bartender bent slightly at the waist. "Mr. Capresi, I was wondering if you needed any help."

"You finish high school?"

"I'm strong."

"You have experience?"

He hesitated, and I could see he was thinking about lying, but then he said, "I'll do anything,"

"Why don't you walk around and make sure everyone has a drink," Anthony said.

This time the bartender bowed, stepping backward out of the bar area.

"I'm in the presence of royalty," I said.

"You're the best man, huh?"

"Seems that way," I said.

"Glad to see that you and Jimmy are talking again."

"You know Jimmy and I weren't talking?"

"Not since you left for LA, right?"

"Word does get around this neighborhood," I said.

"Your brother and I are friends, close friends."

"I didn't know that," I said.

"You haven't talked, so how would you?"

"I guess I wouldn't." He was testing me, though I had no idea in what subject.

Anthony swiveled in the direction of the tables and every head turned away. "We should get the party started, don't you think?"

"Jimmy's not here yet." I lurched forward and knocked my water over, splashing some onto Anthony's suit. He didn't even flinch. "I'm so sorry." I grabbed the cocktail napkin and started to press it against his shirt, royal blue, but the napkin was wet, and I was only making things worse.

Anthony took hold of my hand and said, "It's only water. Not blood." This time when he smiled, I could tell something was very wrong, though I had no idea what was happening.

Moses's one snake swallowed three of Pharaoh's snakes and the big screen went dark. A woman with bold red hair emerged. Her shimmering lime-green minidress clashed so brilliantly against the tablecloths, which now appeared more mauve than purple. She reminded me of an abstract painting I had seen at the LA County Museum of Art.

"A stripper," I said.

"Performance artist," Anthony said.

The performance artist danced to the grotesque rhythms of male moans and groans.

"Now this is a party."

"Take it off!"

"Let it be written. Let it be done. Take it off," called the guest, wearing a blue Armani suit, in a Yul Brynner accent.

The artist made her way over to us and did a backbend over Anthony's lap. "Nice shoes," she said to me.

"I'm Angela," I said casually, wanting her to know I wasn't sitting in judgment of her. I knew a lot of PhD candidates performed to pay for school.

"Nice to meet you. I'm Dawn." Without changing position, she lifted one hand off the ground and shook my hand. Her flexibility and balance were beyond impressive.

Anthony whispered into her ear and stuck a twenty in her cleavage. She straightened, and turning back to me said, "Do you mind? The zipper."

I unzipped her dress, hoping I looked more comfortable than I felt.

"Thanks." She flashed me a professional smile. The fabric dropped to the floor. There was nothing abstract about her appearance now.

"Tell me something, Angela," Anthony said, but the moans and groans and "fuck yeah babys" made it impossible for me to catch the rest of his sentence. I could see he was waiting for my response.

"I can't hear you." I pointed to my right ear.

He said something, but all I could make out was "Hollywood."

"I live in Venice, actually," I said.

"Reporter," he shouted. "*Hollywood Reporter.* I read it."

This I heard. "I read it sometimes. Trade magazine," I said.

He nodded, and the audience's enthusiasm for the now nude performer, dancing on the table in the center of the room, made it impossible to hear anything.

"I didn't catch that." I pointed to my left ear. He got off the stool and shouted, "Quiet!"

The room went silent.

With all eyes on him, Anthony said, "Angela, come with me. The rest of you, as you were."

Anthony picked up my backpack. "What do you have in here? You packing?" He smiled. I squinted at him, trying to understand what he meant. "You know, packing, weapons. Guns. Like in the movie."

"Just saints."

He gave me an odd look. He wanted to know but also didn't want to know. He raised his hand in the air, the show resumed, and I followed him to a back office lined with the same faux wood paneling used to cover the walls of the main hall. The scent of moldy carpet permeated the air. "Have a seat." He gestured to the folding chair in front of a large metal desk. I sat and he took a seat in the swivel chair behind the desk.

"This your office?"

He smiled. "I sometimes borrow the place for business."

"Oh." I took a deep breath. "I need your help."

"Angela, I want to help you, but you got to be straight with me."

"About?"

"I know there's no *Goodfellas II*."

I didn't try and act otherwise.

"This means you don't have the part in some big upcoming movie."

"Anthony, please, I need to talk to Fat Freddy's boss. It's urgent."

"I think I could arrange that, but what's the emergency?"

"It's for Jimmy. He needs help," I said. I trusted Anthony but wasn't sure how much I should tell him.

Anthony picked up the handset of the red rotary resting on his desk, dialed a number, and said to the party at the other end, "Sure, I'll tell her."

"I could hear the dial tone."

"He's ready to meet you."

His mocking me was starting to piss me off.

I stood. "Don't help me. That's fine."

He extended his hand over the desk, and when I refused to take it, he said, "Let me introduce myself. Anthony Capresi, Fat Freddy's current employer."

"You're Fat Freddy's associate?" I plopped back down into my chair.

"His boss."

Anthony in the business of borrowing and lending made sense, but him hiring that loser Fat Freddy was a shock. I thought he was smarter than that.

"You know the expression, keep your friends close but your—"

"Enemies closer," I said.

"Keep the fucking morons on your payroll, so they don't do anything stupid without you knowing, especially if your moms are first cousins. I gave him the job after he dropped out of high school — he failed the GED thirteen times. Fucking moron."

I was afraid anything I said would be held against me, so I kept my mouth shut.

"Don't get me wrong, if he had, you know, a disability, or something. If he was dropped on his head as a baby. I would have more compassion. But the idiot is lazy. He doesn't study. You think you're going to pass the GED without cracking a book? And you show up late?"

"Jimmy owes you a lot," I said.

"We'll work it out," he said.

"Forty-five thousand is a lot to work out," I said.

"Forty-five? Who told you forty-five?"

"At Billy's art opening—"

"Sorry I couldn't make it. Loved the invitation though. I took a class in the art of origami. I wasn't very good but it did wonders for my stress levels." I don't know if I was more surprised that Billy had invited Anthony to his art opening, or that Anthony was a fan of origami. He glanced down at my chest and then quickly up to my eyes. "Sorry, I interrupted you. You were saying?"

"Fat Freddy and two guys, Lip—"

"That stupid-ass cousin of mine drags chicken mouth around and the other moron thinking he's some big shot. He gets them to do all his work and pays them crap. That's their business."

"They call him Lip because he has thin lips. Chicken lips?"

"He was in Grand Union with his mother, he was around eight, and out of nowhere this frozen flying chicken hits him slap in the face, giving him a swollen lip. That's something you never live down. Never heard that story?"

I shook my head.

"You were a few years younger."

"Please, a little more time. Forty-five thousand is a lot of money—"

"Freddy said forty-five thousand?"

"The interest over the original thirty," I said.

"Fifteen thousand over the original quote. That's criminal. I make a living, but I don't extort people. That fat fuck." He punched the desk, denting the metal. I tried to stay calm. "Behind my back. Wait until I get my hands . . ."

I leaned over the desk. "You know I dressed this way thinking that maybe I could seduce the boss."

"You still have the sweetest eyes," he said. The expression on his face wasn't a grandmother wanting to feed me, or an animal wanting to fuck me, it was a boss wanting to kick ass.

"You don't need to deal with that pig."

I sat back and sighed. "Thank you, Anthony. You've saved me again."

"Sweetie," he stood, walked over and sat on the front edge of the desk, and looking down on me said, "Don't thank me yet. It's your brother who owes me. There's nothing I can do for him if I don't get it tonight."

"But Anthony—"

"Believe me," he interjected. "I would love to forgive the debt, rip up the contract, a wedding present, but no can do. Money is tight. I have a reputation to uphold."

"He's in a wheelchair," I pleaded.

"That's my point. If I give your brother a deal, well, folks will talk, and you know what they'll say?"

I shook my head.

"They're going to call me prejudiced."

"Excuse me?" I mumbled.

"They're going to say that I don't treat the disabled with the same respect I give to everyone else, that I pity your brother. So if Jimmy isn't here tonight with the money, I have no choice." He paused and took a breath. "Let's both pray he shows."

Looking into Anthony's shark eyes, I thought about lost Saint Anthony, and I understood why Jimmy had Saint Anthony on his nightstand. He'd been praying to the patron saint of lost souls to save his soul, and to the namesake of this Anthony, to save his ass.

I wondered if one of the saints in my backpack would help.

"You and I are going to join the party and wait for Jimmy," he said. He led us both back to the main room.

Dawn had Sal lassoed to her right breast and some guy in a Calvin Klein business suit on her left. I now wondered if he and the other dressed-to-kill guests were business associates of Anthony's.

"Lick it," the room echoed. "Lick the nipple."

"Don't be a pussy!" someone shouted.

Dawn pushed both heads away, jumped onto the main table directly in front of the blank screen, and spun the two cans of whipped cream in her hands. She was the star of a rodeo show.

"Bring the hubby-to-be up here," she called out.

"He's not here," someone shouted.

"How about the best man?"

"You're being summoned," Anthony said. This time there was no smile. "She's over here." Anthony pointed to me. In one motion, two guys, who I didn't know but were wearing black velour running suits so were definitely from the neighborhood, lifted me into the air and dropped me at Dawn's side.

"Attention, please." Anthony raised his plastic cup in the air, and everyone followed suit. "I know it's customary for the best man to make the first toast, but since our groom is late, his wheelchair probably got a flat." A few nervous laughs echoed around us.

"Not a lot of fans of wheelchair humor," Anthony chortled. "Let's take this moment and toast the best man. I will admit that when I first heard that Jimmy's best man was a girl, his sister, I thought it was, well, fucking weird." This got a huge laugh.

"But anyone who knew Jimmy and Ange back in the day saw they were eggs and peppers." Anthony waited for the laughter to start, someone whispered, "I don't get it." "They are both good on their own, but together they are so good they're dangerous, especially to the waistline." Anthony patted his stomach. I still didn't think the audience understood the joke, but laughter started and then he continued. "But seriously, let's raise our glasses to the woman who abandoned us for Hollywood, but we're glad to have her back, Jimmy's best man, Angela! Salute!"

"Salute!" and verbal clinks, to make up for the paper cups' lack of auditory response, spread through the room.

"You're the best man?" Dawn asked.

"Technically," I said. "I'm not so sure my brother is really wild about the idea. I can't blame him. We used to be close, but we were kids—"

"And now you're all grown up." She pressed her middle finger against my lips. "Follow my lead." She shook the can of whipped cream and said, "Open wide."

"You kidding me?"

"You worry about calories?"

"No, I don't think—"

"Don't think," she said. "I get paid to put on a show and the show is usually around the groom, or if he's passed out, it's the best man." She shook the can and said, "Open." I opened, but instead of spraying whipped cream into my mouth, she sprayed it on my breasts. The audience howled—

And that's when I saw him. There, at the entrance, was Jimmy, and standing behind him was the Fat Fuck himself. It was too dark to see Jimmy's expression, but I was sure he had to be freaked out. Fat Freddy was pushing his chair toward Anthony, who was fixated on Dawn and me. I was certain once Fat Freddy discovered that Anthony knew about the interest he had planned to pocket, he would go after Mommy and me for ratting him out. I had to somehow get Jimmy and me the fuck out of here. I made eye contact with Jimmy, but before I could think about what to do next, our young bartender announced, "Hey, a special bulletin!" The room fell silent. All eyes, including Anthony's and Freddy's, turned away from the performance, to the nineteen-inch black-and-white TV above the bar. It was President Bush. I didn't have to hear him, or read his lips, to know the deadline had passed and we were going to war.

"God help us," Dawn said. And I whispered into her ear, "I have to get my brother out of here."

With no questions asked, she tossed me a can of whipped cream. "Use it if you have to."

"Thanks." I shoved the can in the side mesh pocket of my pack and jumped off the table. With all eyes still on the president, I reached my brother, sitting in his wheelchair – from above I could see most of his roots were coming in gray – when Fat Freddy grabbed the flesh of my upper arm.

"Get your hands off her," Jimmy said.

"Ange and I need to talk." Freddy never sounded calmer and I had never felt more afraid of him.

"About what?" Jimmy had the same tone he used when we were kids and he was face to face with some bully who was much bigger in size. He said that what he didn't have in size, he made up in attitude. Sometimes the bully backed down. Most of the time Jimmy got his ass kicked, which often meant so did Billy and I, who would try to come to his rescue. Bullies usually had entourages waiting to jump in. Jimmy's attitude wasn't going to work this time either.

It was up to me. "Jimmy, I'd be happy to talk with our friend Freddy."

Freddy loosened his grip, I stepped back, pulled the can from my pack's side pocket, and squirted whipped cream right into his eyes.

"What the fuck!" Freddy started to rub his eyes and scream. "It burns! It fucking burns!"

"Jimmy, hold on tight!"

"Jimmy! Ange!" Anthony yelled, but all eyes remained on another boss – the president of the United States.

CHAPTER 25

Pushing Jimmy down Bruckner Boulevard, wobbling in six-inch heels, whipped cream dripping down my cleavage, time was up, bombs would be dropped, and people would die. There was not a thing I could do about that now. Sure as the plastic saints shoved in my backpack, I wasn't going to let anyone hurt my brother.

I took off my heels and dropped them in Jimmy's lap.

"Are you crazy? This isn't LA! It's winter. Your feet are going to freeze."

I started to push harder and run faster.

"Ange, stop. NOW."

I couldn't. We had to get away.

The soles of my ripped nylon–covered feet were burning, and the OJ and vodka was making its way back up my esophagus, which was appropriate. I had never felt so screwed in my life. But I couldn't stop to vomit. I kept pushing Jimmy's wheelchair down the sidewalk adjacent to the parkway and didn't look back until I got to the overpass. There was no one following us – yet. I had to get Jimmy out of sight. The park was our only hope. We could hide in the woods until we figured something out.

Jimmy had given up begging me to stop, but he locked his wheels, and every time I tried to unlock them, he'd whack my hand with the heel of my shoe, so it took all the strength I could muster to push him up the ramp and across the overpass that connected to the park.

We reached the other side. I sighed, relieved the ramp was downhill and would be a breeze, when I stepped on a sharp rock and a violent blast of pain shot through my knee. I let go of the wheelchair. The locks must have broken because Jimmy was flying down the ramp, the way we did when we were kids on our bikes, but Jimmy wasn't a kid and he wasn't on a bike, and I had to catch him before he flipped over.

I tried to run, but the pain was too much, so I hopped. "Fack, fack, fack!" I couldn't let Jimmy's chair hit the bump at the bottom, which had frequently caused us to fly off our bikes and land facedown on the concrete. I lunged forward, reaching for the chair's handles, and tripped. I managed to twist before hitting the pavement, so only the right side of my body hit the ground. Still, I couldn't move. My body was in shock, more from humiliation than pain.

"Angela!" Jimmy came to a smooth stop, and I could see with my left eye his wheels coming my way. I managed to move to a sitting position.

"Theresa Angela! What the hell are you doing?"

"There's still time," I said.

"For what?" he shouted.

"To save you!"

"LA hasn't changed you."

I looked up at him.

"You're still a crazy fuck."

"Please, I know you hate me, but we have to hide, and now."

"Under one condition," he said.

"Anything."

He took off his leather jacket, soft and stylish, and wrapped it around my shoulders and the backpack. "You're going to freeze. A strapless in the winter? Wait a minute." He eyeballed me up and down. "That's Mommy's old slutty red dress. I don't even want to know why you're wearing it, but I beg you, please put the jacket on."

I clutched Jimmy's armrest and tried to pull myself up but couldn't.

"Rest a second."

"We have to get you out of sight. The woods." I tried again to pull myself up.

"The woods? You're planning to murder me and dump the body?" He let out a guttural cackle. I was scared but it still felt good to hear.

"This park is in the record books," he said.

"I know, the largest city park in the country."

"It's now in the top three of where the most murdered bodies are dumped."

"Mafia?"

"What's with you and the Mafia?"

He didn't wait for my response.

"Mostly guys dumping their girlfriends. One guy dumped his older brother after he shot him by mistake, supposedly."

"Tragic," I said.

"I get sibling rivalry, but that's a whole other level." He laughed but this time it wasn't good to hear.

"What was that?" I said.

"What?"

"A car, I heard a car."

"Angela, we're on the overpass of the Bruckner Expressway. It's late, but there are cars."

Panic was rising in my throat. "We need to get out of here now, Jimmy. Please."

Jimmy reached down and, using his upper body strength alone, helped me to my feet. My ankles buckled, but I managed to stop myself from falling. I walked behind his wheelchair, but before I could start pushing again, he spun around so that he was facing me. "What is going on in that head of yours?"

"I don't want you hurt."

"Hurt?"

"There's some good news. I talked to Anthony. You only owe the original thirty."

"You talked to Anthony? You're worse than Mommy." Jimmy twirled around and wheeled to the park. I struggled to keep up.

We passed the swings, which now had underneath protective rubber padding instead of hard concrete, and when we reached the baseball diamond, Jimmy stopped.

At the edge of the woods there were two people standing around a garbage can with flames shooting out. "Who is that?"

"Some teenagers hanging out."

I squinted but still couldn't see their faces from this distance. They definitely weren't tall or wide enough to be Fat Freddy or even Anthony.

"Remember?" Jimmy said. "That was us in the winter. To keep warm, and we loved to watch things burn in the summer."

"And the BCs told Billy the fire was supposed to protect us from the evil spirits," I said. "He believed any bullshit they told him."

"This park *is* haunted," Jimmy said.

He had to be kidding, but then again, Jimmy believed plastic saints could change the course of one's life. I had the backpack to prove it. I was starting to believe it, too. "You saw a ghost?"

The flames from the trashcan shot higher.

"It was a few years ago, first time I could bring myself to come here."

I started to say something, I wasn't sure what, maybe sorry, but Jimmy raised his hand to my face. "Not even sure why I came, but I remembered Miss Carol."

"Our second-grade teacher," I said.

"She told us how the Indians used to bury their people along the shore in the park."

"The Lenape," I said.

"The Lenape," he repeated.

"So, you saw a ghost, of a Lenape?"

"My wheels got stuck. Mud, which was strange because it hadn't rained in days." Jimmy paused and looked over his shoulder and then up at me. "It was close to this very spot, wait a minute, it may have been this very spot. . . ."

"What happened?"

"As hard as I tried," he took hold of his wheels, scrunched his face, and acted the part of a man struggling in a wheelchair. "I couldn't get this thing to move." He let go of his wheels. "I was ready to start calling out for help, when I saw this kid dressed in Revolutionary War garb, the big boat-shaped hat and trousers and all. And he came up behind me and pushed me out of the mud."

"It was probably a reenactment of the Revolutionary War battle that happened here."

"That's what I thought, but when I reached out my hand to thank him, he vanished." Jimmy's voice was a tinge unsteady.

"Come on," I said. "Did that really happen?"

"He spoke to me," he said.

"What did he say?"

"I promised to never, ever, repeat it out loud."

"You're seriously not going to tell me?"

"I'll whisper it."

I crouched at his side, and when my ear reached his mouth, Jimmy shouted, "BOO!" I jumped back, slipped, and fell right on my ass.

"You okay?" He was cackling hard enough to crack a rib.

The cold ground tickled my bottom. We both laughed until all of our lost time was found, and I suddenly realized we were in the same spot where the stadium had been.

"What happened to it?" I asked.

"Tore it down."

"When?"

"A few years ago. It was cracking, falling apart. Too dangerous," Jimmy said.

I should have been relieved that the place where Jimmy fell and was paralyzed no longer stood as a reminder of what I had done, but a deep sadness washed through me. The Rice Stadium grandstand, where we hung out, got shit-faced, and ran to the top like Rocky Balboa (though that was Philadelphia and this was Pelham Bay), was gone.

"You know, Ange, he had a name?"

"Who had a name?"

"Blue Balls," he said.

"That naked statue on the top of the stadium? With balls we spray-painted?"

"You and Billy spray-painted."

"What was it? Ode to Badass Ugly?"

"The American Boy statue." Jimmy lifted his chin to the sky, held his hand over the center of his heart and recited, *"Youth is entitled to freedom. The future of civilization depends upon our children. It is essential if we can hope for human progress that children should be unfettered by the domination and the conventions of the past."* He raised his voice and lifted his fist into the air. *"We owe to youth an untrammeled happiness guided but not stultified by stern obedience to rigid rules set down by their elders. The proper spirit of play must be encouraged: It is the natural instinct of the young. Healthy clean mind in a strong clean body is the idea for which we should strive."* He lowered his fist.

I clapped. It was a gut reaction. I always clapped after Jimmy performed.

"It was the inscription." Jimmy bowed at the waist, in his seat.

"You memorized it?"

"We spent a lot of nights here, and I had to do something while you and Billy were getting stoned." Jimmy said. "I thought about calling you to tell you they were taking it all down," he added.

"I wish you had." I wiped my hand across the dirt.

"I wish a lot of things too," he said.

"Like I was never born," I blurted out.

He reached down and took hold of my wrist. "Don't ever say that."

I smiled and the dam burst.

Jimmy stared down on me. "I blamed you."

"I ruined your life." I was wailing now.

"But we were both fucked up that night."

"You didn't even want to come here. I forced you."

"It was still my idea to climb to the top."

"Jimmy, please, I beg you, say it."

"Say what?"

"I know you made me swear that we'd never talk about that night. But we have to."

Jimmy released my wrist. "It's the past. Let it go."

"I can't Jimmy, I wish I could. I tried. My God, I tried."

"I can't do this now." Jimmy wheeled away from me.

For so long I couldn't understand how people could stand by and do nothing, but watching my brother wheel away, I got it. It was easier to do nothing, to look away, or change the channel, than it was to take responsibility for my actions. But I was no longer the same person who had left ten years ago. I wasn't someone who stood by and did nothing. I was a fucking activist. And there was a great chance my brother would tell me to go to hell, but I still had to try and get us to talk about it. I had to at least try.

"STOP!" I shouted. With my bare swollen feet, I caught up to Jimmy and pulled a Mommy. I lay down in front of his chair.

"Get out of the way," he said.

"Stop protecting me," I said.

"From what?"

"I pushed you Jimmy. I pushed you. Say it."

Jimmy raised his fist, and it slammed it down on his own thigh and there was that cackle, only now at my expense. I hated the sound of it.

"What's so funny?" I sat up.

"All these years you stayed away because you thought you pushed me?"

"Jimmy, I did push you. Say it. Finally say it."

"I jumped. You idiot. I jumped."

For two full seconds my heart stopped.

"I don't understand."

"Maybe I didn't want to go to California."

"But . . . it was your big break."

"And that's what I was afraid of."

"It was your dream."

Jimmy glared down at me and there under his graying hair was the same kid who would hide from our father because he would rather play stickball than become a movie star.

"It was Dad's dream," he said.

Jimmy wiped his eyes with his shirtsleeve. Blue was a good color on him.

He didn't need to say anything more. I knew he couldn't tell Dad, or Mommy. It would have taken away the only hope either of them had of there being more out there in this world, if not for them, for us. A world beyond Pelham Bay. Not to mention that fighting over Jimmy's career seemed to be the only connection they had for years. I turned away. It hurt too much to look at him.

"I'm so sorry, I didn't realize you were in so much pain. You wanted to die."

He took hold of his jacket sleeve and the strap of my pack and pulled me to him. "Hey, drama queen, look at me." I looked.

"If I had wanted to kill myself, I would have chosen a much less painful way of doing it."

"You said you jumped."

"It wasn't so much that I wanted to die, but that I wanted to fly, you know?"

"I get it."

"I knew you would," he said.

"All these years." I hit the back of my hand against his wheel. "I thought that I did this to you. That it was my fault."

"It was," he said.

I glared up at him.

"You reached out to stop me, which caused me to fall the way I did, and I broke my spine, instead of my neck. You saved my life."

I didn't know what to say. I stood up. Walked around to the back of his wheelchair and hugged him.

"Hey, it's all water under the wheelchair," Jimmy said. When he didn't get the laugh he expected, he added, "All that LA sun burned away your sense of humor?" I appreciated his attempt to make me feel better, but I supposed I needed time.

"So what happened to him?" I asked.

"To who?"

"The American Boy."

"I don't know exactly. A museum, I think."

Jimmy had memorized the inscription, I thought with wonder. The only time I had ever noticed the statue was after the parks department periodically painted white over the blue spray paint. "Clean Balls" didn't have the same look or ring to it. Maybe I did get stoned a lot back then.

"*The proper spirit of play must be encouraged: It is the natural instinct of the young,*" Jimmy recited.

I rested my chin on his shoulder and we shared a moment, long overdue, and stared at what was no longer there.

CHAPTER 26

A car horn beeped. I jumped to my feet. Anthony? Freddy? The woods. We could hide there. I got behind Jimmy and tried to push, but the chair wouldn't budge, and the wheels weren't locked.

Together we rocked the chair back and forth until the wheels freed up.

"Start wheeling," I said.

"We are doing this again?"

"We have to keep you hidden until the wedding. Even that fuck wouldn't try something at the wedding, and I know LA isn't ideal, but until Julie's back—"

"What about Mommy? Mike? Billy?"

"They'll understand. They want you to be safe too."

"Mommy's a meddling pain in the ass, but she doesn't deserve to have her legs broken." I took hold of Jimmy's arm to steady myself. "My God. You think Anthony will go after Mommy?"

He shrugged. "That's what those types do, right? The Mafia. They take revenge on the family. Right?"

My heart was pounding loud enough for the undead to hear. "Mommy could come to LA, and Mike and Dad too," I said, but couldn't begin to imagine all of us in my one-room apartment.

"Ange, I'm not moving to LA."

"Jimmy, I want you to be safe."

"Moving across the country to live in one room with our wacky family, as much as I love us, would be equal to shoving a stick of dynamite in my mouth and lighting a match."

He said *us*.

The two figures from the fire ran to the car and they left.

"I guess it wasn't Anthony," I said.

"Let's go home."

I nodded.

"You want these?" He lifted the mauve stilettos in the air.

"Leave them for the ghosts."

Jimmy dropped the shoes on the ground. He wheeled and I tried to keep up.

He reached the pay phone near the parking lot first, and by the time I caught up, he had made the call.

"Our ride should be here soon."

"Hobart Cab," I said.

"A friend," Jimmy said. "Big trunk. The chair will fit." I hadn't considered Jimmy's wheelchair. Something he had to think about all the time.

My feet were killing me. I sat on the curb next to Jimmy's chair.

"Thanks," he said.

"Sarcasm?"

"I'm really glad you came."

"Julie probably not so much," I said.

"She knew what she was marrying into."

"I'm sorry I outed you about the money."

"We worked it out."

"Really? How?"

"We talked about it."

"That's one way of handling it." I smiled.

"For the record, I did want you to come to the wedding."

"Forget it," I said. "It's the past, right?"

"Angela, I wanted to invite you in person." Jimmy pushed against my shoulder. "I went to your apartment to surprise you with a round-trip ticket in my hand. Who knew you would be here?"

"Anyone who watches bad sitcoms," I laughed. And laugh-cried. This time it was impossible to hold back the tears. I couldn't believe Jimmy had gone all the way to Los Angeles to invite me to his wedding.

"I guess I could have mailed you an invite, but I didn't think that was enough, and when I got offered a job in LA . . ."

"You're acting?"

"I occasionally do voiceover work. This was my first job in LA. The money is decent."

"You got the money!"

"Not 'thirty thousand' decent."

"Why keep it a secret?"

"You really have to ask?"

I flashed back to our entire childhood, Dad and Mom, and I got that, but Julie last night at the gallery was angry. "Julie doesn't want you doing voiceovers?"

"Let's say she knows how the 'biz' wasn't something I wanted or that was good for me. She didn't want me to do voiceovers just because of the money. It's actually not so bad, kind of fun. I should have told her what I was doing. She was right about that. But she's even worse at keeping a secret than Billy, though he is getting better at it."

"I knew it. Billy did know where you were."

"I made him promise not to tell anyone, and it would have been no big deal. I would have flown out and been back in time for the wedding, simple. But a surprise visitor here in the Bronx complicated things." He smiled at me.

I nodded. "I guess as long as Dad and Mommy don't find out, it should be fine."

"They will soon enough."

"You're going to tell them?"

"You know what they say – you can't keep a secret in Pelham Bay."

I didn't know *they* said that, but it was true enough.

"Hey, the whole best man thing—"

"Julie thought it would be what I wanted." He paused.

"It's okay, I get it," I said.

"Shut up, she was right. You are my best man." Jimmy kissed me on top of my head.

I looked up at him from the curb. He was being sincere. My mind jumped to Julie. "There has to be a way to stop her from leaving. There must be something we can do to convince her to stay."

Jimmy squinted the way he always had when he was trying to remember a line or choose his words carefully. *"The bigger the heart, the thicker the head."*

A drop of water landed on my cheek. My brother was crying. I wondered if the bombs were dropping yet.

He wiped the tears off on the back of his hand.

"I tried. I really did. So many of us did, but we failed. I let you down, again," I said.

"What are you talking about?"

"We have been organizing and protesting for months, but it was all for nothing."

"Oh my God." Jimmy shook his head. I could only imagine how disappointed he was in me. Then he said, "Stand the fuck up."

"What? Why?"

"Stand the fuck up," he repeated.

I stood.

He took both my hands in his. "If there is anything we know from growing up in Pelham Bay, it's that we can't control our circumstances, but shit, we can't not try. And most of the time, we will fuck things up, but other times, not many, but some, we make things better. So, Ange, listen to me."

"I'm listening."

"We need to get out there and protest. We need to stop this war. We need to get Julie home."

He said *we.*

A horn beeped.

Jimmy looked over his shoulder. "Our ride."

As Jimmy rolled and I walked to the far end of the parking lot, I thought about what I would say to Julie when I saw her next. I thought I would tell her that I understood why she was going. I understood the need to do everything in your control to help save lives. But the truth was I didn't understand that kind of sacrifice. I wasn't sure I would ever have her courage. Or maybe I would congratulate her on her wedding day. I was sure she would make a beautiful bride.

CHAPTER 27

When we got to our ride, standing in front of a Volvo wagon that had been around the block more than a few times, was Anthony, with his arms folded across his chest. And at his side was Fat Freddy. I jumped in front of Jimmy's wheelchair.

"Ange, get out of my way."

Anthony, with Freddy following behind, walked over to us.

"You have to go through me to get to him," I said.

"Then you give me no choice." Anthony wrapped his arms around me, and I thought that was it, he was going to squeeze the life out of me. He lifted me out of his way.

"Congratulations, my friend." He kissed Jimmy on both cheeks. "All go well in LA?"

"They worked our asses off."

"Look at this guy." Anthony smiled at me. "He talks into a microphone and he calls that work. You try cutting blocks of concrete." How could he be so glib about how he took care of the bodies?

"The number of men you have working for you, when was the last time you got your hands dirty?" Jimmy asked. I was surprised that he was so matter-of-fact about Anthony's profession.

"Speaking of the men who work for me," he turned to Fat Freddy, who hadn't lifted his eyes off the ground. "He has a little gift for you."

Freddy stepped forward and handed Jimmy a square white envelope. "Congratulations on your wedding." He hesitated.

Anthony fed him his next line: "I wish you and your wife . . ."

"I got it," Fat Freddy continued. "I wish you all the best in your new home."

Jimmy bought a house?

"Go ahead, open it," Anthony said.

Inside the envelope was a Dollar Store card and inside that was a check.

"This is for fifteen thousand dollars?" Jimmy said.

"What do you say?" Anthony slapped Freddy on the back.

"I wish you and your wife a great life in your new home."

"You already said that." Anthony slapped Freddy again.

"Me and my crew will be working all night to get the house handicap accessible so you and your bride can spend your first night as . . ." Freddy paused.

"Newlyweds." Anthony fed him another line.

"Newlyweds," Freddy repeated.

"Now go wait in the car," Anthony said.

Freddy obeyed.

"Anthony, you're in the construction business?"

He smiled, kissed me on both cheeks, and said, "What'd you think, I was in the Mafia?" He winked. I looked over at my brother and he winked. I could have been mad that he let me believe all this time that Anthony and Freddy were in the Mafia but . . . then again, if he had made the number of assumptions based on clichés and stereotypes that I had, I would have probably let me stew in my own ignorance for a while too. Or I would have called him an idiot and set him straight.

In the past few days, I had been constantly reminded of how long it'd been since I left. But I hadn't felt it until now. I was seeing the place and people I had grown up with through the lens of a Hollywood movie. And I didn't even see *Goodfellas*.

"Hey, Anthony," Jimmy said. "This is not necessary. Julie and I—"

"Want to thank you," I interrupted. It was time for me to stop meddling, but I couldn't let Jimmy give up on getting married tomorrow, technically today; it had to be after midnight.

"Take the check back," Jimmy said. "The pilot got picked up."

"Fantastic." Anthony reached out and patted Jimmy on the back.

"The voiceover work?" I asked. "A cartoon?"

"Sitcom," Jimmy said.

"The Simpsons?" Anthony asked. "Homer, I love that dope."

"Only the lead is animated," Jimmy said.

"That's you." Anthony smiled.

"I'm the voice of Harold, the talking hamster."

"*Paranoid in Pasadena,* a talking hamster who creates chaos in the life of a typical American family," I said.

"You know it?" Jimmy and Anthony said in unison.

"I read something about it in the trades," I said.

"Listen." Jimmy wheeled up to edge of Anthony's black leather wingtips. "I appreciate your help in all this, but Julie and I are okay with waiting on the house."

"Rose isn't."

"What did she do now?" Jimmy sounded resigned.

"She came to me last week and said her son and his fiancé had to spend their first night as a married couple in their new home. It would be bad luck otherwise."

"I never heard that superstition," I said.

"Neither have I," Jimmy said.

"Jim. It broke my heart to pull my men off the job." The remorse showed in his eyes. This was the Anthony I remembered. "She lost your wedding gift on my tip," he said.

"Forget about it," Jimmy said.

"This should have been a sure thing."

"No sure bets." Jimmy forced a smile.

"That fuck goes and declares bankruptcy." I thought the throbbing vein in Anthony's forehead was about to burst. "He screwed over the investors and all his workers, and he walks away as rich as he started. The fuck. Special place in hell for guys like that. So sorry, Jim."

"Hey, man," Jimmy said. "I was the one who told you I had the money for you to finish the job and it turned out I didn't. That's on me."

"The market is all over the place. Up, down. You thought you had it."

"I thought I did."

"You artist types. Making money is your thing. You need to leave the tracking to the pros." Anthony smiled. "Get yourself a financial guy."

Jimmy was a financial guy. He had to be ever since he had his first job. Neither of our parents could balance a checkbook.

Jimmy's face was impassive, his hands clasped and resting on his lap, techniques one of his first acting coaches showed him. "Don't give away anything until you're ready." This became Jimmy's tell when he didn't want to rat someone out, which was usually me. I realized this time he was protecting Mommy. He hadn't gambled his money away; she had. Our mother, who probably still had access to Jimmy's savings because he would never want to put her in the situation of having to ask him for money, borrowed from his account, convinced she would make Jimmy a fortune on this "sure thing," and what would be a better wedding gift than a small fortune?

"January is tough. No one is extending credit on materials. Not to mention, work is slow, so my men are out there doing side jobs, and people can't be generous with their time." Anthony stopped to take a breath, and I remembered Salvation Army Man, and his empty bucket. This was a hard time of year.

"I get it," Jimmy said. "I really do. But this check?" He held up the discount card with the check for fifteen thousand dollars inside. "I don't understand." That part confused me too.

"Well, you know Rose, when she wants something, she doesn't give up easy." Jimmy and I nodded. "She went to Freddy and tried to, for lack of a better word, con him. She told him that if the work was done by the wedding night, she would have no problem getting him the money, because" – he put his arm around my shoulder and squeezed me to him – "our Ange had a starring role in *Goodfellas II.*"

"*Goodfellas II?*" Jimmy's expression had now spread all over his face. "What the fuck?"

"I could have played the Big Boss," Anthony snorted.

Jimmy shook his head at me, and Anthony continued, "That's what mothers do, they help their kids, no matter what it takes. Or at least they try."

And sometimes they make things worse, or they fuck it up altogether.

"But why is Freddy giving me a check for fifteen thousand dollars?"

"Before you rushed off tonight, and by the way, you missed a great tiramisu, thanks to Angie I found out the Fat Fuck was adding fifteen thousand dollars more than what I agreed to – let's say, he and I had a little chat, and he decided there was nothing more he'd rather do than to give his holiday bonus to the beautiful couple, and to make sure all was ready for the wedding night."

"I don't know what to say."

"Send him a thank-you card." Anthony smiled.

"What about the other fifteen thousand?" I said.

"That's a gift from you, Angie," Anthony said.

"Angie?" Jimmy sounded as shocked and confused as I felt.

"Jimmy, give us a minute." Anthony took my hand and walked me away from Jimmy's earshot. "Retribution, Ange. A million dollars wouldn't be enough to make up for what that fat fuck did to you. But this is a drop in the fat fucking bucket."

"Carmela came in before he could—"

"I was talking about when we were kids. The shithead pulled something at Carmela's?" Anthony looked toward the car where Fat Freddy was waiting in the front passenger seat. "I'm going to kill him."

I pulled Anthony back. "I don't need you to save me anymore," I said.

"I may have helped. But I never saved you. You were fighting him off pretty hard. Don't you remember?"

I didn't.

"You kneed him right in the balls."

I didn't remember that either.

"You were about to kick him again. He was going down. Really, I saved him. And superstition or not, they deserve to spend their wedding night in their own home. He will have the house ready. You know, community service."

I kissed him on both cheeks.

"I've been dealing with his shit for too long. He may be my cousin, but he's not my family. The neighborhood never let your family fully into our fold. Instead of keeping you out, we should have been begging you to let us in. You may have your fucked-up dysfunctional family shit, we all do, but at the end of the day, there's love."

"I ran away from that love," I said.

"You ran away because you loved too much, and your heart wasn't strong enough to take it all in. It needed to mature a little." He winked.

"You know you're pretty smart—"

"For a guy who works in construction," he said.

"For a guy, period."

He leaned in and kissed my forehead. "I did get my associate's degree in psychology after all."

"Hey, *I'm getting married in the morning!*" Jimmy's singing vibrated through the parking lot.

"I'll be right there," Anthony called out. "Need to make a quick call," he said to me and walked over to the pay phone. I walked over to the Volvo.

Jimmy had already gotten himself into the front passenger seat. Freddy now sat in the back behind the driver's seat, silent.

"Ange, I'm okay moving to the back," Jimmy said.

"Stay where you are," I said. "I'm good." I opened the back door, got in, and moved so close to Freddy, his cheek was pressed against the window. I could smell his fear, well, his cheap cologne and sweat. I wondered why I hadn't remembered my fighting back when I was thirteen. I was not going to forget this moment.

I reached down and grabbed his balls and squeezed. His eyes were shut tight and his lips pursed. He didn't make a sound. It was hard to determine if I was causing him pain or pleasure. The latter disgusted me, and I caught Jimmy's glare in the rearview mirror. He gave me a slight nod, which I may have imagined, or misinterpreted, but I tightened my fist until Freddy squealed and begged me to stop.

"Please. You're hurting me."

"If you ever threaten me, or any other woman again, I'll yank your scrotum from your body and throw it down the garbage disposal."

"Do you hear her?" Jimmy shouted from the front.

"I hear her!" he cried.

"I'll leave the balls and cut off your dick." Jimmy did his Joe Pesci impersonation from *Goodfellas*. I remembered then, I had seen that movie.

I whispered in his ear: "Remember, there are no secrets in Pelham Bay.

Anthony got in the car. "Ready?"

I released my hold. "Got to put the chair in the trunk."

"Freddy, get your ass out of the car."

I never saw Freddy move so fast. The trunk slammed. Freddy got back in the car. I thanked him. Freddy half nodded. I moved away from him, and when we exited the parking lot, all that had haunted me evaporated into the fire burning in the garbage can.

For the ten-minute ride home we listened to Anthony humming the tune of "Get Me to the Church on Time."

CHAPTER 28

We double-parked in front of the apartment, and standing on the stoop was Mommy, holding on to the banister like she was the one now tethered to it. Anthony got the wheelchair from the trunk, and I rushed over and opened Jimmy's door. Freddy stayed in the car.

"Can I help?" I asked, knowing Jimmy didn't need it, and when he said yes, it felt good. Of course, he did all the real work of lifting himself from the car to the wheelchair, but it felt good anyway.

Anthony went over to Mommy and kissed her ring. It was clear who was the big boss in this neighborhood.

He kissed me goodbye, gently patted Jimmy on the back and said, "No cold feet," and got into his car and drove off, with Freddy still sitting in the back.

Jimmy wheeled up to the stoop with me at his side. Mommy, still standing on the top step and holding on to the banister, looked down at the both of us but didn't say a word. She was waiting for Jimmy, or maybe me, to speak first.

Jimmy let out a deep breath. "This weather is no good for your asthma. You should go inside."

"Don't worry about me," she said. "You okay?" I thought she was talking to Jimmy, but when he didn't answer her, she said, "Angela, are you okay?" She stared at my shoeless feet.

"I'm good, Ma. Feet frozen, but good." I was better than good. I was happy.

"Jimmy, Angela, I know I can be a bit controlling, and maybe even hardheaded . . ." Mommy paused, and when we didn't say anything she continued. "You are both adults and, well, you are more than capable of choosing your own shoes." Jimmy and I both knew that *shoes* was code for Mommy finally owning up to the mistakes she had made. Maybe she was also starting to understand boundaries. "I owe you both an apology."

"Ma, stop, I don't want your apology," Jimmy said. Mommy looked like every last breath had been kicked out of her.

"I will take a kiss," he said.

Mommy couldn't get to Jimmy fast enough. She put her arms around him and pulled me to her.

"I'm so sorry," she said.

"You don't apologize to family," Jimmy said.

"I thought you didn't thank family," I said.

"Same difference," Mommy said.

"You owe them for life," the three of us said in unison.

And while Mommy alternated between kissing my and Jimmy's cheeks and telling us how having both of her children home was the greatest gift she could have ever hoped for, Don C and Son drove up.

"Ma." I tapped her on the back. Dad got out of the van. The passenger's side. Billy exited from the driver's side.

"Ma," I mumbled. "Does Billy know?"

"He knows enough," she said.

Billy waved at us. Mommy waved back.

"I guess you've forgiven him for not inviting you to the opening."

"He's family, can't stay mad forever," she said. "And you should hear how much money he got for the Rat. *Ode to Rose* is what he's calling it now."

Dad slid the side of the van open.

"With his back, Mike should have sat in the front," I said.

"What about my back?" Mike was behind us, on the other side of the screen door.

"Then who's in the van?" I asked.

Mommy was grinning.

"It's Julie," Jimmy said.

Mommy smacked him on the back. "Go to her."

Jimmy and Julie met halfway. I knew they were perfect for each other.

"A sight for sore everything." Jimmy kissed Julie.

"I hope you're okay with seeing me before the wedding," Julie said.

"The one thing that I am more sure about than anything is seeing you only means good luck, and I'm the luckiest man in the world." Jimmy pulled her down to him and they kissed, until Mommy cleared her voice and said, "Let's get upstairs. We don't need to give these nosy neighbors a show."

Sure enough, there was the silhouette in Mrs. Bellini's window.

"Billy and I were on our way back from a meeting," Dad said.

I looked over at Billy. "Miracles of miracles." Billy smirked. "Carmela found the van a few blocks from the shop. Must have been confused about where I had parked."

Dad was about to go Catholic on us and confess, apparently not remembering where he had parked in his drunken stupor, when Billy interjected, "A friend beeped me." He winked at Mommy. "She told me Julie needed a ride."

"It's freezing out here," Mike said.

"What are you talking about?" Mommy said. "We're having a heat wave. It's a balmy thirty-eight degrees," Mommy laughed at her own joke. Like mother, like daughter, I thought.

Mike stepped out of the hallway. "You all coming inside or what?"

"I'm going to head out." Dad caught our glares. "The subway," he said.

"Margaret?" I asked.

"Nice taste in shoes," Mommy said with no hint of hostility or sarcasm, and I imagined Mommy and Margaret might one day be friends, and then Mommy said to Billy, "But she does enjoy her drink."

Billy shrugged. And he was right; there wasn't anything I or he, or any of us could do. If Dad was going to drink, he was going to drink no matter who he was with, but at least tonight he had gone to a meeting, and right here and now, he was sober.

"I can give you a ride to the train," Billy said.

"Great," Dad said, but instead of getting in the van, Dad walked over to Jimmy and kissed him on the cheek. "Good to have you back, son."

"It's good to be back, Dad."

There was so much more I wanted them to say, that I thought they needed to say to each other, but this wasn't the time, and it was up to them to decide when, and if, that time would come. I was learning boundaries too.

"If anyone's hungry, I made gravy," Mike said.

Mommy whispered in Julie's ear loud for all of us to hear, "Marinara, no meat." I knew she wanted to stick her tongue out at me to say, "Ha, ha, I can change."

"Thank you, Rose."

"You don't thank family," all of us said in unison.

Julie looked confused. I hoped for her sake in time she would come to understand us. Then again, I grew up here, and I'm more confused, or maybe the better word is surprised, by this family than I've ever been.

Mommy hooked her arm into Julie's and said, "It's time you call me Mother."

"Mother?" Jimmy said.

"What the hell?" I said.

"She should call me Mommy, or when you're being a bunch of verbal lazy-asses, Ma." She pointed to me, to Billy, and Jimmy. "You're adults. Act like it."

"Yes, Mother," I said.

"Whatever you say, Mother," Billy said.

"Of course, Mother," Jimmy said. We all knew we would be back to calling her Mommy or Ma when we were being our lazy-ass selves. Some things were too hard to change.

"Mother, it's time to eat." Mike went upstairs.

"I could eat a little something." Dad followed Mike.

"I'm leaving in thirty minutes," Billy said. "With or without you." Billy followed Dad.

When the screen door slammed, Mommy hugged Julie and said, "I am so glad you'll be able to spend your first night as a married couple in your new home."

We didn't have to ask how she already knew. There really were no secrets in Pelham Bay, unless it was our mother, holding all of them.

"The house won't be ready." Julie glanced down at Jimmy.

"Jimmy hasn't told her yet, Mother."

Mommy put her hand over her mouth. "I didn't mean to ruin the surprise."

"Don't worry about it," Jimmy said. "We've had enough surprises to last a very long time."

"Would you give me a minute with Angela and Jimmy?" Julie said.

Mommy went inside, and turning to Julie, I said, "Before you tell me what you want to tell me, I want to say something."

Julie waited.

"So say it," Jimmy said.

"Growing up, I thought I knew my brother better than anyone. Turns out, there was a lot I didn't know, there's even more now. But what I do know without a doubt is he made the right choice to marry you." I got down on my ripped nylon-clad knee and asked, "Julie will you forgive me for all the shit I've given you?"

"There's one condition," Julie said.

"I'd be honored to be Jimmy's best man," I said.

"Actually, Billy is going to be his best man."

"He is?" Jimmy said.

"Of course," I said, feeling hurt, but realizing I had no right to be. "I'm grateful you're still allowing me to come to the wedding after the trouble I caused. I am still invited, right?"

"Angela, the first time we met, you were kind of hostile."

"I was a bitch."

"You were a bitch, but last night, at the gallery, you told me not to go to Iraq."

"I had no right—"

"Most people nod or thank me for serving their country. You cared enough to tell me how you felt. This war is complicated for me, but if my being there can help, then I have to believe I'm making the right choice, for me."

"I do get that." Now the drops of water I felt on my face were my own tears.

Jimmy pushed his wheelchair in between us. "Don't you start! If you start, with those big sad eyes, I will lose it and won't be able to stop."

"Jimmy," Julie said. "You've already started." Jimmy and I and Julie took a minute of silence and cried. Suddenly she sucked back her tears and whispered, "I think someone is watching us."

Without having to turn around, Jimmy and I said, "It's Mrs. Bellini."

"Can we go inside?" Jimmy asked. "My wheels are freezing."

"I still haven't asked Angela if she would be my maid of honor."

"You want me to be your maid of honor?"

"You don't have to, but I don't have a sister and, well, it would mean a lot, but you don't have to. . . ."

Jimmy rolled into my foot. "Say yes already."

"Yes already." This time I hugged Julie and didn't let go until I remembered, "I don't have anything mauve to wear."

She and Jimmy smiled. "I hate mauve," Julie said. "You must wear the powder blue tux. I love it."

"I don't think that's going to work," I said.

"I'm sure we can find something for you in the back of Mommy's closet," Jimmy cackled.

"That laugh is the one thing that is still hard to get used to." Julie giggled.

Mommy called down to us. "The food is getting cold. Your feet are going to freeze off, Angela."

"We better go." Julie sounded more anxious about going to Mommy than she had when we talked about going to war. I completely understood.

"You okay?" she asked.

"We're fine," I said. Julie ran up the stairs.

"Can I help?" I asked, looking at the three steps leading to the front door.

"Sure." He backed up to the stoop. I got behind the chair and was going to try and pull him up the stairs.

"Need you to hold the door," he said.

I held it open, and Jimmy pulled himself up the stoop and into the hallway. At the bottom of the staircase, he rolled onto the chair lift.

"You can go up now too," Jimmy said. "This lift takes forever. The one at the new house is a Speed Racer." He winked.

"Where is your new place?" I asked.

"Yonkers," he said.

"Westchester, la-dee-da." My backpack slipped off my shoulder. Jimmy reached out and caught it.

"What's in this?"

I unzipped the pack and showed him.

"Bubble wrap?" Then he got it. "The saints?"

"I needed all the help I could get tonight."

"So someone is a believer," he said.

"Getting there," I said. "Maybe. There's something I need to ask you."

"Still?"

"Archangel Michael, the patron saint of the military, you had him out for Julie, I get that, and I hope you don't mind that I gave him to a Salvation Army guy."

"You took saints off of my dresser." He smirked. I knew he was convinced he had a convert.

"I get that you had Saint Genesius out for the voiceover work."

"He's also the patron saint of converts," he said. "I thought he could help convert you and me from enemies—"

"To friends," I interjected.

"Family too," he said.

"It helped." I pulled him out of the front pocket of the pack.

"Also, you're an activist, not exactly an actor, but you have to work an audience. By the way, your work in Nicaragua took courage."

"How did you know?"

"Mommy's not the only one with her sources."

"We can talk about that later." I pressed the button on Jimmy's lift. He slowly climbed with me at his side. "Saint Anthony was the only saint that made sense. I thought it was because of Anthony the contractor, but you always said you don't pray to a saint because of a namesake," I added before he could. "So you were praying for your sister's lost soul?"

"I misplaced a shirt cufflink," he said. "I was praying to find it. It was a favorite."

"Are you kidding me?" I said but had to admit I felt a little less lost than I had.

"Sometimes the answer is simple."

I hit the stop button on the lift. I took in a deep breath, and before I could confess that I lost Saint Anthony, Jimmy told me to reach into the inside pocket of his leather jacket.

"Saint Anthony!" I was so excited to see him.

"Where did you find him?"

"Eric found him at the gallery the other night and Billy thought it had to be mine."

"I missed you." I kissed Saint Anthony on top of his head and saw there was a thin line fracture from one end to the other. "He's broke. It's my fault. I should have never—"

Jimmy took him from me and after examining him from top to bottom said, "He's better than ever."

"The crack down the middle of his head."

Jimmy brought it up to his eye. "So there is."

"I know you've matured, and you have your life together, and you don't even think it's bad luck to see the bride the night before the wedding, but I can't believe you're not mad about my breaking Saint Anthony."

"He's not broken."

I grabbed the Saint Anthony from him. "Look," I pointed again to the top of his head. "It's cracked."

"That's how the light gets in."

I felt my face flush with confusion.

"Leonard Cohen," Jimmy said.

I shrugged.

"The greatest songwriter of our time."

"I don't know him."

"My big sister, there is so much I need to teach you." He evoked his best Yoda from *Star Wars* impression.

"I am sure there is," I said. "Are you going to be flying to LA a lot?"

"Once, twice a month, for the season. And of course, we will spend time together."

"I'm sure the studio puts you up in a hotel, but if you wanted to use my apartment—"

"Are we back to us living in a one-room apartment?"

"It's called a studio, and it's cozy—"

"Real estate jargon for *small*."

"You would have the place to yourself."

"Where you going?"

"I think I'm going to stay here for a while."

"Ange, we are okay. Dad has his stuff, and well, Mommy is Mommy, and it's going to suck hard until Julie is back, but you don't need to take care of us."

"There's stuff I think I need to be here to figure out."

"What kind of stuff?"

"No fucking idea. I haven't figured it out yet." The only thing I was certain of was I'd be wearing my Birkenstocks.

"Home is where the heart is." Jimmy laughed.

"I think home is where the appendix is," I said, forcing myself not to laugh at my own joke.

"The appendix?"

"You have one, and most of the time you take it for granted. You think you'd be okay without it, but when you feel its pain, if you ignore it, it will burst—"

"And kill you," Jimmy interjected.

"I was going to say send you to the emergency room."

"Having you home wouldn't be your worst idea," he said.

At the top of the stairs, I opened our front door, kissed my baby brother on his gray roots, and said, "I'll be right back."

"Where you going?"

"Forgot something."

I ran down the stairs, opened the front door, and looking up at the shadow in the window across the street, I shouted, "Good night, Mrs. Bellini!"

POSTSCRIPT

Where I grew up, "it fell off the truck" meant someone was trying to impress you. They wanted you to believe their car stereo or home entertainment system was stolen and worth a lot more than they paid for it. The thing was, and everyone who wasn't street-stupid knew, when something really was stolen, you never even implied that it wasn't a legit purchase, but some bargain at Circuit City.

I grew up in the Bronx, New York – Pelham Bay, the last stop on the number 6 subway line. We were all superstitious, never stepped on a crack or walked under a ladder, and many of us wore gold horns on chains around our necks to protect us from the evil eye. Under no circumstances did we celebrate winning the lottery, a trifecta at OTB, or bingo at Our Lady of the Assumption until after the winnings were banked or spent.

In my neighborhood, if someone told you a ghost story, they were trying to scare you shitless. The hauntings usually happened to some relative from the other side – we never asked "The other side of what?" We all knew that meant Southern Italy, or somewhere even farther away. When a person lived their own ghost story, they never spoke of it. Speaking of it was certain to drive you mad. Still, their hollow, sunken eyes and their talking out loud to themselves when they thought no one was listening exposed their truth.

These were not Edgar Allan Poe–or Stephen King–like hauntings, though sometimes revenge was the motivation for a dead wife's return from the afterlife to kick her cheating husband's ass. Every family has their shit, after all. A priest wasn't called in to do an exorcism, though where I grew up *The Exorcist* was considered a documentary. You didn't vanquish family, though sometimes you vanquished yourself.

Where I grew up, I was the girl who didn't see ghosts, the girl who thought holy moths were mythical creatures that adults invented to scare children, the girl convinced that plastic saints promised false hope, the girl who couldn't believe in miracles, so she ran far, far away.

In that distant land, I was the girl who stood steadfast and strove to save the world. Over time, the stories I told myself about where I had grown up spun out of control, and though there were no visible signs, or hollow, sunken eyes, the ghosts I wouldn't let myself see grew strong and fierce, until at almost thirty I was lost and alone in a crowd of thousands. That's the funny thing about ghosts. The farther you run, the harder you resist, the less transparent they appear.

I was the girl who returned home haunted. And when I sat on my stoop, felt the cold, and faced the shadows in the windows from my past, the world stopped spinning. My mother was right to feel sorry for me, but wrong when she said, "You still haven't got a clue."

The clues were all there. They always have been. I was the tough girl from the Bronx, strong willed, hardheaded, and loud, but not a cliché. I was an activist who stood up for others, and I made a difference.

ACKNOWLEDGMENTS

This morning my bathroom flooded right through to the kitchen. It was a mess. Many hours later, with some help, I managed to clean up everything and both spaces are spotless. Better than before.

Last Stop on the 6 was started over two decades ago in graduate school, and was a flooded mess. Years later, and with a lot of help, I've finished.

Ten pages into the first of too many drafts, I heard Grace Paley speak to a room of aspiring writers. She was asked how long it took her to complete a short story. "Some stories took over ten years to finish," she said. After the room flooded with gasps and sighs of despair, she added, "I wasn't working on the story the whole time. I had to grow into the person I needed to be to finish the story." I thought I knew what she meant.

After working on this manuscript for years, I decided to file the flash drive away and move on to another story, which would become my first published novel. About three years ago, one of my oldest writing comrades and dearest friends, the brilliant and respected author Jimin Han, whom I have had the privilege to co-teach with and learn from for years, encouraged me to look at what was on that flash drive. After cleaning out several drawers and cardboard boxes I finally found it. It was a mess, flooded and yet dehydrated. There was too much of what wasn't needed and not enough of what was.

It was then that I truly understood what Grace Paley meant about needing to become the person who could write the story that had to be written. I had finally grown into that person, but it didn't take me ten years to write the story I needed to tell. It took me twenty.

After two decades, there have been countless people who have helped, directly or indirectly, bring *Last Stop on the 6* into the world. I am indebted to all.

There are a few I must thank by name.

I thank Cynthia Manson, my agent, for her passion and her fight for her authors, and being steadfast and never giving up on this book, or me.

I'm indebted to Jimin Han, Alexandra Soiseth, and Marcia Bradley for reading countless drafts and treating my book as if it were their own.

My publisher, Bordighera Press, and its editorial collective for believing in this book, with special gratitude to Fred L. Gardaphe for encouraging me to submit when we met in Cetera, Italy, and to Nicholas Grosso, whose commitment and hard work even under the most extraordinary of circumstances puts beautiful and bold books into the world. He is always gracious and helpful, no matter how many emails he receives from an overzealous author.

They say a cover makes a book, and I am honored to have had the art for this cover created by William Papaleo, an extraordinary artist and most generous spirit, who along with Kathy Curto and I founded the Joe Papaleo Writers' Workshop in Cetera, Italy. Thank you to all the writers who attended the workshop and the people of Cetera for the inspiration and gelato they gave me during the writing of the final drafts of this book.

Thanks to Gary Gershoff, the amazing photographer, who actually managed to take a good picture of me.

I thank Kathy Curto, who introduced me to Bordighera Press and shared her positive experiences with them as publisher of her tremendous memoir *Not for Nothing*.

I thank Nancee Adams, one of the best copy/line editors I've had the honor to work with, for her eye for detail and heart for story.

I thank Caitlin Alexander for loving this fictional family and for her editorial guidance, which was invaluable.

I am forever indebted to my long-standing writers' group, with whom for years I have shared writing and life, and who have supported, pushed, and prodded me when I needed to keep writing no matter how often Mercury has been in retrograde—the sensational seven—Kate Brandt, Marcia Bradley, Jimin Han, Gloria Hatrick, Deb Laufer, Maria Maldonado, and Alexandra Soiseth.

This book was born at Sarah Lawrence College, where I was mentored, inspired, and supported. Very special thanks to Linsey Abrams, Paige Ackerson-Kiely, Judith Babbits, Christina Clohessy, Shirley Degenova, Brooke Duffy, Christine Farrell, Carolyn Ferrell, Maureen Gallagher, Myra Goldberg, Crystal Greene, Susan Guma, Kathryn Gurfein, Kathleen Hill, Leslie Hunt, Joan Larkin, Abby Lester, Gina Levitan, Daniel Licht, Kelleen Maluski, Rita Mastroberadino, Joan McCann, Brian Morton, Sweet Orefice, Nora Reilly, Amparo Rios, Lucy Rosenthal, Marion Scimeca, Joan Silber, and Lyde Cullen Sizer.

Dawn Bartz, Carmela Valente, Dr. Rosalba Corrodo Del Vecchio, Josephine Dorado and Yonkers Public Schools and the Greater New York Chapter of the Fulbright Association, as well as the Summer High School Writers Workshop instructors and the Yonkers, and other young writers I've had the pleasure to work with. Thanks also to the many people who tirelessly keep things running so writers can be writers.

This book and this writer grew up at The Writing Institute at Sarah Lawrence College with a community of aspiring and veteran storytellers of all kinds. It was there that I was humbled into practicing what I preached—write, revise, revise and revise and revise.

A special shout-out to those who read drafts of the book and gave invaluable feedback: Michael Biello, Susan Bolognino, Mary Calvi, Leland Cheuk, Kathy Curto, Gerry Allan Decker, Melissa Faliveno, Cindy Beer Fouhy, Julie (Shoerke) Gallagher, Lea Geller, Veera Hirandani, Lara Katz, Jonathan Kinzler, Jennifer Manchurian, David Masello, Marianela Medrano, Nan Mutnick, Ahmed Nassef, Ayah Nassef, Francesca Nassef, Eileen Palma, Jessica Rao, Ines Rodriques, Michael J Seidlinger, Rachel Simon, Elizabeth Tepper, Mike Tepper, Olivia Worden, and Ali Yunis. And in loving memory of authors Shirley Homes and Muriel Weinstein.

To the activists, artists, writers, lawyers, union organizers, parents, teachers, therapists, doctors, and actors who inspired the character of Angela, and with whom I marched and protested against the war in Iraq, among other causes, who helped me believe we could change the world, though it wouldn't be easy. Special thanks to Lisa Alvarez, Nancy Carson, Jennya Cassidy, Margi Clarke, Jim Desimone, Jeffrey Dillman, Carolyn Shoshana Fershtman, Stevie Gonzales, Addison Goodson, Frances Hasso, Anne Homes, Mary Knight, Cheryl Markham, Sean McNeil, Robert Myers, Baback Naficy, Ahmed Nassef, Matt Nicholas, Lisa Olson, Elena Pop, Leila Rand, Gary McVey Russell, Christian Smith, Scott Snell, Andrew Tonkovich, Lux Tuttle, and Alia Yunis. In loving memory of Gary Stewart and Margaret Zamudio, and the many others.

I have often been asked if this book is autobiographical. It's not. However, it was inspired by a family whose members may argue and shout and have their many quirks, but who have always encouraged the best in me. I must thank from where it all started, my mother, Adrienne Petilli. It is to her I owe my life, literally and figuratively. She loves me unconditionally, believed in me when I couldn't believe in myself, and never stops believing in or bragging about her children. I love you, Ma.

My sister Trina Dunn and her husband, my second brother, Thomas Pendergast. My brother, John E. Dunn, and his wife, my second sister, Alix Dunn. My nieces and nephews and godchildren, by order of age: Carmela Leo, Alex Gaylon, Jack Dunn, Katie Dunn, Julia Dunn, Daniel Knight, Kaj Soiseth, Kai Pendergast, Zavia Pendergast (Z-Girl), Amina Rand-McNeil and Ash Rand-McNeil.

My aunts and uncles: Robin Chance, Dennis Dunn, Madeline Dunn, Angela Fekete, John Fekete, and Kathleen Worthington, Dennis Dunn, and all of my cousins in the United States and Italy, with special gratitude to Tiffany Ziegelhofer, Federica Forlini and Carmillo Aranci.

And to my goddaughter, Carmela Leo, my oldest friend from the neighborhood, and her beautiful family, who have always welcomed me and fed me and showed me love and kindness and never made me feel like I didn't belong.

Thanks to Steve Kardos, Ayah Nassef, Elizabeth Tepper, and Mike Tepper, my daughters and sons by marriage and by birth, for their patience, love and teachings, and for their courage to be true to themselves, to take risks in their creative endeavors, while showing empathy and love to others.

To the people of Pelham Bay, where I wrote my first stories and continue to find inspiration for a lifetime of others.

Last, but not ever least, I thank Allan Tepper, my life partner, manager, home-front editor and the love of my life. I don't have the words to adequately express my gratitude to him, but I do know without him I wouldn't be writing today, and most words would be spelled wrong, and don't let me get started on the misplaced commas. His faith and belief in this book kept me from saying goodbye to these characters and giving up on their story. *Last Stop on the 6* is not my book, but *our* book.

ABOUT THE AUTHOR

PATRICIA DUNN is the author of *Rebels By Accident*. This Italian American, Bronx-raised rebel has traveled the world. These days, she can be found on her living room couch, with her dog Butterscotch, working on her next novel or meeting with aspiring and established writers.

VIA FOLIOS
A refereed book series dedicated to the culture of Italians and Italian Americans.

MICHAEL PARENTI. *Waiting for Yesterday: Pages from a Street Kid's Life.* Vol 90. Memoir.

ANNIE LANZILLOTTO. *Schistsong.* Vol 89. Poetry.

EMANUEL DI PASQUALE. *Love Lines.* Vol 88. Poetry.

CAROSONE & LOGIUDICE. *Our Naked Lives.* Vol 87. Essays.

JAMES PERICONI. *Strangers in a Strange Land: A Survey of Italian-Language American Books.* Vol 86. Book History.

DANIELA GIOSEFFI. *Escaping La Vita Della Cucina.* Vol 85. Essays.

MARIA FAMÀ. *Mystics in the Family.* Vol 84. Poetry.

ROSSANA DEL ZIO. *From Bread and Tomatoes to Zuppa di Pesce "Ciambotto".* Vol. 83. Memoir.

LORENZO DELBOCA. *Polentoni.* Vol 82. Italian Studies.

SAMUEL GHELLI. *A Reference Grammar.* Vol 81. Italian Language.

ROSS TALARICO. *Sled Run.* Vol 80. Fiction.

FRED MISURELLA. *Only Sons.* Vol 79. Fiction.

FRANK LENTRICCHIA. *The Portable Lentricchia.* Vol 78. Fiction.

RICHARD VETERE. *The Other Colors in a Snow Storm.* Vol 77. Poetry.

GARIBALDI LAPOLLA. *Fire in the Flesh.* Vol 76 Fiction & Criticism.

GEORGE GUIDA. *The Pope Stories.* Vol 75 Prose.

ROBERT VISCUSI. *Ellis Island.* Vol 74. Poetry.

ELENA GIANINI BELOTTI. *The Bitter Taste of Strangers Bread.* Vol 73. Fiction.

PINO APRILE. *Terroni.* Vol 72. Italian Studies.

EMANUEL DI PASQUALE. *Harvest.* Vol 71. Poetry.

ROBERT ZWEIG. *Return to Naples.* Vol 70. Memoir.

AIROS & CAPPELLI. *Guido.* Vol 69. Italian/American Studies.

FRED GARDAPHÉ. *Moustache Pete is Dead! Long Live Moustache Pete!.* Vol 67. Literature/Oral History.

PAOLO RUFFILLI. *Dark Room/Camera oscura.* Vol 66. Poetry.

HELEN BAROLINI. *Crossing the Alps.* Vol 65. Fiction.

COSMO FERRARA. *Profiles of Italian Americans.* Vol 64. Italian Americana.

GIL FAGIANI. *Chianti in Connecticut.* Vol 63. Poetry.

BASSETTI & D'ACQUINO. *Italic Lessons.* Vol 62. Italian/American Studies.

CAVALIERI & PASCARELLI, Eds. *The Poet's Cookbook.* Vol 61. Poetry/Recipes.

EMANUEL DI PASQUALE. *Siciliana.* Vol 60. Poetry.

STANISLAO G. PUGLIESE. *Desperate Inscriptions*. Vol 31. History.

HOSTERT & TAMBURRI, Eds. *Screening Ethnicity*.
Vol 30. Italian/American Culture.

G. PARATI & B. LAWTON, Eds. *Italian Cultural Studies*. Vol 29. Essays.

HELEN BAROLINI. *More Italian Hours*. Vol 28. Fiction.

FRANCO NASI, Ed. *Intorno alla Via Emilia*. Vol 27. Culture.

ARTHUR L. CLEMENTS. *The Book of Madness & Love*. Vol 26. Poetry.

JOHN CASEY, et al. *Imagining Humanity*. Vol 25. Interdisciplinary Studies.

ROBERT LIMA. *Sardinia/Sardegna*. Vol 24. Poetry.

DANIELA GIOSEFFI. *Going On*. Vol 23. Poetry.

ROSS TALARICO. *The Journey Home*. Vol 22. Poetry.

EMANUEL DI PASQUALE. *The Silver Lake Love Poems*. Vol 21. Poetry.

JOSEPH TUSIANI. *Ethnicity*. Vol 20. Poetry.

JENNIFER LAGIER. *Second Class Citizen*. Vol 19. Poetry.

FELIX STEFANILE. *The Country of Absence*. Vol 18. Poetry.

PHILIP CANNISTRARO. *Blackshirts*. Vol 17. History.

LUIGI RUSTICHELLI, Ed. *Seminario sul racconto*. Vol 16. Narrative.

LEWIS TURCO. *Shaking the Family Tree*. Vol 15. Memoirs.

LUIGI RUSTICHELLI, Ed. *Seminario sulla drammaturgia*.
Vol 14. Theater/Essays.

FRED GARDAPHÈ. *Moustache Pete is Dead! Long Live Moustache Pete!*.
Vol 13. Oral Literature.

JONE GAILLARD CORSI. *Il libretto d'autore. 1860 - 1930*. Vol 12. Criticism.

HELEN BAROLINI. *Chiaroscuro: Essays of Identity*. Vol 11. Essays.

PICARAZZI & FEINSTEIN, Eds. *An African Harlequin in Milan*.
Vol 10. Theater/Essays.

JOSEPH RICAPITO. *Florentine Streets & Other Poems*. Vol 9. Poetry.

FRED MISURELLA. *Short Time*. Vol 8. Novella.

NED CONDINI. *Quartettsatz*. Vol 7. Poetry.

ANTHONY JULIAN TAMBURRI, Ed. *Fuori: Essays by Italian/American
Lesbiansand Gays*. Vol 6. Essays.

ANTONIO GRAMSCI. P. Verdicchio. Trans. & Intro. *The Southern Question*.
Vol 5. Social Criticism.

DANIELA GIOSEFFI. *Word Wounds & Water Flowers*. Vol 4. Poetry. $8

CPSIA information can be obtained
at www.ICGtesting.com
Printed in the USA
FSHW011715111021
85295FS